Also by George Byron Wright

Baker City 1948
Tillamook 1952
Roseburg 1959
Driving to Vernonia
Newport Blues, A Salesman's Lament
In the Wake of Our Misdeed
I Am Ned Pine

YOU ARE ENTERING
SUMMATION
A NOVEL
GEORGE BYRON WRIGHT
STATE HIGHWAY DEPT.

[signed] G B Wright

C3 Publications
Portland, Oregon
www.c3publications.com

Copyright © 2024 by George Byron Wright.

All rights reserved. No part of this book may be used or reproduced in any manner whatsoever without written permission of the publisher except in the case of brief quotations embodied in critical articles or reviews.

Library of Congress Cataloging-in-Publication Data has been applied for

Names: Wright, George Byron—author
Title: Summation: a novel / George Byron Wright —1st ed.
Description: Portland, Oregon: C3 Publications
Identifiers: LCCN (print) | LLCN (ebook)
ISBN 9780986362811 (trade paper) | ISBN 9780986362828 (ebook)

First Edition

Cover and interior design by Abbey Gregory

This is a work of fiction. Names, characters, places, and incidents are the product of the author's imagination or are used fictitiously. Any resemblance to actual persons, living or dead, events, or locales, is entirely coincidental.

Printed in the United States of America.

For Betsy

SUMMATION

"I see my dad when I look in the mirror and I'm terrified I'll repeat his mistakes."
—Lawrence Ware, Philosopher

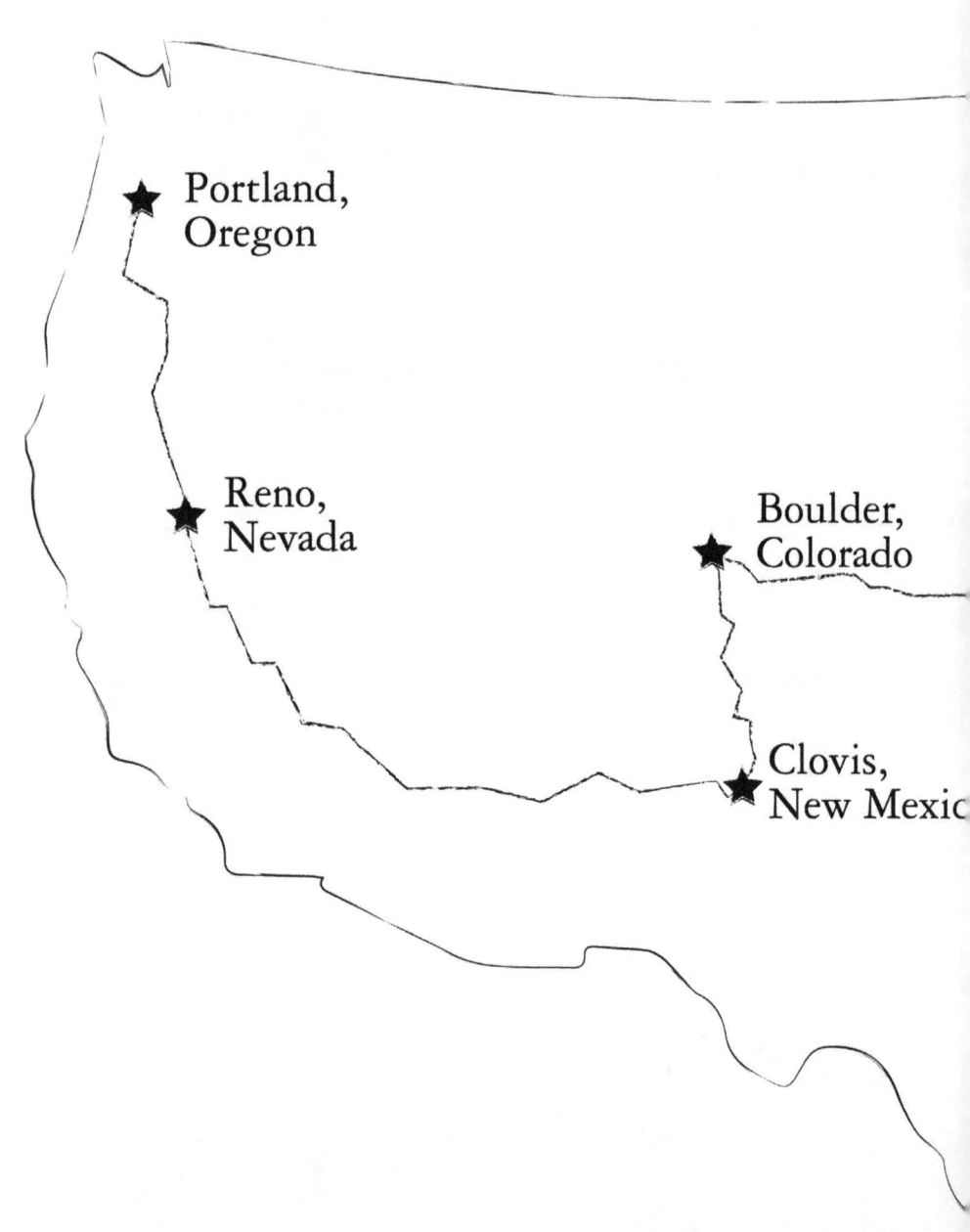

Chapter One,

So, he was dead, my father. He succumbed when my thoughts were elsewhere. It hit my gut like food poisoning. Thus began the fulfillment of a cryptic bargain he and I struck last September; it had been six months, as he had predicted. In a moment of resignation, a son studying the face of his moribund father, I had agreed to carry out his crazy scheme. I'm drawn to tell you what occurred following his death because it was so unforgettable.

Three days after he died, I boarded Northwest Airlines flight 102 flying out of the Portland International Airport on a DC-6. It was March 12, 1952; I was headed for Jupiter, Florida. Rain speckled the glass of my window seat, the fuselage shuddered as the plane surged down the runway and we lifted off in a cacophony of Pratt & Whitney radial engines clawing the air. My father's remains and the pledge I made to him awaited.

We were never close, my father and I, not really. I mean, I bore him no malice; I just never took the time to care that much. He was…hell, he was a cardboard cutout to me. Randolph Evers Sanborn was merely ordinary. I guess that's how I'd put it—so ordinary it seemed a waste, the space he took up. That, and he was unkind to my mother. He didn't abuse her he tolerated her, walked past her as if she were a lamp post. Imagine a life of merely being an object to the person you were wed to.

Do I think he loved her in his way? No, that emotional attribute was not a part of his primeval nature. I was about to find out who he really was. A strange summation of his life, the ploy he'd planned and coerced me to complete had to reveal something more of him. It must. Otherwise…otherwise what?

I had gotten the word last year, just after Labor Day. I was at my desk at Painmayer Timber going over some financials. The last time I'd heard from my father was when he called to tell me my mother's fragile heart had given out. We brought her home, grieved, and did all the proper things. She's buried out at River View Cemetery. I've been out there once since the funeral. She deserved better. Dad, he went back to Florida; we hadn't shared even a postcard for better than a year, nothing until his call.

When I heard his voice in my ear, it was small, uncertain even, very unlike his usual self-assuredness, that of a used car salesman closing a deal, insincere but confident. I laid my pencil down and leaned back in my chair; something wasn't right.

"This is a surprise," I said, massaging my forehead with the free hand.

After some hissing on the line, he answered, "I know, Michael. Sorry for not...you know, calling more often."

"Or at all." I inhaled then confirmed, "Same from my end too, though." When he didn't respond, I added, "Well, it's not my birthday."

He chuckled. "Not sure I know when that is."

I laughed back. "Nor I yours."

"Aren't we a pair."

I considered then concurred, "Were we ever?"

"Damn," my father uttered, sounding far away. "And now it's too late."

"Meaning what?"

"Michael, I...I've got the cancer."

I felt a chill just then and leaned forward onto my elbows. Was that sensation for him or for me? Losing my mother was the crushing blow every child gets when the woman who bore them reaches her expiration date. Still, I had put my sadness behind me and moved on, as we all must. And now, the man who'd been cast as my father had perhaps been sentenced as well.

"That's no good," I said.

"No. No, it isn't." I heard him inhale and let it out on a groan. "Too damn many cigarettes, Michael."

"You're sure about this?"

A hum. "Yes. I've known for a while now. My doctor diagnosed it several months ago. It's confirmed, lung cancer."

"But they're treating it, aren't they?"

"Look, Michael, I need you to come on down here. Come see me. Can you do that? As soon as possible?"

I sat up, reached out with one hand to shuffle the papers on my desk, and cleared my throat. "I don't know. We're in the midst of a big timber buy."

"I see." More distortion on the line. "This is the end point for me. Like to clear some things up. With you."

"Uh-huh."

"Look, the short of it is, I have maybe six months. If you come, I'll pay your way, whatever it takes."

"It's not that, Dad."

"I heard you, business. Been there myself."

"Six months?"

"They're giving me the radiation and some kind of new drugs they're trying out these days, but yeah, six months."

So I went. I'd never been to Florhaven before, or Florida for that matter. After a long day in the air and a ninety mile rental car ride from the Miami airport, I arrived in Jupiter just after dusk. It was still warm, seventy I'd say, unlike Portland's likely forty degrees at that hour. Florhaven Estates was one of those new retirement communities, sprawling over 600 acres, with hundreds of cottages and even a 30-bed convalescent hospital. My father chose Florhaven because of medical care being close at hand, what with my mother's deteriorating health. I guess maybe he did care for her more than I figured, or just wanted to cover his bases.

When I pulled up to his cottage that evening, the car's headlights revealed a small box of a place, white stucco, pitched roof, with a palm tree on one corner, a patch of grass, several flowering bushes, and a screened little patio. He met me at the door and smiled deferentially, his often haughty manner nowhere evident. He looked like hell. He'd lost even more hair and was nearly bald maybe due to his treatment. His once crystal clear blue eyes were watery and faded, and the tissue beneath them was puffy and dark. Befittingly we shared no embrace. He led me through a sparsely appointed living space. None of the decor was from Portland; they'd left everything behind. They had deeded the house to me, made the break to Florida, and left Nadine and me to purge the vintage foursquare.

We ended up out on the patio, where we sat on flowery padded lounge chairs. The warm air felt good. He asked how the trip was; I said fine. He nodded and went off to get refreshments. His clothes, lightweight chinos and a yellow and blue Hawaiian shirt, literally hung on his emaciated frame. He had never been bulky, but his physical appearance right then was startling. He returned with a tray carrying a pitcher of iced tea, glasses, and a plate of lemon cookies. I stood up and shed my sport coat. The air was close.

I sipped sweetened cold tea. "Mom liked it here?"

He blinked. "She did. Missed her friends but made new ones and loved the weather."

"And you, you like it?"

He bit off a piece of lemon cookie and looked at me. "Not really. Did this for Melba. Thought it would be easier on her heart."

"That didn't work for long."

"No, didn't." He looked off through the patio screen; the light was fading. He reached above his head and switched on a floor lamp. "And now I'm going to croak too." He smiled a bloodless smile.

"Why not come back to Portland?"

He shook his head. "Nah, not wanting that. Just as soon end it here."

"So, why am I here?"

He smiled an indulgent smile. "Came to me some time back, after I'd been given the hard news, that I'd better get my house in order, as they say."

"Paperwork? You could've mailed it."

He maintained the wisp of a smile. "If that's all there is, you'd be right."

"What more is there? You wanted me to see this place?" I looked around. "Not interested in it. Anyway, it will be a long time before I'd need or want this kind of retirement holding pen. Not my kind of future."

"Understand. Wasn't mine either." He held out slack-skinned thin arms. "Yet, here I am."

We fell quiet and consumed more tea and cookies. When the last cookie was finished off, he asked if I wanted more; I shook my head.

"Well then," he said finally, "might as well get to it."

I didn't know what to say, so said nothing.

"First off, you're right, most of what needs to happen…after I'm gone, that's all been taken care of. I've made it easy for you. Will is written and in the hands of my lawyer in Portland. This bungalow is yours, fully paid for. Sell it if you want. As our only child, everything goes to you except for some charitable donations your mother wanted to make—a few hundred is all. I was frugal, invested pretty well, so you'll receive a nice inheritance, minus the cost of what I'm about to reveal."

I had bitten down as he unraveled all of that. "Whatever that is," I said. "So what is your real agenda? Why have I come all this way? Just to have tea and cookies with you? There must be more."

He wiggled his sandaled feet on the lounge chair and folded spare arms across his chest. "I really made a mess of it with you, didn't I?"

"If you mean is my tit-for-tat payback for a father's neglect? Okay. You're right, I'm here merely because I feel obligated to be, especially as you are facing the end of your life. Beyond that, there's not much to add."

"Fair enough." He drew his lips in and bobbed his head. "Fair enough. You know I was thinking the other day that one thing I managed to achieve was surpassing life expectancy. I saw an article on that very topic recently, and guess what? Here I am, sixty-six years old, and I broke the barrier. Life expectancy for men right now, in 1951, is sixty-five and a half years. I've broken that barrier. Not bad, huh?"

"Quite an achievement." I gave him a tight smile.

"Yeah, well, without the smokes I'd still be going strong. So, small victory."

"Now what?"

"How's Nadine, by the way?"

"She's fine, sends her condolences," I fibbed.

"Sweet girl."

I huffed out a grunt. "Hell, you rarely saw her."

"You did well, lovely woman."

"Okay, she's nice. Let's get on with it. I have a return flight tomorrow."

"All right, let's do get on with it then." He scooted over, rose from the lounge chair, and wandered off into the house, emerging moments later with a small box. He settled back down, sat up straight, and placed the box on his lap. "I'm about to make a proposal. Afterwards, I'll cook up some grouper, and we'll dine Florida style." He unfolded the flaps and laid his hands atop whatever was in there.

And he did, have a proposal. Or rather cornered me into a bargain the likes of anything I could've expected. The crazy thing is, I agreed to do it, and I have no idea why, other than it seemed harmless enough. And I knew he would be dead by then, so there would be no further contact with the man—ever. Now you may think I was nuts to agree to what he asked, and you'd be right. Yet there I was flying back down to Florida again. But this time I wouldn't be flying back.

Like I said, he was gone, deceased, and the deal I struck with him would go into effect as soon as I returned to Jupiter. I had a two hour layover in Chicago before catching a connecting flight to Miami.

She was supposed to be there waiting for me. Her name was Johnnie, Johnnie Gates. I soon learned what she'd actually been named at birth, Jonalynn, but it never took: she was Johnnie from the very start. And Johnnie, she'd be a big part of the bargain I'd struck with my father. We'd never met before, even though she lived in Portland.

I got off the plane and started looking for her.

Chapter Two,

Within fifteen minutes of retrieving my luggage, I heard my named being called out emphatically over the clamor. I don't know what I was expecting, but she was unique—both in body and personality. Later she would declare that she should have been a boy. I could understand why: stocky build, maybe five foot eight, shoulder-length blonde hair, blue eyes, prominent Romanesque nose, square shoulders, strong neck, and angular jaw line. She was wearing a man's style white shirt with the cuffs folded up on her forearm, chino slacks, penny loafers, and no makeup or jewelry. She was different from the outset.

If she even gave a thought to it, she was seeing me as a forty-one-year-old male, dressed in a dark blue suit, burgundy tie, and black shoes, totally unsuited for Florida, but that's what I was used to wearing. I wondered how I appeared to her, all six feet of me, with thick brown hair, sort of a square face, on a lanky frame decorated with ears I'd never been happy with.

She didn't waste time on formalities, just said she had a car outside and made for the exit. I loaded my suitcase into the trunk of the sedate Chevrolet sedan she'd rented and slid into the front seat next to her; she drove.

"So here we are, Mr. Sanborn," she said while pushing the cigarette lighter button in. "You ready for this little adventure?" Her voice was low and throaty.

"It's Michael," I replied.

"Okay, then, Michael. Call me Johnnie." The lighter popped out, and she lit a Lucky Strike. "What next?"

"First, have all of the arrangements been made? For my father?"

"They have."

"Good. I need to go by his place, at Florhaven, a retirement village they call it. Have to check in with a real estate agent about the sale of the property."

"Okay, just get me there."

The light was fading when we arrived. Our headlights lit up a sign that was stuck in the ground in front of the bungalow: For Sale, Florhaven Realty. I let us in with the key I'd taken with me six months before, turned on the lights, and called the number for the agent. He was having dinner but said he could come by in half an hour. While we waited, Johnnie and I sat out on the patio and discussed what lay ahead. Neither of us could quite fathom the trip we were about to take—with my father.

The real estate agent, a short, portly fellow with no hair, wearing a bright yellow shirt that billowed over his bulk, showed up fifteen minutes late. He apologized, then told me there was already good interest in the property. He boasted that quick sales at Florhaven were usually the case. Very popular, he emphasized. I didn't bother to tell him of my dislike for the place. I told him we'd be staying overnight and leave the key behind. Arrangements had been made for the furnishings to be sold and the house to be cleaned. My father had taken care of most everything; he'd even packed up family memorabilia and shipped it to me some time ago.

Johnnie and I brought in our bags and prepared to stay over until morning. I gave her the bedroom and took the couch. There was nothing to eat in the house, so we drove around and found a small diner that was still open and over shrimp Po Boys talked more about our pending road trip together.

Before bedding down on the sofa, I called Nadine to let her know that I'd arrived okay and everything was moving ahead as planned. She still couldn't believe that I had agreed to what she called my father's preposterous stunt. I demurred that what was done was done. I didn't tell her that I'd be spending the night with an unattached female in the other room.

The next morning, as Johnnie and I were leaving Florhaven for good, a woman in a housecoat came over from an adjacent bungalow. She asked if I was Randy's son. Randy? No one ever called my father Randy. When I said yes, she lamented my loss and told me that a few of the neighbors had held a little informal reception in his honor. A real charmer after all, I thought. I thanked the woman, gave her a big smile, then Johnnie and I skipped going to breakfast right then and drove directly to Lundberg's Funeral Home, an imposing old mansion that had been serving as a mortuary for decades. Johnnie pulled around back of the place, killed the ignition, and gave the steering wheel a thump.

"Okay, here we are. You all set there, Michael?"

"I guess."

"All right, let's go meet this Lundberg fella."

Albert Lundberg was the third-generation owner of the funeral home. Thin fellow, gold rimmed glasses, neatly trimmed head of brown hair, and attired in a very nice light tan suit with a bland blue tie. When we met him in his office, he sat rather stiffly at his desk, hands clasped together on a green ink blotter pad, and offered us a flat-lipped smile.

"Miss Gates, good to greet you in person. Mister Sanborn, sorry for your loss." Spoken with the aplomb of a professional griever.

With a practiced hand, Lundberg pushed his bill for services across to me; the amount was greater than I had expected. His face reddened.

"On such short notice, our staff worked overtime to meet your deadline."

"I see." I looked at Johnnie. "Did you view their work?"

She nodded. "Excellent."

I paid the man. My father was waiting. I visited the viewing room where he was at rest, hands folded across his midsection, eyes closed; a bit of color had been added to his lips and cheeks. He looked not much different than the last time I'd seen him, more gaunt, but the application of cosmetics downplayed the pallor I had expected. He had asked to be buried wearing a selection from his Florida wardrobe, so there he was in a flowered shirt and light beige slacks. I reached out and touched the back of one hand but withdrew when I felt the coolness and sensed the lack of a heartbeat.

You've probably assumed some of the story, but here's the crux of it. When my father had me come visit him last fall, it was to oblige me to carry out a scheme he'd contrived in the months leading up to his death. A plot that would be carried out after he had expired, and only if I agreed.

To begin with, four months prior to his death, my father contracted with the Gates & Collier Funeral Home in Portland to convey his body back home by funeral coach. He spared no expense, I learned. Johnnie's father, Clarence Gates, had drafted his daughter for the task, considering it purely a transport job. Gates and his daughter received full details of my father's plan: chauffeur his remains cross-country and incorporate seven stops along the way—simple. The final requirement was that I, his son, would ride with the driver and carry out a planned series of visitations.

I had the seven envelopes in my possession, as my father had mailed them to me before his death. They contained letters to persons known to him in life; they were to be personally delivered by me. I'd read each letter and was both moved and dismayed by what my father had put in them. Every letter was typewritten on rag content ivory paper. Below the closing lines of each letter was my father's signature handwritten in black ink, usually just Randolph. He had given much thought to not only the content but also the appearance of the letters. By their very nature, each message declared: Take this seriously, very seriously.

Per the agreement outlined by my father, I was to meet face-to-face with every designee, divulge that Randolph Sanborn was deceased, and hand over the letter he'd written specifically to them. Each letter revealed that his remains were parked nearby. And yes, I could imagine reactions ranging from acceptance to displeasure and regret, even rage.

And now the show was about to hit the road.

Our ride was waiting for us out behind Lundberg's, sitting next to an ambulance. It was a glistening black 1950 Cadillac Meteor Landau Statesman funeral coach; a metal nameplate appeared in the side windows: Gates & Collier Funeral Home. The vehicle was Johnnie's pride and joy. It had a massive eggshell chrome grill, the large V hood emblem with Cadillac crest, and was long and sleek with side coach lamps and landau S shaped moldings just behind the rear windows. It was all tied together with rear fins inspired by the P-38 war plane. Johnnie was an encyclopedia when it came to statistics about that vehicle. It had everything but a radio; her father thought it undignified for music and announcer chatter to emanate from his fine funeral coach during somber moments of loss and pain.

Johnnie backed the Meteor up to Lundberg's rear entrance, and two men wearing comparable gray suits opened double doors and rolled out a casket carriage. Johnnie and I stood back as the men lifted the casket and pushed it in until it engaged with the casket rollers. They used a bier pin to hold the casket in place.

Hello Dad, I thought, ready to hit the road?

Johnnie confirmed with the Lundberg staff that they would see that the rental car was returned; then she slid behind the wheel onto the plush two-tone gray bench seat next to me. She looked over, smiled, and turned the ignition key. The big V8 engine under the hood came to life.

Before hitting U.S. 41, we stopped off at a diner, parked the coach right close, and over a late breakfast, studied a AAA road map. Our first stop would be in Clarksville, Tennessee, nearly 800 miles. I couldn't help but wonder who was waiting for me there. I knew his name but not who he was. Johnnie had mapped out the entire trip, nearly 4,500 miles. Folding the map, she innocently wondered if I was going to travel the entire trip looking like a mortician. I did look like a stuffed shirt, so upon leaving the diner I found Burdine's Men's shop and did some quick shopping for a new wardrobe. I emerged wearing chinos, a sport shirt, even a pair of Thom McAn brown and white two-tone wingtips: the new me.

I stored my retired clothing, along with the new, in the space in front of the casket and gave my father a pat. Johnnie was holding her arm out the open window with a cigarette between her fingers. She nodded her approval of my improved look and pulled out into traffic; several vehicles paused or stopped to let the hearse go ahead. Johnnie laughed. It was a common occurrence, being given the right of way.

The seven-letter road trip was underway.

Chapter Three,

It was midmorning when we left the city limits of Jupiter behind. Johnnie had scheduled our first overnight stop to be Macon, Georgia, halfway to Clarksville. We stopped only to refuel and grab sandwiches and coffee to go. It was late, after dark, by the time we pulled into Macon and located Wiggins Funeral Home. In spite of the hour, the owner, Charles Wiggins, a tall, dignified Black man, cheerfully drove us to a nearby motel and offered to come get us early the next morning to retrieve the Meteor. He refused any payment as a courtesy of the profession.

Early the next morning, Johnnie jolted me awake by thumping on my door: time to move. After a quick shower and shave, I stood at the ready when Charles Wiggins appeared and ferried us back to the coach. On the road by seven-thirty.

Handing off the letter in Tennessee would be my debut performance. I tried to imagine intruding on the unsuspecting lives cast in my father's drama—but no luck. Johnnie suddenly broke into my train thought and involuntarily began reciting details of the trip.

"For instance, how do you think we got the Meteor here?" She patted the dashboard.

"Drove, I guess."

"Not on your life. Wasn't gonna run empty miles on her. I wrapped her up snug and put her on auto transport. She was waiting for me at a truck terminal in Miami. Perfect condition."

By the time we'd gone another couple of miles, I knew every detail of how she'd orchestrated our trip: road maps, AAA TripTik planner with routes and milage, arranging to store the coach each night, occasionally even where to sleep and eat—must have taken many hours and phone calls.

When the dashboard clock above the glove box read just after four o'clock, she flipped the stub of a cigarette out her wing window and looked over at me. "Getting close. Clarksville coming up. You ready for this, whatever it is? Your dad, he didn't tell us much. Just curious. You okay with it?"

"Not sure." I reached out and stretched my arms toward the dashboard. "There's no dress rehearsal for what I'm about to do."

She hummed but didn't say anything.

"Okay," I said when she slowed for a speed limit sign. "Suppose I should fill you in." I opened the glove box and pulled out the packet of envelopes and snapped the wide rubber band that held them all together. I extracted the first envelope and waved it at her.

"This one's for Clarksville. Delivery number one. For every stop there'll be an envelope, just like this one."

She nodded. "Okay."

"This first one here is addressed to a Cordell Jones. Before he died, Dad wrote this Jones a letter. I'm supposed to make an appointment and deliver the letter in person. No mention of the funeral coach; they'll read about about it in the letter."

"Holy smoke," she choked out a laugh. "So you've read 'em? The letters?"

"I have. I'll tell you about it later. Let's park the coach."

The people at Rickle's Mortuary were of the more serious type than Charles Wiggins in Macon had been, and they wanted a fee. A staff mortician took three five-dollar bills from me, gave us permission to come and go on their lot, and called us a cab—there would be no courtesy ride. Duke's Cab, smelling of cigarettes and body odor, dropped us off at Thackeray's Inn, which claimed to be air conditioned and had its own restaurant. We checked in and I went off to our rooms to freshen up. I shaved off my day-long shadow and put on fresh clothes. Wearing my new duds and two-tone shoes, I felt as ready as I ever would be. I'd never shown up with a dead man in tow before.

Johnnie knocked on my door; she'd changed into a fresh version of the same outfit she had been wearing.

"You called the guy?" she asked.

"Not yet."

She raised her eyebrows and dropped into an upholstered side chair. "Nervous?"

I ignored her and flipped open the spiral notebook containing contact information, located the number, and dialed. It rang several times before there was an answer. It was a female voice.

"Yes, ah, is this the Jones residence?"

"It is. Who is this?"

I hesitated, inhaled, and knew that this was the beginning. "Mrs. Jones?"

"Yes."

"I...I am Michael Sanborn." When she didn't respond, I added, "I am Randolph Sanborn's son."

"I see."

"I wonder if Mr. Jones, if Cordell is available to speak."

The pause was long. "No, he isn't."

"When will he be home?"

"What is it you want?"

"I have something I need to give him. From my father. Would that be possible?"

There was a pause. "Are you in town, in Clarksville?"

"Yes."

"When can you come by?"

"Anytime. I'll need directions is all."

She told me how to find their house and hung up. Johnnie sat wide-eyed while I quietly calmed the flutters in my gut and wondered just how round one of the funeral express would play out. Duke's Cab returned us to Rickle's Mortuary to pick up the Meteor.

Other than confirming street directions, we didn't speak on the drive to Dodd Street. The house was a tidy one-story bungalow; a large maple tree stood on one corner of the yard, the grass was mowed and edged, and the flower beds contained what appeared to be bright white and purple pansies. I'm not good with plants. When Johnnie parked the Meteor at the curb, it was nearing seven o'clock; she waited calmly while I gathered my thoughts. Finally, I sat forward, held the envelope tightly, gave her an insincere smile, and got out.

The woman answered the door in the merest of a moment after I rang the bell and stood staring up at me. She was a Negro, a fact that wasn't addressed in my father's letter. She was a pleasant-appearing women, somewhat ample but not heavy, graying hair, with a calm demeanor. She was light brown, lighter than the few people of color I'd seen around predominantly White Portland.

She wore browline glasses with dark upper frames and peered at me through heavy lenses. I put on a salesman's smile; she did not reciprocate.

Chapter Four.

The envelope in my right hand seemed to have gained heft and heat.

"Mrs. Jones?"

She nodded and stepped back. "Come in, please."

The pleasant aroma of something cooking filled the air, like a comfort food casserole or goulash, the kind my mother used to fix. It was a nice though modest house, matching furniture, not new but appealing, among the assorted things that make space worth something: pictures on the wall, family photographs, house plants, table lamps—it felt inviting. I particularly liked a watercolor painting of an aged red barn on a green field.

When I stopped gawking around, I turned and saw her watching me, hands clasped at her waist. She had on a light green housedress with a white collar; over that she wore a white apron decorated with small flowers and big patch pockets. I broadened my smile.

"I like that painting."

She turned her head to look at it. "Cordell painted that. He was good at that, painting. Gave him a way to relax."

"Very nice." The past tense, I missed it at first. "Is he here, Mrs. Jones?"

"Marlena," she answered. "No one calls me but Marlena."

I nodded and said okay.

"Sit down, Mr. Sanborn."

"Michael. Please call me Michael."

It was her turn to nod. "Fine." She waited until I sat in a platform rocker then took a seat herself in an armchair. "Why are you here, Michael?"

I held the envelope in one hand. "My father, Randolph Sanborn, asked me to come see Cordell and deliver this letter."

"Yes, I knew of your father," she said.

"Well, you see, he recently passed away, my father. Lung cancer."

Her hands remained in her lap. "I'm sorry for you."

I smiled. I guess it was more of a grin. It felt ridiculous. "Before he died, my father asked me to make a number of visitations after he was gone. To give certain people a personal letter he had written to them." I held up the envelope. "This is a letter to your husband, to Cordell. That's why I have to see him."

"You can't."

"Oh?"

She looked down, then back up right at me. "He's gone too, these past three years." She squeezed her hands.

Just then, the front door swung open, and a middle-aged Black man stood in the open doorway. "What's that hearse doing out front, Mom?"

Mrs. Jones sat up straight, eyes widened. "Hearse?"

"Yeah, big shiny black one." The man caught sight of me and stared. "Who's this?"

Marlena Jones rose. "Mason, this is Michael Sanborn. Michael, this is my son Mason."

The man was square-shouldered, had striking masculine features with a thin mustache; he was darker than his mother. His expression went from curiosity to sober judgement in an instant. I'd read the letter. I knew the underlying tale and could sense that all three of us knew the history. I kept my smile on though it sorely wanted to quit.

Mason Jones shut the door with a solid thrust. "Sanborn." He looked toward his mother. "Not that Sanborn."

"Yes," I answered for her. "That Sanborn."

He took several steps into the living room. "Why are you here?" It wasn't a question; it was an accusation.

"Mason." His mother's tone suggested restraint. "Michael's father has passed."

The man stared at me then turned and went to a window. He looked out. "You mean...?"

I nodded. "That's right. He's with me."

Mason Jones looked out again and came up shaking his head. "What the hell is this? You telling us you have your old man's...body out there?"

Summation

"I am."

"What the fuck for."

"Mason," his mother admonished.

He waved a hand at her. "Why?"

"I'm taking him home, back to Portland."

The man shook his head, turned in a circle, and rubbed a hand over his mouth and jaw before coming around to stare me down some more. "Portland, that whitey hellhole we escaped from. And you just decided to stop by here and rub our noses in your old man's dying. Well, so what? Do we give a shit? No!"

"Mason, why don't we hear the man out now? He has something for us. A letter, he has a letter to Daddy."

"A letter." He gave me a bitter laugh. "A letter from the grave…no, from the coffin. Still hafta bury the bastard." He raised an arm. "Well, give me a shovel."

We, all three, stood in a clutch, saying nothing after his tirade. Where do I go from here, I thought. Damn you, Dad. That's what was going through my head.

"And who's that big White woman standing out there by the hearse? Your wife?"

"Our driver."

"Mom, this is insane, isn't it?"

"Mason," I broke in. "May I give you and your mother this letter? If you don't want to read it, fine, tear it up. But my father put some thought into it, you may find something in it, some solace, or not. It's not something through rose-colored glasses. I'm just delivering it." I held the letter out.

He looked at it, then at his mother, and shrugged. Finally, Marlena took a step toward me, and I handed her the envelope. She saw Cordell's name typed on it. I told them I'd wait outside. If they wanted to talk with me, let me know. If not, we'd be on our way.

She was prying the envelope flap open when I closed the door. Here is what they would read:

RANDOLPH E. SANBORN
FLORHAVEN ESTATES
JUPITER, FLORIDA

February 1952

Cordell Jones
1001 Dodd Street
Clarksville, Tennessee

Dear Cordell,

You've just met my son, Michael. And he has explained why he's calling on you, with me being deceased and my remains parked at your curb. You see, I've coerced him into becoming a unique messenger after my passing. He has been charged with visiting a distinctive list of people with whom I interacted during my life. As he begins this journey, you are the first person he has been directed to approach.

I know this is all very unusual. But one day as I agonized over the malignancy that would do me in, I was brought up short by several penetrating questions: My life, had it meant anything? Would my presence in the world have been considered worth the air I breathed? Had I lived an exemplary life? As I contemplated the sum and substance of that, the short hard answer was no.

There was no way for me to make up for my many shortcomings, but while I couldn't ask for forgiveness, at least I could express my regrets. This attempt could easily be considered a cowardly way to make up for something long overdue. Why did I wait to speak from the grave? Hell, I was protecting myself from ever having to correct the miserable treatment of my fellow man face-to-face.

```
Cordell, you are a man of integrity, a man of
talent and much potential. While at Natron Insur-
ance, there were opportunities which should have
gone your way. They didn't largely because of my
racial bias. My father was a bigot, and I was a
carrier to some degree. So, as I assessed my sins
of commission, there you were. I cut off what was
rightfully yours because I had the authority and
influence to do so. Looking back on my regrets, I
know your gifts were far greater than mine, let
alone your qualities as a human being. I ask not
for your forgiveness because you lost too much that
should have been. Only know that this coward took
his shame to the grave.

With high regard,
```
Randolph

I passed Johnnie waiting at the curb and walked down the sidewalk about half a block to clear my head. Just before I turned back around, an elderly Negro came out from his house and hobbled toward me all bent over, leaning on a large wooden cane.

"You there," he said on the raspy whisper of a voice. "What happened, Mrs. Jones pass?" He was focused on the coach as he spoke. "Can't be, she's too young. Lordy."

I raised a hand to calm the man. "No, sir, she's fine."

He looked at me, finally taking his eyes off the funeral coach. "What? Why's you here then? Scaring folks to death, you are."

What could I say? "A visitation." That's what I conjured up.

"A visitation? What's that?" He looked again at the big black vehicle.

"Visitation." He repeated the word, trying to decipher its meaning.

I smiled, what else?

"You means like the grim reaper?"

We stood there in the shadows, and I let the growing darkness camouflage my inability to further define the moment. And I knew damn well that such encounters could happen at every stop. Finally the old man moved off grumbling to himself and climbed the stairs, stabbing his cane on each step, until back into his house.

I watched him disappear behind a heavy wooden door and decided that if no one came out of the Jones' house in another couple of minutes or so, we'd move on. I had my hand on the door handle of the coach when the porch light came on and Mason came out. He waved. I waved back and returned to the house. The good smells were still in the air, so was the tension. There was a sofa in the room; Mason and his mother were seated on it, side-by-side. The son asked me to take a seat; I settled into the rocker again. We all exchanged looks at one another for a short time before Mason leaned forward on his knees and looked directly at me.

"I'm wanting you to know our side of the story," he said. "You up for that?"

I nodded and shrugged. "Seems fair. Sure."

Mason turned to his mother. She remained still. "Okay," he said, looking back at me. "We read the letter." He had it in his right hand and held it up. "A dead man's apology? Doesn't mean a thing."

"I can understand."

"Can you? How? How old are you?"

"Forty-one."

"Okay, I'm forty. Never met you until today. And I'm betting that your old man never spoke of the smart-as-hell Negro working at Natron, pushing the mail cart around and doing low-level paper work, am I right?"

I nodded.

He leaned out even farther. "Your father's acknowledgement of my dad's potential—that really cuts into my gut. He knew, the bastard knew, that Cordell Jones had what it would take to make a place for himself. I was eighteen when we packed up and left Portland. And I remember how much he resented the racial bias he felt. How depressed he was. He felt he was a failure. When we returned to Clarksville, it was still the Depression, and the only job he could get was at the foundry. Dirty, hot work around casting furnaces. He did that as long as he could, until it got his health." He stood and came to stand over me. "You getting this, Michael?" He leaned down. "I said, are you getting this!"

I felt the heat in my face. "I'm getting it," I answered as calmly as I could.

"Mason," his mother's voice came up. "He isn't his father. Those are not his sins."

The man backed off. Turned in a circle, came back around to look at me again. "Let me show you something." He went to a lamp table and picked up a framed photo and brought it over to me. "Here, hold this. It's my favorite picture of Dad. Look at it."

It was a black-and-white photograph of a smiling man. His expression was warm, his features striking, his color close to that of his son. The resemblance was obvious. Cordell Jones was probably about his son's age now when it was taken.

"He was a handsome man," I offered.

Mason took the picture back and looked at it. "Yes." He put it back. "He didn't look that good after all of those years at the foundry. Even after that he still had to work. During the war, while I was serving in the Army, he took a job at Fort Campbell, the Air Force base. As a carpenter. Best job he ever had. He loved it there.

"After the war, I used the GI Bill, went to Howard University, got a business degree. I was just getting started, hiring out that shiny new diploma, when Dad fell off a scaffold at the fort. He was gone. I had to come home, be here for Mom. The woman I was going to marry wouldn't follow me here. Guess that says something. Got on at B. F. Goodrich making soles and heels. Now I work at Kraft making cheese. So much for my big career, guess it runs in the family."

"Mason, stop such talk," Marlena Jones said.

"Now, Mom and I have dinners together and try to forget what might have been." He raised his arms. "So you see, Michael, your father's letter of regret means nothing. Nothing. Not a damned thing. So what if he took his sins to the grave? Absolute bullshit." He looked at his mother then went over, leaned down, and kissed her gently on the cheek.

When he stood up, his back still to me, he said, "Now, we would like to you leave."

When he didn't turn around, I rose and left the house without further comment. Johnnie got out of the coach when I came down the steps from the house. She was standing with her hands in her pockets. "How'd it go?" she asked.

I sighed a pathetic laugh. "If they're all like this, I'll need therapy by the time we get back home."

She pointed. "It may not be over."

It was Mason. He'd come out and was approaching us. "Your dad, he's in there, really?" I nodded. "I want to see him."

I looked at Johnnie then back to Mason. "Him, or the casket?"

"No, him. I want to actually see him."

"Why?" I asked.

"I just do. Will you agree?"

"Can you do that?" I asked Johnnie.

She said yes. I agreed to do it. We waited while she got a flashlight out of the glove box and opened the right side door of the coach. I held the light while she opened the rear door to locate the casket key and unlock the lid. When she came back to the side of the coach, she looked at me, questioning. I nodded. She reached in, used the key, and lifted the lid while I aimed the flashlight. There he was, my father, looking the same. Mason stepped forward, peered in for a long moment before stepping away. Johnnie went through the process in reverse and closed up the Meteor.

I reached in to put the flashlight back into the glove box, and when I stood back up he was right there, in my face. He knocked me down with a wild punch—I ended up sitting on my ass on the parking strip grass, head swimming.

"That's for bringing all of this back into our lives." He walked off. Marlena Jones was waiting on the porch under the light; she was watching what had just occurred but stood still as a statue. I looked at her and she at me, but neither of us acknowledged the other.

When I struggled to my feet, my butt damp from the sod, I saw several men and women standing outside their homes, clustered on the sidewalk, beneath a streetlight, quietly staring at the scene. One woman raised a hand of concern to her face. I swiped a hand across my wet rear end and considered that she had likely never seen a Negro hit a White man before. I felt like saying it was all right, I had it coming.

As she drove away, Johnnie said, "Well, that was something." I touched my jaw and agreed.

Summation

Chapter Five,

The trip back to Rickle's Mortuary was driven in silence, other than Johnnie asking me twice if I was okay. I said I was all right though my face was tender when I flexed it. We parked the coach and used the night bell to rouse the mortuary attendant on duty; he called us a cab, and we were in a booth at Thackeray's restaurant an hour before they closed. We agreed on the Salisbury steak special and that we both needed a drink; while I enjoyed the medicinal qualities of a Sidecar, Johnnie downed a Gin Rickey. Equally anesthetized, we put away a meal that wasn't the best or the worst, but it fell into my stomach like a miracle drug. We ate in silence. When I leaned back, my plate stripped clean, Johnnie was staring at me. Her meal had also gone missing.

"Did the trick, huh?" I said and wiped my mouth with a napkin.

"Was okay," she answered. "Drink was better." Then she leaned forward and on a hoarse whisper said, "Seriously, Michael, you telling me that you're gonna do that, what we just went through, that you're gonna be doing that six more times?"

"Next stop Pine Bluff. And I ain't bluffing." She didn't laugh. "It's what I agreed to do."

"Yeah but, you expecting combat at every stop? Are these all people your old man did wrong?"

The waitress dropped the dinner bill on the table, and I dug for some cash. "Not all, but some…maybe even most. He's making amends in some cases, or trying to. Besides, we're just getting underway. What happened today was likely an aberration."

"So you say. But he's dead, and you're out running the gauntlet putting yourself between his remains and some possibly vengeful folks."

"You brought a gun, didn't you?"

"Funny. And no, I didn't bring a gun, or any kind of weapon. That industrial weight flashlight we used could give a good head-knocking. That's it." The waitress cruised by and swept up the bill and the money. Johnnie waited then said, "But really now, Michael, tell me at what point would you pull the plug, pat your father on the lid of his casket, and go home?"

"You're getting well paid, aren't you?"

She hesitated. "We are, yes."

"And I took you for a strong, take no guff woman from the first day I met you. Am I wrong?"

She sat up straight. "What's that got to do with anything? I can take bullshit as well as the next person, but does that mean I have to?"

I smiled but felt irritated just the same. "Look, here we are several thousand miles from home base and just getting started. Now that I'm into this, I'm more fascinated than I thought I'd be. The Pine Bluff stop will be a most interesting rendezvous. You won't want to miss it. Might be another unwelcome welcome. Should we pick up a baseball bat?"

She patted the air, and we called it a day.

The next morning was Sunday. It was 360 miles or so to Pine Bluff, but we agreed to take it easy, sleep in, have a late breakfast before moving on. It was a spectacular day, clear skies, heading toward temperatures in the high sixties. Johnnie hosed off the coach at the mortuary and dried it with her chamois until it shone like black glass.

Before we'd left town, I had called Nadine to tell her I'd made the first stop. How'd it go? she asked. I told her. She groaned, said my name three times in a row, and questioned my soundness of mind. I left out the part about being socked in the jaw. Best that way.

The ebony Meteor coach was a commanding presence on the road, moving us along smoothly behind its hydramatic transmission at the head of its own ceremonial parade. When Johnnie would come up on a car or truck, often the driver would pull off the highway, allowing the specter of past life to move by.

We stopped for lunch in the town of Jackson at an eatery called The Hut, boasting the South's Best Bar-B-Q. There was a row of dancing pigs on the roof, each one outlined in neon. After downing orders of barbecued spareribs, we were back out on the street in less than thirty minutes.

A local cop was on the sidewalk standing next to the coach, giving the vehicle the once-over and jotting something down in a notebook. When we approached, he slipped the notebook into his shirt pocket, eyeballed the coach once more, then turned to us.

"This here your vehicle?" He tipped his head toward the coach.

Johnnie said it was.

He nodded and pulled at his nose. "Where y'all heading? I see you got Oreygone plates on this…hearse."

"That's where we're from. Transporting the remains of a deceased gentleman back to Portland."

"You don't say. That's a right long haul, right long haul." He looked my way then back at Johnnie. "Suppose you have papers and all."

"What would you be wanting?" Johnnie asked. "Have my funeral director's license from Oregon and receipt from the Lundberg Funeral Home in Jupiter, Florida, transferring the remains to us."

"Jupiter? Never heared of it." He looked at me again. "And what's your part in all this?"

"The deceased is my father."

He blinked at me and opened his eyes wider. "You don't say. And you're riding along?"

"I am."

"That a fact? Never heared of something like that before."

"I agreed to accompany him back home before he passed."

"Uh-huh." He pulled on his nose again. "Tell you what, if you'd just show me your license, lady, and give me a peek in there so I know you're not hauling pigs to market…"

"Pigs to market?" Johnnie spoke right up. "That's uncalled for."

"Sorry, meant no offense." He hesitated, looked at his shoes, and said, "Just give me a look inside, and you can be on your way."

Johnnie looked at me, and when I nodded, she stepped to the curbside casket chamber door. By that time, a handful of onlookers had stopped.

Johnnie said something to the policeman and he waved an arm and the curious moved on. After the officer had been given a peek, he touched the brim of his hat to Johnnie and meandered off down the sidewalk to his patrol car.

Once back in the coach, Johnnie pulled out the map and shook her head. "The morbidly curious. Goes with the business, but I never get used to it. Pigs to market, for cripes' sake."

"Never been accused of that before?" I couldn't help laughing.

"Not funny," she grunted then she raised the open map, hiding her face, and began to laugh. "Guess it was."

She folded the cranky map and laid it on the seat between us. "Pine Bluff, who we gonna harass there?"

"Fellow name of Ripley."

"You mean like Ripley's Believe It or Not?"

"Different Ripley."

"Well, we'd best put some miles on the odometer. This Ripley, he know we're coming his way?"

I shook my head. "Not giving the scoundrel any advance warning." She turned her head and leveled dubious eyes on me. "I read the letter," I said.

Johnnie said, "I thought we'd be getting a breather on this next one."

"Not yet."

She turned the ignition key, the big engine came to life, and pulled away from the curb. On the way out of town, we passed the pigs to market cop, who was seated in his patrol car a couple of blocks away. He waved as we cruised by. Johnnie said a curse word under her breath and reluctantly returned the wave.

Before we cleared the city limits, she pulled the coach into an Esso gas station; an acned teenage attendant filled the tank. He stared in at us nervously as he washed the windshield but looked away quickly when I flashed him a smile.

After we caught U.S. 79, Johnnie checked her side mirror and said, "You gonna share the details of letter number two? A scoundrel, you said."

"Uh-huh. I did." That's all I said.

She cruised up and slowed behind an old flatbed farm truck. Through the cab's rear window, a man's head was silhouetted; he was wearing a brimmed hat, looking side-to-side, checking his rearview mirrors, and

Summation

slowing even more until he steered the truck off to the side of the road. As we passed, he leaned out the window and held out his battered fedora in what I assumed was a gesture of respect.

"So," she said, ignoring the man's intent and accelerated back up to speed. "This guy, what'd your old man do to him?"

I had a vague memory of Ripley Miller. From what I'd learned, mainly from my mother, he and my father had a vainglorious alliance: they played golf together, drank together, belonged to the Elks—self-absorbed men who seldom included their wives in any of their pleasures. It had been all about them. While Ripely was a small man plagued with early hereditary baldness and a non-athletic body, he'd made up for it by his sartorial touch; I remember him as a dapper dresser. That's all I recalled, except that I thought he was an arrogant twit, all toothy smiles and fake charm. Funny what a young mind plucks out of early life and holds onto.

We drove on. The bright sun shone in on us for a long stretch. We pulled the visors down, and after a few miles I took the envelopes out of the glove box, stretched the rubber band, and extracted the Ripley letter. Johnnie glanced over as I unfolded the thick paper, scanned the first paragraph, wondered how Miller would take it, and then read my father's message to his old friend aloud.

Afterward, Johnnie held her hands at ten and two on the bone-white steering wheel and looked straight down the highway. "What a snake," she said as we approached the small town of Marianna, Arkansas, just as dusk came to call.

Chapter Six,

We rolled along Marianna's main street beneath the watchful presence of a spraddle-legged water tower inscribed with the town's name. In the center of the small business section, Johnnie pulled to the curb and stopped. She left the engine running and leaned over the steering wheel.

I looked at my wristwatch; going on six o'clock, still marginally light out, but from what we saw of the town, it had already shut down for the day.

"What now?" she asked.

"How much farther?"

She reached up to turn on the dome light and lifted the map beneath its yellow glow. "Educated guess, couple of hours, give or take."

"Maybe we'd best find a place to eat. How are we on gas?"

She squinted at the fuel gauge. "We'll make it."

"Okay, let's look for chow."

We found the Walnut Ridge Grill still open. We walked in unnoticed until a middle-aged waitress pointed to an empty booth. "Watcha want?" she challenged. Under pressure, we chose pulled-pork sandwiches and a couple of Dixie beers. The waitress blew at a strand of hair drooping down from her forehead and lumbered off with our order.

"She didn't even notice how special we are," Johnnie muttered.

I snorted a laugh, raised my arms, stretched, and looked over at Johnnie: at her square face, her determined jaw, and the straw-colored hair.

"What?" she said. "That look. You were going to say something. What is it?"

"Nothing."

"Hell, you say. Now I know there's something. You don't like my driving, my nose, the fact that I don't wear perfume?"

I laughed out loud. "What the heck, where'd all that come from?"

She looked at me unsmiling, her blue eyes locked on. "I'm waiting."

I leaned forward on my elbows and smiled at her sober expression. "Okay. We have a very long way to go."

"And?"

"Since we'll be spending all this time together, I'd like to know more about you." When her eyebrows went up, I added, "All we've been doing up to this point is checking the map, parking the coach at night, finding places to sleep, and eat, like right now, and onto the next stop."

"That's what your father paid us for."

"You're right...you're right, it's just like..."

"Like what?"

Our pork sandwiches appeared suddenly, followed by the beers, stalling my response. Our cheery waitress pulled a church-key out of her apron pocket and pried the caps off our beer bottles. We each took a swig.

"Like what," Johnnie repeated and took a bite of sandwich.

I set the cold-sweat beer bottle down. "It's...I don't know...knowing more about the seven people we're tracking down than about my fellow traveler seems not right—rude even."

She put her sandwich down and wiped her mouth, all the while looking at me, her eyebrows arched. Then she laughed into her napkin. "Rude?"

I took a sizable bite of bun and pork and barbecue sauce, and nodded.

"All righty then, I was born in 1920 in Portland, makes me 32. I'm five foot eight. You can see my not exactly svelte body type..."

"No," I said, raising a hand. "I know all of that, or can guess most of it. Tell me about you, not the statistics."

She leaned back in the booth. "Okay, like what?"

"Up to you," I said. "Whatever you like."

"No." She shoved her half-eaten food aside and pointed a forefinger at me. "You started this."

I nodded. "Okay, tell me who you are."

She took another swallow of beer and squinted at me for a long moment. "Damn," she said at last. "Never had such a question put at me before." She spread her arms out and then laid her open hands on the table. "Criminy."

"Never mind. Too personal, sorry."

"Well, I'm not the person I wanted to be. Had plans when I was in high school, never happened. Mom died, right away making me the woman of the house and the one to tend to my little brother Danny." She paused. "He was brain damaged when mom had him. That's when she died. I was a junior in high school at the time."

She closed down. Clasped her hands and squeezed; her eyes began to glisten. I gave her the moment and didn't say a word.

"We not only lost our mom. My dad lost his secretary, receptionist, and all-around partner at the mortuary. I got those jobs too." She drained her beer. "You know I haven't thought about all of that for a long time, at least not run together like that. Dang, there's a hole in my gut where I keep it all. Still hurts when it gets stirred up."

"I didn't mean to have you stir up bad memories."

She smiled. "Probably good to drag it out and dust it off every now and again. Besides, no one has ever told me they wanted to know more about me." She contemplated and smiled. "Ever."

I winced a smile back at her. "May I ask if you feel trapped in all of that?"

"Hell yes. I'm a goddamned body snatcher, fill-in homemaker, with a damaged brother to care for. Sound fun?"

I regretted asking.

"On top of that, I was supposed to be a boy." She laughed. "That's why my folks named me Jonalynn, my father's idea. He started calling me Johnnie from the day they brought me home from the hospital. Hell, with this body I almost was a boy. Until I was a senior in high school, I could take on the boys and beat them regular...at anything. Course puberty changed that overnight. I was popular for athletics until it came time to date."

"You have someone in your life now?"

She chuckled. "Oh sure. There's a hot market for a block-bodied female who messes with cadavers, gets called to pick up a body in the middle of a date or a distress call about her impaired brother."

I paid the bill, left a tip for our charm school waitress, and we exited Marianna, Arkansas; I wager no one noticed we had been there. Johnnie quietly drove the coach with one hand draped loosely over the steering wheel. Nothing was said for a stretch of miles. I'd glance over off and on and see her face highlighted by the dashboard light; she was focused, off somewhere thinking her own thoughts.

"Thank you, Michael," she said after about half an hour. She glanced over at me. "Like I said, no one has ever asked me anything like that. To know about me, that is."

I laid my right arm on the window sill, repositioned my behind on the nap of the upholstery, and let her self-examination ride. Fact is, I searched my own head and found no recollection of interested parties wanting to know more about me either. Decided to not go into that with Johnnie, least not until I'd ruminated on my own past a bit more.

When we cut past the Pine Bluff city limits, it was shortly after nine o'clock.

Johnnie pulled the coach into a Sunoco gas station that was still open, and a kid ran out wearing a billed cap and a blue shirt with letter stitching on it. When Johnnie opened the door, I heard him ask her if there was a dead person in there. She ignored the question and told him to fill her up. We used the restrooms, I paid for the gas, and Johnnie asked the attendant for directions. The kid waved his arms around, and we drove off in search of a motel and our next host funeral home.

Chapter Seven,

Johnnie drove straight out Main Street, hung a left at the courthouse, its tower clock eyeballing us, and found the Southcliffe Funeral Home right where it was supposed to be. It was a colonial two-story house with a canvas canopy jutting out over its front walk.

Johnnie bucked the coach into the drive and parked alongside the mortuary's own vehicles. She groaned, rubbed her eyes, swung out of the coach, and approached the main entrance. A porch light flared on after a few moments, and a woman dressed in a gray skirt and matching dress jacket stepped out to look over at the coach. She mouthed a few words to Johnnie and stood stark still.

Johnnie nodded and walked back to the coach. I got out and walked around to meet her, "What's up?"

She smiled and shook her head. "She's the attendant on duty: Mrs. Crouch. One cold fish. She's irked that we're late. She wants payment now so she can close up and go home. Guess the night calls go to her house. Anyway, need ten bucks. So much for courtesy among undertakers. Oh, she did agree to call us a cab."

I pulled the money out of my wallet and noted that I'd need to go to the bank and cash some traveler's checks. As Johnnie walked back, I gave the woman a wave and received nothing in return. She closed the door and killed the porch light—we had been summarily dismissed. Johnnie parked the coach where instructed, and we stood obediently in the driveway until a white Checker Motors taxi with a black hood pulled up, Calvin's Cab emblazoned on its doors. The driver was a middle-aged thin man sporting a flat-top haircut wearing a red tee shirt that had a seen better days. A nearly spent cigarette was crimped between his lips. He dropped us at the Moss Motel without ever saying a word en route. After we'd taken luggage to our rooms, Johnnie knocked and stood in the open doorway.

"What?" I asked.

"This Ripley guy, how you gonna handle him?"

"I don't know. Just call. See if he's home. If he is, drive over and do my duty."

"But he's god awful...what your dad said he did." I nodded. "You gotta do something. Turn him in."

I sat on the edge of the bed, on a beige and blue striped bedspread. "Pretty sure the span of time during which Ripley could've been charged ran out a long time back."

"So that's it? What are you gonna do then?"

I raised my hands defensively. "Take Dad by for a visit and deliver the letter. After that we drive to Kansas."

She waved a hand in disgust and left, shutting the door with force. I called my wife.

"Where are you?" Nadine's voice was flat. Ours wasn't a blissful marriage, but it was respectable, even fond on a good day. These interchanges from the road weren't.

"In Pine Bluff."

"Where's that?"

"Arkansas."

"Who's there?"

"Fellow name of Ripley Miller."

"You see him yet?"

"No, we just got into town an hour or so ago."

She paused. "We, who's we?"

"Me and the coach driver, Johnnie Gates."

"Oh, the driver." She didn't ask anything more, so I left the gender part alone. Probably regret it.

We fell silent. I sat on the bed, the phone wedged under my chin, and unlaced my shoes. Finally Nadine sighed into my right ear. "Michael, this is a travesty. Frankly, I haven't told any of my friends what you are really doing. They all think that you are just being a good son taking care of your father's passing in Florida. But not that you are running around the country with his dead body on some sort of crazy last rites tour in a hearse."

"It will be over soon." She didn't respond. "I did promise him that I'd do this."

"You weren't even close. You never had anything good to say about the man. Never."

"I know," I said. "Look I'm beat, heading to bed. I'll call you in a couple of days." She hung up without commenting.

When Johnnie knocked on my door the next morning, it was not yet seven o'clock. She was famished. The motel desk clerk suggested breakfast at a cafe two blocks down and one over. We each ordered a basic breakfast and returned to the motel. In spite of having to take on Ripley Miller, it was going to be a nice day; we stood on the walk in front of our rooms feeling the sun on our faces while I picked at my breakfast residue with a toothpick.

"Before we check out, I'll call Miller."

Johnnie raised her eyebrows. "That ought to be interesting."

I laughed. "Yeah, well he's older than me. If he tries anything physical, I think I can handle him."

"We shoulda bought us that baseball bat."

After making myself presentable, I referred to my list of phone numbers and dialed the one I had for Ripley Miller. It rang several times until a woman answered in a soft, almost timid, voice. I asked for Ripley; whoever she was, his wife likely, told me he was already at work. Where was that? Anderson Real Estate, he was an agent. I wrote down the number, hesitated while I considered how this man I hadn't seen for two decades would react to my father's letter.

Finally, I squared up the black Bakelite phone on the little desk, lifted the receiver, and circled the rotary dial three times: 774. After several rings, a man answered and blandly declared Anderson Realty. I hesitated before asking if Ripley Miller was available. Whoever it was dropped the phone without saying yes or no. Moments later someone put their ear to the receiver and spoke.

"This is Ripley. What can I do for you?" The voice was one I didn't recall, just an ordinary voice, nothing notable about it, no southern accent.

I leaned back in the desk chair and looked at the framed print on the wall, a nature scene. When I didn't answer immediately, Ripley Miller said hello like he was speaking into a dead line.

"Ripley Miller?" I responded.

"That's right. What can I do for you?" he repeated.

"My name is Michael Sanborn."

"Do I know you?" he asked, my name evidently ringing no bells.

"You did...some time ago."

I could almost detect his smile when he said, "Oh, I sold you a house? You in the market again?"

"No, no, not in the market, at least not here in Pine Bluff."

"Okay." His tone had withdrawn its warmth. "You selling something?"

"No, not selling anything."

"Look, fella, I'm busy here, so unless you get to the point I'm—"

"I'm Randolph Sanborn's son," I spoke over his voice.

There was no response. It was as if the line had gone dead, except that someone in the background said, I'm showing it this afternoon. A second later, Ripley Miller hung up. I called back, but he was unavailable, had gone home. He only worked short days was the response. That was all right. I knew where he lived, at least I had an address.

The Calvin's Cab was waiting when I carried out my bag. Same driver, flat top, smoking, and as taciturn as the last time. He drove us straight to the funeral home like a homing pigeon. I paid him exact change, no tip; he noted the slight, looked at me with deadpan eyes—he got it, my message. Johnnie went inside to alert whoever was on duty that we were reclaiming the coach. No one followed her out.

She slid behind the wheel. "So. Where now?"

"Find a bank. I need to get some more cash. Then we'll go visit Ripley Miller. Think I spooked him."

"How's that?"

"Got him at work. When I identified myself as my father's son, he hung up on me. I called right back, but he had already vamoosed."

"Does sound spooked. Bastard."

I visited the Pine Bluff National Bank, cashed $100 in traveler's checks then we went looking for number 10 Idlewood Street. We stopped a letter carrier and asked for help. Over by the country club, we were told; he gave his directions by sighting down an extended forefinger.

The street was a roundabout route of wide well-tended lawns, trees, groomed hedges, and stately houses. And then, there it was, number ten. It was a big two-story house constructed of red brick with white woodwork, perfectly symmetrical, with four large windows on the first level and an arch of ivy framing the entry; four smaller windows graced the second floor. There was a driveway on the left going out behind the house. Johnnie eased the coach up to the edge of the front lawn; there was no curb.

"Too bad they're slumming," she said.

I opened the glove box and pulled out the letter. Johnnie looked at the envelope in my hand and shook her head.

"Well," I said while palming the thick paper. "Number two, here I go."

"Shoulda bought that bat," she repeated.

I ignored the comment, stepped out of the vehicle, and walked across the lawn to the front door. Two concrete urns with plantings in them bracketed the slab porch. I used the brass knocker and stepped back. When the door opened, I was facing a woman whose physical presence was different than I'd expected from her voice over the phone. She was tall, big boned, and her smile revealed a set of prominent teeth.

"Yes," she said. "May I help you?"

"Mrs. Miller?"

"That's right."

"I'm here to see Ripley, if he's in."

"Yes, he's here, please come in." It was then she saw past me to the street where the coach sat, all gleaming black and chrome. She inhaled quickly. "My goodness, is anything wrong?"

"No, don't be alarmed. I can explain things to Ripley."

She hesitated, her smile gone, face transformed. She took a step back, allowing me to enter, then moved off to go after her husband. I closed the door and remained standing in the foyer holding onto the envelope. My stomach was expressing the unease of the forthcoming confrontation. Several minutes passed before I heard footsteps, and a short, mostly bald man, with dark eyebrows, small mouth, reddish nose, and a jowl, came up

Summation

to me. He was dressed casually in tan slacks, an open-necked dress shirt, and brown wing-tipped shoes.

"It's you, then," he said.

"Yes, I am Michael Sanborn, if that's what you mean."

"What do you want, and what's this about a hearse parked out front?"

"I can explain everything if we can perhaps sit down somewhere."

Ripley Miller looked up at me, his pale blue eyes evaluating what was going on. "No, I don't think I will do that."

"And why is that?"

"Better yet, why should I?"

I held up the envelope. "Because I have something for you." He looked perplexed. "A letter. From my father."

"A letter from Randolph?"

"That's right."

He stepped to one of the side light windows by the front door and peered out. "What about the hearse?"

"It's in the letter," I said and held it up once more.

He looked out again before walking off and waving a hand for me to follow. We ended up in what would have been called a parlor when the house was built. An effort had been made to furnish the room as it might have been in the early part of the century. Ripley didn't sit down, nor did I.

"All right," he said, eyeing the envelope in my right hand. "Let's have it."

I nodded and held it out to him. He hesitated but finally took the envelope from me, held it in both hands, and turned it over several times before lifting the unglued flap and gingerly removing the sheet of paper. After a moment he sat down in a wingback chair and began to read. I remained standing and watched.

RANDOLPH E. SANBORN
FLORHAVEN ESTATES
JUPITER, FLORIDA

February 1952

Ripley Miller

10 Idlewood Street
Pine Bluff, Arkansas

Hello Ripley,

I always wondered where you landed after leaving Portland in the dead of night. Your former colleagues at Sidney & Mayer very kindly told me. Pine Bluff, no less. Charming town with a storied history. I have wondered though, do any of its residents know who you really are?

But let me back up. My son Michael who you may remember has just arrived, and you've likely noticed the hearse parked out front. I'm in it, or what's left of me as I died recently from lung cancer. I know you're just as sorry as hell to learn that. Anyway, before I expired, I made a deal with my son to transport my body back to Portland, and I asked him to go along for the ride so he could make a number of stops along the way. You are his second assignment.

I'm sure you know why I'm on your doorstep, don't you, Ripley, old chum? As I sat down to write this letter, I recalled our long, self-indulgent friendship. We shared so many things, didn't we? From golf to our views on life and the pursuit of success by whatever means. Our politics were of the "we have ours but we want more" persuasion. We shared everything from cocktails to bigotry. And as I faded away I had more regrets than a man wants to take to his grave.

But none of my shortcomings match the day you told me of the death of Agnes Thompson. That moment still hangs wretchedly in my mind. I recall those years when you were her guardian doing the noble task of overseeing her financial affairs for a

standard fee. For Mrs. Thompson, a widow without
anyone to care for her as her mental capacity dete-
riorated, you were a godsend—or so it seemed. But
the day you met me for a drink and gloated that
you had purloined $200,000 in bearer bonds from
her estate haunts me still. Then, after closing
out your affairs, you took those negotiable, anon-
ymous instruments and vanished like a thief in the
night, which you were. But then here I am taking
aim at your depravity when it is now beyond forfei-
ture and punishment. Am I then any better than you?
Likely not, but then you still have to live with
your guilt, don't you?

Yours in mutual disgrace,

Randolph

As he read, Ripley's facial expression was eerie to observe. His right cheek twitched, and his eyes narrowed. He read it, looked over at me, at the letter again, then tipped his back against the chair, eyes closed. After a long moment his eyelids popped open, and he sat up.

"He's out there then?" He waved the letter in the direction of the front door. "In that thing, the hearse?"

I nodded and looked down into an anxious face.

"Egad, that is something. His body is truly outside my door?"

"Yes. You want to confirm that fact?"

"God no. Morbid." He stood and waved the letter "And what he says... in here, in this letter—never happened."

"That so?" My smile was meant to mock his assertion. "He went to a lot of trouble to get that letter to you. In his dying days, no less."

He stepped close, looked up into my face. "Believe what you want. I am well thought of in this community, if you want to know."

"Are you now?"

He read my face, drew in his thin lips, and looked again at the letter in his hand. "I have position here. I do," he added when he saw I was not impressed. "I'm on the chamber of commerce executive committee, I'm a director on the Pine Bluff National Bank board, a member of the Elks..."

I raised my right hand to stop his recitation. "What's that have to do with Agnes Thompson?"

His face grew red. "Because," his voice turned guttural, "because, you oaf, no one of my stature could ever be accused of what's written here." He stabbed a forefinger against the page.

"This is a beautiful house. Must have cost a pretty penny." He glared. "As I recall, you were a run-of-the-mill bean counter in Portland. A bookkeeper. That right?"

He stood straighter. "I was a CPA."

"Still, you wanted to be a partner with Sidney & Mayer, but that never happened. Right?" He grimaced, so I added, "You know, I never had many heart-to-heart chats with my dad, but he did tell me of the time you went on a binge when you were turned down for a partnership back in, what? Sometime in 1930?"

"That's plain bullshit!" Spittle sprayed off his lips when he barked those words. "Your old man never told you any such thing. Not a word of truth to it."

"That was the year I went to college."

"So?"

"Before I left home, my dad and I, we had this leaving-the-nest talk, I guess you'd call it." When Ripley just blinked and drew his lips tight, I went on. "I was going to Oregon Agricultural College in Corvallis. Guess he had a hint of pride with me going for a business major."

"That's just damn swell. You and your reluctant father hit it off for five minutes once."

"Thing is," I raised a forefinger and pointed at him. "The thing is, he advised me to get smart and stay smart to move ahead. Then he told me a story...about a guy who didn't and was aced out from advancing. You."

"Bullshit."

"So, you had no real money it seems. But here you are, selling real estate as a cover no doubt, but living in a luxurious house, right next to the country club, serving on all those boards you mentioned. How'd you manage that?"

He licked his lips but didn't respond.

"I never heard of the allegations laid out in that letter. About Agnes Thompson. But if it's true, and surely it is, you are one loathsome human being. Come on, Ripley, there's no way that a man with your frail financial history could abruptly leave town, move thousands of miles away to another town, and arrive awash in cash." He glared at me with enmity. "Your wife, Marsha isn't it? Didn't she ever wonder how you and she were so abruptly well to do? Quite a feat, pulling that off. How'd you do it?"

Ripley shuffled his feet but kept looking at me with a dead cold expression; again he made no attempt to respond.

"What? An inheritance from a distant uncle? Or…"

"Shut up," he growled. "Shut up, shut up, shut up!" With each utterance, his voice rose, and the veins in his neck bulged. "Get out. You've completed Randolph's assignment—now get the hell out of my house."

"You mean Agnes Thompson's house, don't you?"

The man's face had a rosy red hue, his eyes grew cold, and he tore my father's letter in little bits and let them drift to the floor. "Okay," he said from the back of his throat. "You've done his bidding." He stepped to the side window again and peered out. "Now drive his moldering body away from here and on to wherever your next victim resides."

"Kansas. Emporia."

"That right?" His face was a mask of cynicism. "Deranged," he muttered. "Absolutely insane."

Chapter Eight,

When Johnnie jockeyed the Meteor coach around and headed it back down the roadway, Ripley Miller was standing in the doorway of the house that Agnes Thompson had paid for with her last breath. Ripley's wife appeared beside him and said something while watching us pull away. Ripley shook his head and said something in return. He was not a happy man.

"I think we ruined his day," I said.

"Wasn't that the idea?"

"My dad's intent, without a doubt." I stared straight ahead as we moved along Idlewood Street. "But I did find pleasure in facing him down—eye to eye, nose to nose, both of us knowing that he was a crook." I coughed a laugh and socked a clenched fist into an open hand. "Thought he was going to have a heart attack. His ruddy nose turned beet red, I tell you."

"So, that's it then? We deliver the letter like we're from Western Union, go on our way, and that weasel gets away with robbing an old woman's kin before she was even cold?"

"He already has. Gotten away with it."

"Your old man must have wanted him to be held liable." She coasted up to a stop sign and looked both ways. "The SOB."

"I don't imagine my dad was thinking Ripley would be ever held accountable. Too late for that. What he wanted…most certainly…was to confront Ripley, his co-conspirator in many small sins, and smack him upside the head from the hereafter. Let him know that his despicable act may be long gone but not forgotten. He wanted me to meet Ripley face-to-face, goad him into reading that letter of accusation while his son looked on, and watch him wallow in disclosure of his criminal act."

Johnnie made a wide left turn; the coach rolled modestly against it shocks while the hydramatic transmission hummed through the gears. "Pisses me off."

I knuckled my eyes. "It's okay. It's done. My father gave Ripley what he had coming. Too damn bad that he didn't do it while he was alive, chest-to-chest. I would have paid to watch that."

"Was he too spineless to do it when he was still living?" She saw me look her way and squinted. "Your dad, I mean. Couldn't do it?"

I considered my father's temperament. "Could be that, I guess. Suppose we all have wrongdoings we'd prefer to take with us, unrevealed. Too cowardly to fess up and clean the slate. My dad just found his own way of cleansing his worst cases of guilt, leaving me to be his bearer of bad tidings."

She nodded above the steering wheel. "Yeah." She laughed. "I've looked at a lot of the pasty, inanimate faces of the recently departed. Laid out in their Sunday-go-to-meetin' clothes. I often wondered what secrets they took with them, stuff they left floatin' around. What was on their minds just before…the end?"

"Now there's a thought," I said. "Grim though it may be."

She laughed. "Guess everyone's got secrets. Like you say, the kind we'll never admit to. You?"

My mind stalled. Sure, I had regrets. There had been transgressions. I hadn't revisited them for a long time. But they were there, or rather there she was. I'd always blamed it on the war. In Los Angeles, away from my wife and home, serving in the routine job my business degree had gotten me, that of a naval cost inspector. And there she'd been, a young civilian clerk, lovely to look at, unattached. And there I'd been, a bit older than she, in my uniform, and unscrupulous.

"How about gassing up?" I dodged. "Grab a bite down the road? Where we bunking tonight?"

"Springfield. In Missouri."

It ended up being a sluggish drive. Just out of Pine Bluff we were hit by a rain squall. Traffic slowed and bogged down; we merged with a long line of cars and trucks and muddled along. This time, with wipers going and rain pounding, drivers were less inclined to pull off and to let a hearse pass. An hour and a half out, we hit the outskirts of Conway, Arkansas. Our hunger pangs drove us off the road, past the Conway City Limits sign, declaring itself the City of Colleges. Johnnie cruised in slowly until we found a cafe called Moll's. She parked, we heeled-and-toed across the wet street through the easing downpour, and I shouldered the door open.

Johnnie finger-combed her tangle of damp hair and crawfished into a booth.

The wrinkled mimeographed paper menus colored with coffee ring stains offered up food that one never saw in Portland. I ordered fried catfish, and Johnnie a pig meat sandwich; that food had character. The rain had ceased by the time we left Moll's. Johnnie grumbled at the mud spatters on the coach and got us back on the highway.

I was lost in thought and dozing when Johnnie used a curse word and swerved the coach onto the right shoulder of the highway. She skidded the vehicle to a stop, totally rousing me. When I asked What the hell, she slammed the gearshift into park, gyrated around, and thrust her body out of the coach. By the time I got my brain working and stepped out, she was facing two men in dark business suits and giving them what for. A big four-door burgundy DeSoto, with a windshield visor and whitewall tires, was blocking our way.

A tall, fat man with a sagging jowl and wearing a fedora was patting the air and trying to calm Johnnie when I walked up. "What is all this?" I said with as much gravitas as I could muster.

"Run me off the road, will you?" Johnnie was right in the guy's face.

"Clam down, Lady. This is not about you." He had a high-pitched voice for his size.

"That right?" she responded. "Who then?" She raised a thumb over her shoulder. "Our passenger?"

"Him," said the other man, pointing a forefinger at me. He was as tall as the fat one but younger and thinner, and he had a shock of black hair.

"Really?" I answered. "If you're needing the services of a mortuary, you wasted your time running us off the road."

"Funny," the big man said.

"Don't get smart with us, Bub," said the younger man.

"So, spill it," I said.

The thin guy came toward me. "You made a call today on Mr. Ripley Miller in Pine Bluff, that right?"

I nodded. "We did."

The younger man squared his shoulders and seemed to take the lead. "Well, he didn't much like it."

"That right?" I looked over at Johnnie. She tightened her lips like she was wishing she had the baseball bat she'd been arguing for. "Just a personal visit," I responded.

The fat one spoke again. "Not the way he took it."

"Can't see as it's your business, but I was delivering a message from my deceased father. They knew each other, Ripley and my father. And as you can see, we are leaving the area."

"That don't draw no water. We got business with you," the younger man said, squaring his shoulders.

"What kind of business?" Johnnie challenged. Made me smile.

The younger man paused, looked over at his partner who nodded, then flexed his shoulders once more. "Whatever it was you said, or maybe delivered, he don't want any of that…what'd he call it," he asked his partner.

"Disseminated." Came the answer.

"Yeah, he don't want it dee-sseminated."

"What's that mean?" I teased.

When the younger man look perplexed, his partner stepped in. "You know what it means, Jackass. Now, do you get the message?"

"Do you know whatever it is that I'm not supposed to disseminate?" I looked straight into the big man's eyes. He didn't blink.

"You know damn well what it is. I don't know because it's confidential from Mr. Miller. We've been directed to make a point on the man's behalf. The point being, as you know, that you will forget what you discussed with Miller and never give, share, or disseminate such information with anyone." He stared hard. "Do you get the message?"

I smiled, but my stomach was fluttering. "Let me get this right, my father's belated greetings to Mr. Miller are the cause of this kerfuffle? That is strange."

The big man studied me for a long moment then took a step forward. "Listen fella, be clever if you want to, means nothing to me, but we're here to get Mr. Miller's message across—emphatically."

With the background of passing traffic, tires throwing up roadway mist from the rain, and two guys from out of the blue threatening me, I burst out laughing—couldn't help it. "You don't know a damn thing, do you? What if I agree to your demand? You going to follow me all across the country to make sure I don't tell some gas station attendant Ripley's secret—a secret you don't even know?"

The younger one took three quick steps and jabbed a forefinger into my shoulder. "We ain't needin' to know...whatever it is. It's you needin' to know we'll put the slug on you if Mr. Ripley tells us to 'cause you didn't listen to us."

We all stopped talking and turned when an Arkansas State Patrol car pulled in behind our quartet of humanity; red lights mounted on the roof on either side of a chromed bullet-nosed siren were flashing. Our two antagonists locked eyes, and the big man patted the air for the younger one to stay calm. He looked back at me, uneasy. I gave him a low-level smile. The four of us turned in unison to see a stocky, middle-aged state patrolman slide out and stand next to his official vehicle, all the while keeping his eyes on us. He paused to settle his campaign trooper hat on this head and hitch up on his holster belt. Eyes still on us, he closed the door on his black-and-white Ford patrol car and came forward; the emergency lights continued to flash behind him.

"Afternoon." He spoke openly. "You folks having problems here?"

No one spoke, so I smiled at the hired muscle and said, "Hello, Officer. No problems. We'd pulled over to check our road map, and these gentlemen stopped to see if we needed help."

The officer stood calmly in his creased khaki shirt, whipcord dark blue pants, with a Sam Browne belt crossing diagonally over his right shoulder. He hooked his thumbs in his holster belt and looked at the coach, eyeballing the Oregon license plate.

"What's this all about?" he said, nodding toward the coach.

Johnnie turned to look at the rain-spattered Meteor hearse. "We are transporting the remains of this gentleman's father back to Oregon."

"That so? From where?"

"Florida," she answered.

He asked for her driver's license, studied it carefully, and handed it back with a polite tip of his head. Then he turned his eyes onto the funeral coach and sauntered over. After peeking into the rear window, he came back and said, "I suppose you have some documentation for all of this."

I suddenly felt like laughing again. Instead of pouring over financial data at my desk back in Portland, there I was standing on a gritty highway shoulder in Central Arkansas chaperoning my father's body back home, the hearse carrying his remains parked askance off the tarmac, the driver of said vehicle standing with her arms folded while two trouble makers looked on, with a curious state cop giving us the once-over.

I swallowed my urge to laugh while Johnnie pulled her funeral director's license from her wallet and went to the glove box for paperwork from Lundberg Funeral Home. The cop, his forehead wrinkled in concentration, studied the documentation thoroughly before handing it all back to Johnnie. He stared at the coach again and then looked at each of us in turn one more time.

Finally he stepped over to the two goons. "I think you gentlemen can be on your way now."

The fat man gave a hard stare back but didn't break the policeman's poise nor intent. After a long moment, the big guy nodded, tipped his head to his partner, and they moved off back to the DeSoto. The cop watched until they'd gone then turned back to us.

"So, what's the story?" When we just stared back, he added, "With them? They causing problems?"

I glanced at Johnnie, she shrugged. "Yeah, they were," I said. "How'd you know?"

"Things looked odd when I passed going the other way." Then he pointed to the roadside. "Skid marks. Your hearse there, it didn't just glide to a stop, did it? Thought not. And their car, the way it was sitting, I'm thinking they cut you off."

Johnnie nodded. "Yeah, they did."

He looked at the coach again. "Do you know them?"

We both shook our heads.

"They threaten you? Why did they stop you?"

I motioned him farther off to the side of the highway, away from the traffic and airborne grit. We all turned our backs to the road, and I told the officer enough to get the picture. He listened without comment, looking mostly down at his feet. When I'd finished, there was a long period of no reaction before he turned to look at us.

"Helluva story," he said finally. "And it's really your father in there? His... remains?" When I nodded yes, he said, "Those characters were serious. Followed you quite a ways before running you off the road. You think they'll hassle you anymore?"

"No idea," I answered. "Never seen them in my life. Mostly, I think they were hired to give me a scare. You know, bluster and threats."

"Where you headed from here?" he asked.

"Staying the night in Springfield, then on to Emporia, Kansas, our next visit."

He asked us to wait while he returned to the patrol car, turned off his emergency lights, and got on his radio. He returned, pulled up on his pistol belt again, and said, "You should be okay all the way into Springfield." He had arranged for the Arkansas State Police patrolling that stretch of highway to be on the lookout for us and the DeSoto. From the state line on into Springfield, the Missouri State Highway Patrol had been alerted to keep the coach under protective surveillance.

Our favorite patrolman followed us for maybe ten more miles before another police car picked us up. We were under precautionary guard.

Chapter Nine.

It was just after six o'clock and heading toward dusk when we hit the outskirts of Springfield. The Missouri State Highway patrolman who'd been behind us gave a chirp of his horn then pulled away at the city limits. We were on our own.

Springfield, Missouri, another place I'd never been. The city limits sign proclaimed a population approaching 90,000 citizens and boasted that the town was the birthplace of Route 66. Johnnie slowed the coach, pulled off the highway, and idled along on a busy street looking for a place to catch an early evening meal.

"Lookie there!" she spouted and drew the coach to the curb. "We just gotta eat there." She leaned forward over the steering wheel and giggled.

There sat a stretched-out corrugated Quonset hut on the corner of Glenstone and Seminole streets; atop its arched steel body was a sign declaring it to be Casper's Chili Hut. Johnnie coaxed the coach over a lumpy cement driveway and parked in a gravel lot next to a three-quarter-ton red Diamond T pickup with Olson's Electric painted on its doors. We exited, stretched our backs and looked around as two men in coveralls came out of the restaurant probing their teeth with toothpicks. The older of the two men paused and shoved his right hand in behind a bib shoulder strap.

"Funeral today?"

I shook my head. "No, we're not from here, just traveling through."

"That right? Well, you picked the right stop." He tipped his head toward the intersection and chuckled.

And sure enough, kitty-corner from the cafe was a wide expanse of green dotted with granite monuments, inscribed headstones and a scattering of deciduous trees—Hazelwood Cemetery according to the name emblazoned on the sign arched over the entry onto the grounds. We all had a laugh, and they assured us the food was good.

Casper's chili was full bodied, for sure. We sat at the counter on spinner stools and had full-to-the-brim bowls of chili sprinkled with shredded cheddar cheese and onion, served with sturdy cornbread coated in warm butter. A man seated next to us whispered that the chili's secret ingredients were Mexican chocolate, nutmeg, and beer. Whatever, it was damn good chili.

Afterward, Johnnie petitioned for a drive-through of the cemetery, a sort of busman's tour. In the receding light of daytime, as we cruised around the paved roadway, my stomach began to tighten. Could've been the chili, but more likely it was the meandering among the chiseled stonework, coupled with the presence of my expired father. I'd mostly compartmentalized his death—but traversing those grounds made his demise suddenly indisputable.

I leaned forward. "Please leave this place," I said on a soft breath.

Johnnie eased the vehicle to a stop. I saw her peripherally studying me. "You all right?"

"No." I gestured with a hand for her to move on.

She nodded, coaxed the beast forward, exited out onto Seminole Street, and drove without speaking. I sagged back; I wasn't even seeing the town. At some point I felt the coach roll a bit as Johnnie pulled into a wide driveway. I roused and saw an illuminated monument sign set on a green manicured lawn; we had arrived at Elmwood Mortuary.

Johnnie pulled around to the rear of the building to a phalanx of wide garages. She pulled up to the only open door revealing an empty bay and killed the ignition.

"Been wondering," she said.

"What?"

"When it would hit you for real." She draped her hands over the steering wheel. "You've been too...what? Custodial like, I guess. A mere delivery person."

"That's what I am."

She was quiet for a moment, then said. "Just been wondering where you've been keeping it."

I stared through the windshield at nothing. "I never knew him. Not really." I cranked the window down and rested my elbow on the sill. It was still warm out. I inhaled. "Or liked him. I never even liked him."

She hummed softly. "So why'er we doing this again?"

"Made a deal."

"No, my dad and I made a deal. For money. Your deal was for something else. What?"

"You going to let somebody know we're on the premises?"

She pointed to the dashboard clock. "We're early. Police escort musta gained us some time."

"So, why'd I agree to this? You try looking your terminal father in his eyes and telling him no deal."

She reached across my legs, popped the glove box open, and rummaged around, coming out with a crumpled pack of Luckies, extracted a slightly bent cigarette, pushed the lighter button in, and waited for it to pop back out.

She touched the glowing tip to the cigarette. "Yeah, but this deal with your dad can't be a binding contract—can it?" When I just looked at her, she said, "You know we could be home in two days. Your father's past caring."

I wanted to grab her shoulders and shake her. Right then a matronly women in a flowered dress, walking on low-heeled pumps, appeared out of the shadows. Her face carried a practiced smile. Johnnie got out to meet her.

She introduced herself as Constance Herd, co-owner with her husband. She stepped away from Johnnie and around to me and extended a hand through the open window.

"Mr. Sanborn, how very nice to meet you," she said, her self-same smile intact.

I took her plump hand in mine and squeezed gently. "Thank you. We're most appreciative of your hospitality."

"Of course, of course. So sorry about your loss. We're honored to help you on your way." She turned to Johnnie again. "Miss Gates, please feel free to use this open bay."

Johnnie thanked her and asked if she could borrow a hose to wash the grime off the coach. The woman acquiesced with a flourish of generosity, and before long Johnnie had a bucket, sponge, and even a chamois. Mrs. Herd turned on floodlights above the garages and agreed to call us a cab.

The coach was washed and stored by the time a bullet-nosed, yellow Studebaker cab arrived. The driver didn't get out, just waved an arm out the window. It was up to us to load our bags in the trunk. We did, and he took us where we wanted to go and departed quickly and without comment. Dark was closing in by the time we checked into a flat-roofed motel called the Caldwell; we each settled into our rooms having agreed to call it a day. I decided to call Nadine. She answered on the second ring, her tone that of someone who'd been interrupted.

"Hello there," she said, a shade of surprise in her voice. "Where are you?"

"Missouri. Springfield, Missouri."

"That right? Springfield, Missouri. Heard of it, never been there. Anything special about it?"

"Ever heard of Route 66?"

"Oh sure, guess everyone's heard about it, the long highway."

"Well, this is where it began. It's the birthplace, they claim."

"You delivering another letter there?"

"No. Just laying over. Then on to Emporia, Kansas, tomorrow."

"Yes, I know," she said. "I called Clarence Gates...at the funeral home? Just to check in with him, see if he'd heard from you. Asked me how you were doing on the road. Hasn't heard from his daughter, Johnnie, in a few days."

My scalp tingled. "That right? I'll remind her to call."

Her laugh in my ear was biting. "Yes, why don't you do that. He'd love to hear from Jonalynn." She upped her voice a notch. "Funny, you never mentioned that your driver is a female."

"Really. Thought I had," I said in a flat-out lie. "She's doing a great job."

"I'll just bet."

"Did all of the planning, got the coach shipped to Florida, mapped out the entire trip, scheduled stops in every town. Good driver."

"Guess your father is serving as chaperone for you and the young lady."

"Funny," I said.

"No," she said. "It's not funny. My husband off on a cross-country road trip transporting a dead body while in the company of an unattached young female."

"Nadine," I said, dropping my voice, "You can't believe that anything… well, anything improper is taking place."

Her laugh wasn't one of levity. "Oh, really? And how would I know that?"

"She is a decent person doing a good job. Nothing's going on."

She fell silent; we both did. I was seated at a small desk, leaning on an elbow, holding the receiver in the opposite hand. I felt regret for not telling her about Johnnie, but that was slight compared to other missteps. Missteps I'd put away, stored in my mind's attic. My father's revelations, the good and the not so good, had triggered an unpacking of the worst of myself.

"You still there?" Nadine said.

"Yes," I answered. "I am."

"So, she's a decent person, you say. I'm sure she is, still…"

"Nadine, please stop it. There's something else."

She fell quiet. I knew her. I knew her eyes had narrowed. "What is it?"

I twiddled the phone cord in one hand. "Like you said, Dad and I, we were never close. And on this trip I'm compounding my estimation of his failings. Chasing after his errors and his wrongdoings."

"So, why are you doing it?"

"Because I promised I would, made a pact."

"That's no reason. He's gone."

"There's more."

"Like what?"

I bit down before saying, "Like me. Like my own mistakes. I could write seven letters."

She huffed a little laugh. "And ruin your mister by-the-book image?"

I ignored her. "We drove through a cemetery here today. Johnnie's idea. It was right then, on those grounds, that I had a chilling sense of finality—my father is truly deceased. Actually dead. I felt almost faint." She started to speak. "Just hear me out," I said.

"Okay."

"At that moment, things came into my head. Thoughts and memories I haven't had in years. Recollections of times gone by when I wasn't at my best."

"Come on, Michael," she said. "What on earth are you talking about?"

"For one, there was this woman," I said, feeling trembly. "Her name was Maria. It was when I was in the Navy, in Los Angeles, you remember, during the war. I was a cost inspector. She was a civilian clerk." I hesitated, expecting an outburst. None came. "I was…attracted to her," I said. My eyes watered; I blinked and rubbed at the wetness with a forefinger. "Damn, this is loathsome."

"Michael…" she said, but I cut her off.

"Wait," I said. "I need to get this out." I heaved two breaths and saw my dark image in the mirror. "There you were, my wife, holding things together while I was assigned to the war effort. And…and out of your sight and presence, I fell victim…to hell with that, I cheated on you. I don't deserve you…"

"Michael," she said on a raised voice. "Listen to me—just listen, will you?"

"What?"

There was a moment's hesitation. "I know about this. I know about Maria."

"No," I said. "How could you?"

"Because…because one day she appeared at our front door."

I stopped breathing. There was dead silence except for a slight thrum on the line. I was unable to speak.

"Are you still there?" she said.

I squeezed the receiver handle. "Yes."

When I didn't say more, she said, "You understand what I'm saying?"

"Why was she there?"

"Why did you think? For you. She came looking for you, Michael."

"My god, why?"

Nadine was calm, she didn't yell at me or curse, she merely said, "I'm not sure what she expected to find when she rang the doorbell. Not really. She was very shy, I guess you'd call it, and sweet and pretty, but you knew that."

"What did she say to you?" I said on a whispered breath.

"She asked for you. I told her you were at work. Then she introduced herself and told me she'd met you when you were in the Navy and that you had worked together. I could tell it was awkward for her when I said I was your wife." When I sighed, she said, "You can relax, Michael. She said nothing about what I assumed may have happened between you. She just said to tell you hello and left."

Summation

"You never did," I said. "Tell me." Again no response. "How can you not hate me?"

After a moment, she said, "You came home to me, didn't you?"

"Yes, but…"

"Michael, finish this thing and get on back here."

The line clicked; the receiver was a dead thing in my hand.

Chapter Ten.

I didn't sleep. I lay flat on my back, arms at my side, still in my clothes, and stared up into the dark—Maria. I couldn't erase the image of her sweet face from my head. The only illumination in the room seeped in around the edges of thick curtains from an exterior porch lamp; even in that semidarkness I couldn't sleep. Once in the middle hours, I got up to go pee. Still unable to sleep, I gave up about five, took a shower, and got dressed. I turned on the desk lamp, sat down and wished I smoked; that would have been the time. I found myself considering how my father had plotted while he awaited his own death, calculating how to take responsibility in absentia for his own transgressions while homing in on the wrongdoing of others and serving up retribution from the grave. He had devised a way to evade the face-to-face repercussions of the seven souls by sending me to stand in as his surrogate. It was an act resemblant of what Shakespeare had written on the subject, something akin to a father's sins being laid upon his children. Right out of my college English Lit class and the Merchant of Venice.

Comfortable in my own exaggerated sense of self, I had easily assumed myself to be immune from my father's end-of-life manipulations of his iniquities. But my own wrongs, the ones I had shoved aside, were being resuscitated. Maria, she was the first one to be exposed—but what of others? They would rise up now, I realized. Dad, what I would give for another ten minutes with you, just time enough to engulf you in my outrage for using me to paint over your long-held sins—after the fact, even. I did not succeed at clearing my head of those concepts.

Around seven-thirty, there was a light rap on my door; I found Johnnie standing there all fresh and scrubbed—and hungry. We jaywalked against morning traffic, pushed our way into Moxley's Cafe, inhaled the aroma of morning food, and each ordered the chalkboard special: cowboy eggs on toast, link sausage, and coffee. Afterward, I laid money on the table, and we were back at the motel in less than thirty minutes. Johnnie had called for a cab, and by eight forty-five she was backing the coach out of the Elmwood Funeral Home garage. We passed through Springfield's Wednesday morning traffic and merged onto the highway. I reached into the glove box and pulled out the packet of letters and plucked the next envelope off the top.

Johnnie glanced. "Who's number three?"

"Fraser Hayes," I said. "A professor in the School of Business at the Kansas State Teachers College."

"Professor? Suppose I'll be needing a bat for him?"

I considered the fault line of the letter. "I don't think so."

"No matter," she said. "I bought one yesterday after we got into town. Found a hardware store a couple of blocks away and got us an actual Louisville Slugger." She grinned and looked straight down the highway. "Ash, made out of the best ash. Good balance. Those thugs better not come around us again."

I hummed a chuckle. "I think you'd actually like it if they did show up so you could brandish your hunk of lumber."

"Maybe," she said. "Least ways, I'll be ready. But your not thinkin' there'll be another dustup like we had with the last one? That Ripley guy?"

I refolded the letter and stuffed it back into the envelope. "No. More likely the reverse. Seems this Fraser is the one aggrieved this time."

"Aggrieved. Now there's a word."

I glanced at the dashboard clock. "How we doing on time?"

"Got a while yet. Next town's Ottawa. We'll stop there for lunch and gas up. That'll leave us just shy of an hour and a half until we hit Emporia."

My thoughts skewed onto Fraser Hayes. The man hadn't left Portland of his own volition; it said so in the letter. Then here I'd come, barging in uninvited, resurrecting a long-forgotten chapter of his life. Letter number three would be no different than the others in that way. How would he react to the words of a dead man? Of course, it was a setup, entrapment. I didn't like it, but I would do it and in a curious, even shameful, way looked forward to the encounter.

Next, we hit Ottawa, Kansas, a small town founded in the late 1860s according to a billboard at the edge of the town. Come to find out Ottawa was mainly famous for flooding. The historical notes on the back page of the Granary B-B-Q menu stated that because of its location straddling the Marais Des Cygnes River, the town had flooded every fifteen years or so since 1844. The 1951 flood had been the worst. We missed it.

As I perused the menu I made mention of the floods to our skin-and-bones waitress. "Yeah, ain't that somethin'," she said on a cigarette smoker's voice. "Instead of the sights and the good fishin', our claim to fame is that dang river coming right up to our navels reglar-like."

We sympathized, washed our beef brisket sandwiches down with Pabsts, and left with full stomachs. We were maybe fifteen minutes out of Ottawa when Johnnie sniffed, checked the rearview mirror, and said, "You know, I'm no head doctor, but something's eating at you."

"That right? What makes you think that?"

She shrugged and glanced over at me. "Just a feeling."

The big motor was thrumming methodically; traffic was light. She was assuredly guiding the vehicle with one hand.

"You think so?"

She kept her eyes on the road. "I do. I guess I do."

At first I didn't respond. What could I say to such an insinuation, even if it was close to the bone? I let it hover between us while I picked at the scabs of bad memories I'd packed away and forgotten. She had that right. I had no doubt that when we sat on his patio in Florida, my father knew that his son thought him less than an honorable man. But had he ever suspected that I had my own cluster of unprincipled acts? Probably. But it made no matter because we had never discussed anything deeper than the Portland Beavers baseball team or the Dewey-Truman election.

I scooted forward, reached out, and planted open hands on the dashboard. "In a sense you're right."

Just then a Ford sedan roared past, horn blaring, a car full of teenagers with arms waving from open windows.

"That was me once," I said. "Full of piss and vinegar and no sense."

Summation

"Crazy, that's what they are," she said. "We've buried kids like that. More'n I like to recall. Nuthin worse than young ones dying ahead of their time."

"I can imagine."

"So," she said, returning to her assertion, "you wantin' to air it out… whatever it is?"

I leaned back against the cushion, the carload of kids but a glinting speck well out ahead of us. "It's a list."

She looked away from the road directly at me. "A list?"

"My dad," I began, "he never treated my mother like my friend's fathers treated their wives. No hugs or kisses or words of affection. Never saw him do any of that except on special occasions…in front of witnesses: anniversaries, family gatherings—only then. And never with any warmth. My mother lived a life of domestic isolation while my old man enjoyed his own self-centered version of life. Mom and I, we were, what? Props, that's it, we were props in Randolph Sanborn's orchestrated method of living. Systematic, that's what it was. Just like one of his actuarial tables predicting the probabilities of life: the variables, the likelihoods, the extenuating factors, hell even the prognosis of an extended life, happy or not."

"Your mother? What did she do—with her life? With her time?"

That was an arrow to my chest. I checked the dash clock; in twenty minutes we'd hit Emporia. Mom. What had she done every day of her bland life? "I can't answer that, not really."

"Did she have a job?"

"No. My father wouldn't allow his wife to work outside the house."

"Why not?"

"Appearances. Heard him say that once when Mom came up with the idea of taking a position at the library. She loved books. Wanted to be a resource librarian. She was educated, so it would have been a good fit."

"Too bad."

Yeah, I thought, too bad. Just too damn bad. "The worst thing," I said, "the very worst thing was that I did nothing. I stood on the sidelines while she tiptoed through constrained life." I squeezed my thighs. "I never stood up for her. I didn't challenge my father when he denounced almost everything Mom wanted that would have enriched her life. Like that job at the library. A trip to visit her sister: too expensive. Anything she wanted was denied."

"Hell, you were just a kid, what could you do?"

"Still, I saw it and felt it, how she was being treated. Could have said something. Damn well should have intervened. Besides, I wasn't always a kid. Worse yet, I felt her pain less the older I got. Easier to ignore."

Johnnie rotated her neck stiff from driving and asked, "What does your wife do…for herself? To, how'd you put it, enrich her life?"

I pinched the bridge of my nose and clamped my eyes shut. "Wow," I said on a slow breath. "You laid me open with that one."

"I didn't mean to…"

"I know, I know. But you hung me out to dry. Me spouting off about my old man mistreating Mom, and I can't answer your question. Nadine? My god, what is her life like?" I twisted in the seat to half face her. "You know what I would have said if someone asked me, what's your wife up to these days? First I would have said some inane thing like, Oh, she's keeping busy, redecorating the house, has several clubs she belongs to, loves to garden, all that nonsense. Then whoever it was would say, Nice, and we'd move on."

Johnnie said nothing more. We drove on—Emporia lay just ahead. One more posthumous attempt at redemption was in the offing.

Chapter Eleven.

I read the Fraser Hayes letter again; my father's words fared no better. His feigned regrets for unresolved sins expressed belatedly, it was a hell of a thing.

Johnnie took Highway 99 into the city, which became Commercial Street and aimed us right at Kansas State Teachers College. I asked her to pull to the curb when I saw a pay phone, and I made the call. A female voice announced School of Business and said Yes, Sir, when I asked for Professor Hayes. Moments later, a resonant male voice was in my ear.

"Professor Hayes?"

"That's right."

I hesitated as a garbage truck lumbered by before saying, "Professor, my name is Michael Sanborn. You knew my father."

"Is that right?" Wariness had crept into his voice. "Is he affiliated with the college here?"

"No." I hesitated. "He's deceased. Passed away recently."

"I see."

"Yes, well, that's why I'm making this call." Hayes didn't react. "Like I said, you knew my dad. Randolph Sanborn?"

Another pause, longer. "Oh. And you say he has passed?"

"That's right. Just recently." I could almost hear his mental gears tumbling. "Cancer."

"Not a nice way to die." We both fell quiet for a long moment. "Pardon me for asking, Michael," the man said, finally, "but what is the reason for your call?"

I gave Johnnie a wave that I would be done soon. "You see, Professor,

I'm here…in town."

"Really? Here. Here in Emporia?"

"Yes. To see you."

A light chuckle came into my ear. "To see me. Why on earth…"

"I have something for you," I cut in. "From my father. I was wondering if I might see you? Come by the college, or your home…maybe this evening." When he didn't respond, I added, "It won't take long. If it wouldn't be too inconvenient."

"And if I don't want to see you?"

I paused then pushed out a small breath on a smile. "Well, I hadn't figured on that. Then I guess I'd mail the envelope—it's a letter—I'd mail it to your home address on Constitution Street. That's right, isn't it: Constitution?"

"Yes—1020 Constitution." He cleared his throat. "What's in it? You say it's a letter. What's in it?"

Johnnie was lighting another cigarette. I watched her go through the ritual, then said, "It's a personal letter—to you. Something he wrote while he was under treatment for his cancer and knew he was dying."

"My word," Hayes spoke softly.

After a lull, he agreed to see me that evening at seven o'clock at his home.

Johnnie was just stubbing out her cigarette when I returned to the coach. She looked at me and arched her eyebrows. "So, how'd that go? Will I need my Louisville?"

"Not sure. We're dropping by his house around seven. Where are we bunking the coach tonight?"

Our venue for the coach was Plumb Brothers Funeral Home out on State Street, which had obviously been a farmhouse in decades past. With their two garage bays already occupied, the Meteor was stowed inside a barn at the rear of the property. Malcolm Plumb, the skeletal older brother, with a stand of straw-like white hair, provided a quilted tarp to cover the coach, and gave us a ride to the Swan Motel. On the way, he confessed that because they had an early service the next day, we'd be on our own once he'd dropped us off.

"A local woman, known to be mentally defective, walked out onto the state highway the other night and just lay down in the middle of the road. Run over twice before anyone saw her. The family wants an immediate service, so we'll be tied up tomorrow."

"Completely understood," Johnnie said. "All of us in this business have had to react to sudden and violent deaths."

"It's what we do," Plumb said as he swung his car into the Swan Motel lot and pulled up to the drive-through.

Johnnie waited until the man had driven away before saying, "Michael. That DeSoto. I just saw it."

"No. You sure?"

"I'm sure. Same color, had the visor, whitewall tires, sedan. Same car."

We stood beside our luggage and looked up and down the street—as if expecting a car the color of a bruise to suddenly appear. Finally, we checked in at the motel and agreed to some personal time to shower and change before catching dinner at the motel's Swan Lake Cafe. Another night, another meal. This time it was a blue plate special: meatloaf, mashed potatoes, and green beans. Since there was no alcohol due to Kansas's prohibition of on-premises liquor sales, we settled on coffee and apple pie instead.

Just before 7:00 p.m., Johnnie maneuvered the coach up to the curb in front of 1020 Constitution Street, turned off the ignition and the headlights; the engine shuddered. The only light was from a vapor street lamp on a nearby corner and a porch light. We sat quietly looking out at the house. It was a modest-sized, white, two-story, probably built in the late teens, with a deep, covered front porch and a hipped roof. The glow of interior lights shone out through sheer curtains.

I withdrew the envelope from the glove box. When I turned to bid Johnnie farewell, she was holding up the baseball bat and smirking. I waved her off and slipped out of the front seat, closed the door with a click, and thought, Here we go again, Dad.

On the porch I turned a brass bell twister. Its clapper chattered, and summarily the frosted glass door with a stag deer etched in it swung back. A tall, slender man, square of jaw, with a swath of rich dark hair and an angular face, stared at me. We were nearly of equal height, though I thought him to be maybe ten years older than me, probably mid-fifties. I smiled. He was still dressed in a white shirt, blue tie loosened at the neck, and suit pants. I felt too casual in my road clothes.

"Professor Hayes?"

"Yes," he answered.

"I'm Michael Sanborn."

He peered over my shoulder. "Uh-huh." The coach was clearly visible. "Is that..."

"Yes, it is."

After a long moment of inspecting the Meteor, he said, "I guess you'd better come in then."

He stepped back and let me pass, entering a modest foyer. I held the envelope in my right hand and followed him into a spacious living room, where one wall was covered with a floor-to-ceiling wooden bookcase filled to capacity. There was a brick fireplace bracketed by dark wood paneling. It was a comfortable room, with matching upholstered couch and armchair covered in what looked to be brown mohair.

Hayes looked about, seeming to inspect the room himself, then turned to me. "Would you like to sit down?"

I nodded and chose the armchair. He stayed standing and looked down at me. Neither of us said anything. After a minute or so, he walked to the windows and pulled the curtain aside and looked out.

After a long look, he stepped away and came back to face me. "Would you like some coffee?"

I smiled. "All right, sure."

"I'll ask my wife to make us a pot." He disappeared, and moments later I heard an exchange of voices.

No challenge, no questions, no sign of angst or irritation. I'd risen and was studying the spines of the books on the wall when he returned—with his wife. The woman carried a tray with cups and service items, and Hayes held a chrome percolator pot. They laid out the items on a low table and each assumed a duty: she setting out the cups and saucers, he pouring the coffee. I stood back until Hayes held out a cup and saucer for me to take.

"Cream or sugar?" he asked.

"Black is fine," I said, countermanding my usual coffee preparation.

He waited for me to be seated. "Mr. Sanborn, this is my wife, Juanita.

I've explained to her who you are...at least my assumptions."

The woman was striking, with high cheekbones, olive skin, gracefully combed dark brown hair, and matching deep brown eyes. She wore a simple dress the color of coral, pleated below a belt at her waist with buttons below a collared neck. I smiled, thanked her for the coffee, and waited for them to be seated; then I sat down again. We each sipped from our cups, and I waited for Fraser Hayes to run out of patience.

He did. "I was baffled to get your call." He set his cup on the table and leaned back. "I did the math, and it's been nearly fifteen years since I left Portland. Fifteen years. And out of the blue I get this strange phone call from you."

"I know," I said. "I'm on this very peculiar journey."

Hayes looked to his wife and smiled while shaking his head. "That's an understatement. That is a hearse sitting out in front of our house, isn't it?"

"Yes it is."

"You told me that your father passed away recently?"

I gripped the envelope. "Yes."

Hayes suddenly stood. "Okay," he said holding both hands out in front of him, "Am I right in assuming..."

"Professor Hayes, before you go any farther, let me give you this," I said, holding up the envelope. "It's the letter I mentioned, from my father to you."

"What's in it, this letter?"

I stood and took a step forward. "Here, best you read it for yourself."

He looked straight at me. "I think not."

I froze, holding the envelope out. What now? The man continued to stare at me, his face a blank mask of resistance. His wife looked up at Hayes in puzzlement, a smile on her lips. Her expression made me wonder if the woman had ever witnessed her husband being so adamant.

"All right," I shrugged, "I'll just leave it then."

"No. Take it with you." I continued to hold the letter out. "I don't want it," he insisted.

"It's just a letter," I said. "His last words...to you."

"Exactly. That's why I don't want it...don't want to read it." He waved me away. "Please, just leave."

"Fraser," Juanita Hayes spoke up. Her eyes were wide, and she had a sweet smile on her face. "Like he said, it's just a letter."

Hayes spun around and glared down at her. "Stay out of this, Juanita." He dropped his hands to his side. "Just be quiet."

"But Sweetheart…"

"Stop!" His bark caused her head to tip back and her smile to fade. "You don't know anything about this, so be quiet. Please."

I stood stark still and lowered the envelope. It was quiet. Neither he nor I spoke; his wife folded her hands in her lap and studied her husband as if seeing him in a different light. And we all remained as we were until Hayes inhaled deeply and spoke.

"He's really out there? His…remains?"

I lowered my chin and raised it. "Yes, that's right."

"My god, how morbid. What compelled you to do such a thing?"

"It was his wish that I do this. There are other destinations and other letters."

"Truly? How many?"

"Seven in all. You are our third stop. We have four more to go."

"We?"

"There is a driver with me."

The smile he formed was not born of humor. "How bizarre. Juanita, there's…a dead person outside. This man's father."

She turned her head my way and gave me a sympathetic smile. After a moment, she stood and collected the coffee service items and carried them from the room. Hayes and I stood where we were.

Chapter Twelve,

The two of us stood in place; neither of us spoke. I circled a thumb over vellum paper's toothy surface and noted that the coffee had made its way downstream.

"Professor? I wonder if I might use your restroom?"

"What? Oh." He swung an arm out. "Down the hall on the left."

It was a small guest restroom: a toilet, a basin, and a mirror. A fragrance I took to be lavender rose from an aromatic bar of soap on the edge of the washbasin. While rinsing my hands, I noted my face in the mirror. The image was of someone unnerved.

When I returned to the living room, Hayes was at the window again, looking out. He stepped back quickly, letting the curtain drop. Our eyes met again.

"Professor," I began, "regardless of your determination to not accept this letter, let me assure you…"

"I don't need your assurances, sir."

I continued. "I understand, but I'm confident that in this envelope you will find a letter which is no way vindictive or whatever else you're thinking. I've read it, and I found it the opposite of those things. Perhaps you might see it even as a statement of regret."

He snorted. "No, never that."

"And why not?"

"Because the man, your father, had not a speck of what you call empathy or remorse in him."

I cringed against that certain reality, a reality I knew. "As his son, I can concur in your assessment. I'm sorry to say that I witnessed his inability to recognize his own guilt many times."

"Then how can you pursue this ridiculous journey now?"

"That was then."

"And this is now? How convenient."

"No." I clipped the word. "Not convenient at all. You think I wanted to do this? Drive all over hell's half acre with Randolph Sanborn's body in tow?" I stepped forward, closer to him. "I have a job, a wife,...my own life. I've never been to Emporia or most of the other places I have to visit. And...and," I raised my hand holding the envelope, "I've never heard of you, Professor Hayes."

The man started to say something, but I cut him off.

"Wait," I said. "Do I care if you don't want to read this blamed letter? I do not. What I came to care about was one man's end of days. Yes, the cancer took him, but before that he wanted to go out on his own terms." I jabbed the air with the envelope. "His own terms. And you know what that means, as I read those seven letters? Rightly or wrongly, he is attempting to clear the deck of his moral offenses on the one hand. On the other, he felt there were those who he needed to be called out for their own transgressions—those he knew well, maybe even abetted. So it's not all one-sided: what a bad boy am I."

At that moment, Hayes turned to see his wife standing in the doorway to the kitchen. They exchanged looks of, What is happening here? from Juanita, and Leave this to me, from him.

I made one final attempt, holding up the envelope. "Your decision," I said.

Fraser Hayes' shoulders slumped, and he reached out. "All right, give me the damn letter." I hesitated, he reiterated, "Go on, give it to me."

I held the envelope out. He took it and reached out to his wife. She came to him, and they sat beside each other on the couch. He kissed her on the cheek, extracted the letter, and opened the folds. I stood back while they read:

RANDOLPH E. SANBORN
FLORHAVEN ESTATES
JUPITER, FLORIDA

February 1952

Professor Fraser Hayes
School of Business
Kansas State Teachers College
Emporia, Kansas

Dear Fraser,

Pardon me for dropping into your life like this. As my son Michael has told you by now, I left this world a short time ago, lung cancer. But before that terminal date, I revisited my life and came away knowing that I had fallen short in many ways. Left me wondering if I was ever an asset as a human being. That's why my remains are parked outside, to make an attempt at amends to you, at least in my mind, before I died.

As I recalled, it was nearly 15 years ago. That was when the head of Natron, Ralph Chapman, asked me to pick up his wife at the Municipal Airport. I forget the date, but surely you remember it well because I asked you to go in my stead. As our head financial manager, you were a very busy man, but you agreed to pick up Mrs. Chapman in my place. I doubt that I ever even thanked you. I was like that, wasn't I?

Fraser, it churned my gut to remember the terrible accident that day. As I remember, you were avoiding a truck, as you related, and as a result crashed into a bridge abutment. The horror of your course correction was that Ruth Chapman died at the scene.

I could barely make myself write those sentences knowing that it could have easily been me instead of you. But, and damn this is wrenching, as devastating as her death was, that is not why I write to you. I barely knew the woman, but I knew you and knew full well the hell you went through then.

In spite of my debt to you, I never supported you, not once. I have no right to erase my failure to stand up for you, joining the ranks of those shunning you. Not only that, Fraser, I supported the accusations that tied your long-past teenage driving history to the woman's death. There was no citation by the police that you were driving recklessly, but no matter. You were the scapegoat, and so it would be. And then you were gone. After a brief period of wondering who would take your place, I moved on. All I can offer you now is that I know you were never at fault, and I have taken the shame of my part in your treatment down with me. But owning my guilt now is meaningless, isn't it?

Hoping you are living a fulfilling life,

Randolph

Fraser Hayes lowered the letter to his lap and turned to look at his wife. From where I stood, I saw her sweet expression of solace. She reached up to place a hand on the back of his neck and tilt her head against his shoulder. They sat that way for some time until finally Hayes rose from the couch and turned in my direction. He raised the letter and examined its content one more time.

"You've read this letter."

"I have."

"Yes. But my wife…Juanita…this is the first time she's heard any of this." He smiled down at her. "I want to tell her those things I've kept to myself."

"I understand. I'll be on my way. Thank you for…"

"No," he said, "I want you to stay while I tell her of that time. Will you sit with us while I explain things?"

I acquiesced, and after a quick trip out to the coach to rouse a dozing Johnnie and alert her of the delay, returned and settled back into the mohair armchair. In my absence, Juanita had gone back to the kitchen to brew more coffee; Hayes and I waited without further discussion. She returned carrying the tray with the addition of an array of Vienna fingers cookies. I was grateful for something to do with my hands.

When we were all settled, Hayes and Juanita side-by-side on the couch, Hayes laid the letter on the coffee table and sat back. He turned sideways on the cushions and looked at his wife. Her lovely face wore curiosity and uncertainty, but with the trace of a smile. I could tell she wanted to support and believe her husband, whatever he was about to tell her. I settled back with my coffee and a cookie and wondered of my role right then. I decided—none.

"Juanita," Hayes began, "Sweetheart, I've told you little about my past, except that I was from Portland, Oregon, never married, and had worked in the insurance industry before coming to Kansas. Isn't that right?" She nodded, her eyes wide and searching. "Well, there was much more, but I chose to ignore that in favor of us having a good start to our lives together.

"At the time of that wretched collision, I held a good position with the Natron General Insurance Company. I was on my way—I was advancing. Or so it seemed." He glanced at me and waggled a finger. "You undoubtedly heard of the accident that day—from your father."

When I shook my head, he shrugged and said, "In any event, from that day on, I became an outcast at Natron in spite of the tragedy being ruled an accident a...misfortune." He reached up to pinch his nose. "This is hard. The letter. It's all coming back."

"Sweetheart, you don't have to do this," said Juanita touching her husband on the arm.

"Oh, but I do...I do." He drew forefingers across his eyelids, relieving the moisture there. "You know, Michael, I despised your father—for a very long time." I said nothing in response. "Oh, I tamped it down as best I could, the anger, but it never truly went away. Now your showing up brings it all back.

"But you know, this is good. I finally get to cut it away, to rid myself of your father and my loathing of him. Let me tell you why. That year, after the crash, I kept hoping that Randolph and the company president, Ralph Chapman, would relent. I wanted a moment of what? Amnesty, I guess. It never came."

"He knew that," I said, when I should have stayed quiet. "Says so in the letter."

Hayes waved a hand at me. "I'm not done here." He turned to Juanita again, took up one of her hands and kissed it. "I have more to say, and you are my witness so the sweetest person in my life knows of my pain and my anger and where it comes from."

The woman's face was taut with concern and uncertainty. She looked over at me; I was sitting up straight, my elbows on the arms of the chair. I did not react.

Hayes took in a breath then leaned forward on his elbows and went on. "Like I said, I wanted to be absolved, to be accepted back into the lineup. But that never came to be. In fact, they put me on the bench, began turning over my major duties to an associate: a guy name of Norval Lewis, slow, not particularly adept, gradually took my place.

He looked at his wife again. "I decided to quit, to…to hack myself free. But doing what and where? Well, I was sitting at my desk one day feeling useless when my best friend, Leroy Case, calls. Leroy taught accounting at Holmes Business College in Portland at the time. He knew all about my impasse and had somehow gotten word that a college in Kansas was seeking a candidate for its business school faculty with corporate-level financial credentials. Leroy, bless him, had made inquiries and primed the pump, so by the time I got a call from the dean of the Business School for Kansas State Teachers College, I was ready to pack."

Hayes turned to me, losing his smile. "Michael, let me tell you, it gave me such gut-level pleasure to throw my resignation at them, to disengage from what had become a daily round of torment. On that final day, I purposely strode past your father's office, stopped to look him in the eye before walking out. Damn, that felt so good." He stood, pulled his loosened tie completely off, tossed it aside, and wrapped his arms around himself, a determined smile his lips.

"It was late July, 1937, when I arrived in this town," he said, a faraway look on his face. "I rented an apartment and huddled with the dean and the head of the department to frame a course of study based on a new academic concept just emerging around the country—corporate finance.

"I wandered the streets of Emporia and felt as an imposter. I was lonely as hell." He turned his eyes back on Juanita. "That was until the day I ate lasagna for lunch in the college cafeteria."

"And peach pie," Juanita said.

"Yes, and peach pie. I was in the cafeteria food line when I noticed the person passing the food across to me. A vivacious woman with beautiful brown eyes and a smile that made my face tingle. I put the lasagna and that piece of pie on a tray—and just stood there smitten. After that, I ate every meal I could in the cafeteria.

"I finally asked the cashier who she was and learned that the woman I already loved was Juanita Flores. It took me a while, but I guess I convinced her that I was a reasonable risk, because we've been married for thirteen years. And we have a daughter, Olivia. She's twelve and at a friend's house this evening."

"Congratulations," I said. "How did my father close the letter? Something about a fulfilling life?"

Hayes rose, took two steps forward, and stood over me. "So, I should be grateful for his despicable treatment because look at my life now? Because of my forced departure I am now blessed by my loving wife, a beautiful daughter, and my rewarding academic career? Is that it?" The smile slid off. In its place was a cheerless face with pulsating jaw muscles. "Well, damn you to hell and damn your father to his grave. You can't trade in what he did with a visit of his deceased self and a letter of contrived remorse." He looked toward his wife and nodded to alleviate the apprehension written on her face and in her eyes. "Yes, I have a fulfilled life. A better life than I deserve. But some scars never go away."

He stopped speaking. We all took turns looking at each other. Hayes finally stepped back and shuffled about in a circle. "And your journey verges on the hideous. And now I would like you to leave our home."

I pushed myself up from the armchair and stood looking at the man. Nothing more was said. They were in an embrace when I let myself out.

Chapter Thirteen.

Johnnie was sound asleep lying across the coach's front seat. I roused her with a gentle poke of a shoulder, and she sat up yawning, cuddling the baseball bat. I slid into the coach, sat with my right leg out of the open door, and looked back up at the house. Two silhouettes were framed in one of the windows behind the sheer curtains. I didn't gesture neither did they.

"How was it?" Johnnie asked.

"No different. Not taken well."

"Should it have been?"

"I don't know, just thought the outcome might be better this time."

"Because you wanted it to?"

I looked again up at the window; they were no longer there. "No, it was more owing to how his life has turned out—for the better, it seems. Lovely wife, a child, academic career, position in the community..."

Johnnie grunted a laugh. "So, this fellow, Hayes, he should have just shrugged off the bad stuff because life turned out all good after all?"

"That's what he said."

"I'll just bet he did. He was run out of town wasn't he?"

I pulled my leg in and shut the door. "His choice, leaving Portland."

"Really?"

"Really."

"If you say so."

I was annoyed by her attempt at intuition. "Let's get out of here. Look for a phone booth, and I'll call a cab to meet us at Plumb's."

She had turned the ignition key when there was a tap on the window.

It was Fraser Hayes leaning over, peering in at me. I cranked the window down and looked up into his lean face.

"May I see it?" he said. "Him?"

I thought about it for a moment then nodded and looked over at Johnnie. She turned off the engine, and we both exited the coach. Johnnie opened the curbside door; the interior bulb revealed the casket in a shadowy light. Fraser Hayes stood back with his hands in his pockets and stared.

Finally, he nodded and said, "That's it, over and done."

I watched as he returned to the house and closed the door without looking back.

By the time the cab dropped us off back at the motel, it was right at nine o'clock. If it hadn't been for the no on-site liquor sales law, I would have been in the mood for a drink in the lounge—but then there was no lounge. Instead, we opted for a quick soup and sandwich meal in the cafe, which was preparing to close. When I was still grumbling about needing a drink, Johnnie laughed and admitted that she had a bottle of bourbon in her luggage. We adjourned to my room, which radiated the typical flat stale smell of a space that belonged to no one and everyone. I retrieved two water glasses from the bathroom and held them out while Johnnie poured us each two fingers of Old Crow.

"Maybe too much," I said.

"Nah," she answered. "Like my Uncle Gerald used to say, Comes a time when only a big slug of whiskey will set things right."

"Okay." I raised my glass. "Let's make things right." And I did—three times; Johnnie was more restrained. When I heard her voice after making things right, it was muffled as if through a closed door.

I thought she had said, "What does that mean?"

I shook my head and braced my left arm on the spindly wood table between us. "What does what mean?" My pronunciation was less than crisp.

"You said, It's in the blood."

I blinked. "Blood?"

"Yeah, in the blood. You said it a couple of drinks ago."

I licked my lips and leaned over on my elbows. "My father was an unprincipled man. We're confirming that, are we not?"

Johnnie looked at me, her face calm, shoulders erect on her blunt body. "Isn't that the point of all this?"

I laughed with no humor. "All we're doing is forcing these people to bear the bitter pill of having known my old man." I stood, wavered, sat back down "Tonight, I drug two decent people over foul ground, exposing sour memories to satisfy Randolph Sanborn's intent to fake a clean slate."

"Why you feeling it so much this time?" I looked over at her, and she added, "I mean, you treated the first two stops like you were delivering a telegram."

I looked down at the brown, low-grade carpet. "That's what I'm doing, isn't it, just making deliveries? It was different somehow…with Hayes and his wife." I raised my head and looked across the room at an ugly orange and green abstract piece of art on the wall. "It was just different."

"Different."

"Yeah. The first person was dead. Cordell Jones, he was deceased. The message was shameful, but I didn't have to look the man in the eye."

"What about his son, the one that hit you?"

A bubble of gas suddenly erupted on the fusty dregs of bourbon. "Yeah," I said, "what about him? Mason was his name. Had every right to clout me."

Johnnie studied me, then nodded. "Uh-huh."

"Now Ripley Miller. There was nothing to feel sorry for. He was an evil doer."

"Like I told you, that car, I saw it again. The DeSoto."

I looked at her, noted the seriousness in her face, and said, "Probably just another purple car. Can't figure why they'd still be following us."

She shrugged. We both went quiet, and the room took over with its blandness. She held up the bottle of bourbon. I shook my head. She re-corked the bottle, set it on the table, and seemed to wait me out; anyway she didn't pick up the conversation. Neither did I until remembering her question and what I'd meant.

"It's in the blood. I said that?"

She nodded. "Yes."

"Uh-huh." I stood. "I'm thirsty." I took one of the water glasses into the rest room and filled it from the sink. I came back out, drank it all down, and dropped back down into the same chair. "Guess it means I'm tainted,"

I added. "By him. By his vital fluids."

She tilted her head to one side. "You really think that's true?"

"I do. Now, I do."

"Now?"

I knuckled my eyes; my head was still swimming a bit. "Yeah, since the very first letter." I opened my eyes and found her staring at me like I was addled. "Damn it, Johnnie, he's dragging me through my own wrongdoings."

"Guess we've all done things we'd like to forget," she said, her tone one of tolerance.

"Tonight," I said, "tonight, while Fraser Hayes was reliving the backstabbing he had endured, my mind was assaulted by the recollection of a nearly duplicate sin of my own."

"Duplicate? Wait a minute." Johnnie sat up and looked straight at me. "You know something?"

"What?"

"Right from the start, I've been on the sidelines. I'm doing the driving and organizing, but otherwise I'm watching the game from the bench. But now, you're going off the reservation. So far I've been like so much wallpaper. I can listen to this duplicate sin business, but is that what you want?"

I studied her face, saw into her eyes, nodded, and then told her of my comparative act of betrayal. She listened, her face unmoving, as I recounted my double-crossing of college classmate Dick Charles. Dick had more talent, more sheer brilliance, than anyone I knew, and it came to him effortlessly. He was a year behind me but still known as the superior student in the school of business. He was all promise, no downside. Painmayer Lumber, like a lot of companies, annually came to Corvallis to the Oregon Aggie College in search of promising business graduates. That's how I had come to be recruited by Painmayer myself.

"That next year," I told her, "Painmayer pegged Dick Charles as a top candidate to recruit for the finance department. Since I was a recent OAC business grad, they asked me my opinion of Charles." She was staring hard at me. I pinched the bridge of my nose and inhaled. "Like I say, it's in my blood."

"What'd you do?"

"I betrayed him. Lied about his integrity, that he was known to cut corners and drank too much. That's all it took."

She continued to stare at me, licking her lips and sitting rigidly. "Why?"

I coughed my response. "He was too damn good."

She nodded once slowly. "I see."

"A mirror image of my father's transgressions. Get it?"

"What happened to him, that Dick Charles?"

"You mean, how did I disrupt his life?" She merely blinked. "He landed a plum job in Chicago at Sears Roebuck headquarters. Came up a winner anyway."

She pushed her chair back and stood. "Well, we got six hundred miles betwixt here and Boulder. Best we get some sleep and roll out early." She picked up her bottle of bourbon, likely taking it so I wouldn't drink more, and looked down on me. "That is unless you're thinking of changing the route. Heading home maybe."

I considered her suggestion. "We'll go on."

"Okay," she said. "Seven o'clock." She tipped her head and left the room, mercifully taking the bourbon with her.

Chapter Fourteen,

Several times during the night, my mind plowed back through the act of deceit I'd waged against Dick Charles. I had long ago packed away the regrets for my behavior, but now they were back. When I couldn't feign sleep any longer, I turned on the night stand lamp, and looked at my watch: 5:45.

I stood in the tub shower for a long time, arousing flat suds from the motel's ridiculously small bar of soap, feeling the hot water slither down over my body. I cursed my father several times. He'd set me up—I knew it. I dressed for the road in a pair of rumpled chinos and the third wearing of a long-sleeved sport shirt; by then it was still only 6:30. I decided to take a walk to the cafe and wait for Johnnie and was met by a wall of cold, dry air; I quickly grabbed my sport coat, though it did scant little to warm my torso. The Swan Lake Cafe was open and serving breakfast to its road-warrior guests. I took an empty booth, ordered a cup of coffee from a smiley, thin-lipped waitress, and scanned through a copy of the local Emporia Gazette Times someone had left behind. I'd just read the front page: the number of polio cases nationally had increased to 58,000 and Eisenhower would make a presidential campaign stop in Emporia on June 12. Then Johnnie slid in across from me.

"Morning." I held up the paper. "Ike's coming to town," I said.

"That right?" She pulled a menu out from behind the sugar jar and napkin dispenser. "Not much into politics."

"Okay, ready for the road?"

She looked at the menu.. "Taxi'll be here in thirty minutes. Better order something quick and easy."

I agreed to eggs over easy and toast with coffee.

"Long day?"

"Can't get to Boulder in one day. We'll lay over in a burg called Colby. Looks to be near on six hours of watching the yellow line to get there."

Our food came. We ate in silence and were waiting in the motel office when a taxi rolled up right on time. A balding middle-aged man stowed our bags and chattered all the way to the funeral home. In the wake of the departing taxi's exhaust, we saw evidence of the funeral service that would occur later that day. The funeral vehicles stood polished and at the ready. Johnnie sauntered over to a long, black funeral coach, walked around it slowly, and returned. "Never seen one of them up close before," she said. My eyes widened, demonstrating my lack of understanding. "That's a Packard Henney coach. We considered getting one but stayed with the Caddy's cleaner lines."

I bobbed my head like I knew what she was talking about, then walked out to the barn. Johnnie removed the padded tarp, pulled a towel from behind the driver's seat and did a quick wipe-down; we were ready to go.

As we were rolling out the driveway, Malcom Plumb came out from the mortuary and waved us down. I asked about the funeral for the woman who had died on the highway; her name was Zuly, I learned. They were expecting a modest gathering for the service. It saddened me to think of that. Of course I was certain that my father's interment would also be sparsely attended.

We left Malcom Plumb to his duties and drove into the town to refuel. While the coach was having its oil and tire pressure checked, I squeezed into a phone booth and called Nadine collect.

She accepted my collect call with a laugh to the operator. "Of course. Hello, Michael," she said, her voice rising in a slight lilt.

"Nadine. How are you?"

"Fine, just fine. Just reading the paper. Did you know that Portland will have its own television station this fall? Says here that it will be the very first UHF commercial broadcast in history. Whatever UHF means."

"Interesting."

"They aren't calling it a station, like radio. Instead it will be called a channel, Channel 27."

"How are you?" I asked again.

"Oh, just up, still in my bathrobe, enjoying my darjeeling and wheat toast with marmalade. How about you?"

"Getting ready to hit the road on our way to Boulder. A long haul."

I could hear her munching. "How did it turn out in Emporia? Your delivery?"

I hummed my unease. "Predictably."

"Meaning?"

"Professor Hayes, Fraser Hayes is his name, he wasn't thrilled to see me or read Dad's letter. Even though it was an apology."

"An apology?"

"Uh-huh. A confession and an apology."

There was a long pause. I heard the clink of what was evidently her tea cup being set in the saucer. "Michael," she said, her voice the sound of someone who was likely shaking her head. "How much longer?"

"Four stops to go. A week maybe."

"Another week." There was a pause. I waited. "So," she said finally, "how is this all going for you, really? According to plan?"

"Plan?" I looked out at the coach; the attendant was cleaning the windshield, and Johnnie was watching like a momma bear would her cub. "It's Dad's plan. I'm just unwrapping it."

"What's that like?"

"Like opening the wrong present at Christmas. You know, expecting one thing and getting another."

"A lump of coal then."

I laughed. "Yeah, like that." Johnnie was looking over at me; she was ready to go.

"Damn it, Michael, forget this journey of regret. Drive on back here."

"I have to finish this."

"If that's what you want." She sniffed. "How's your chauffeur doing?"

"Johnnie's okay. She'd be more likely to side with you on this though."

She laughed. "I like her more already."

"And she's waiting for me, ready to get back on the road." I paused a beat then added, "Thanks for enduring all of this, even though you're not."

"Well, nothing lasts forever, even this crazy trip."

I pulled the door open and waved to Johnnie. "Nadine, please know that I love you."

"My, my," she said. "And it's not even our anniversary."

I sighed and hung up. Express my regrets later. The attendant accepted three dollars and change with a smile as Johnnie ignited the V8. On the way out of town, we stopped at a food market where I purchased a sack of portable food and a Thermos vacuum bottle for coffee, which we had filled at an adjacent cafe. We left town later than planned.

We'd gone maybe five miles before anything was said between us, and that was Johnnie asking me to pour her a cup of coffee. She sipped from the red Thermos cap, kept her eyes on the road, and nodded her thanks. It was chilly, so I fiddled with the heater controls until warm air began to come out. I settled back in the seat. The road was clear, not much traffic and lots of highway stretched out before us with no end in sight.

I poured myself some coffee. After my first sip, I said, "Got a sack full of edibles. Interested?"

She glanced at the bag on the seat. "Like what?"

"Oh, apples, bananas, vanilla wafers, even some Dolly Madison Zingers."

"Sounds good, but it'll have to wait. The DeSoto's back." She had her eyes on the side mirror.

I spun around in the seat and squinted out through back window, peering past the casket. "I'll be damned."

"Been back there for a while but too far away to recognize. They're closer now, and it is definitely a purple car. I'm sure it's that DeSoto."

"What are they doing?"

"Nothing, just hanging back, but they're closing the gap."

"Maybe they'll pass us. Maybe a different car."

"No, it's them. I can make out their bodies. The big guy's on the passenger side; the skinny one's driving. It's them all right. Same car, has the visor, same one."

"Unbelievable. I mean, totally unbelievable. This is Ripley Miller's doing."

She nodded, her eyes still on the side mirror. "Of course. That guy's a baddie."

"Yes, but why this? Why put hired muscle on our trail? Especially after being run off by the state police. They staying close?"

"Uh-huh." She slowed down. "Yep, they fall back when I cut my speed. They're doggin' us all right." She accelerated. "Give me some of them vanilla wafers. I'll just keep driving unless they try something."

I dug out the box of cookies and handed her several and took another look back. The car was still there. There was hardly any traffic, an occasional car or truck going the opposite direction, and once a big sedan passed us. The DeSoto was still there. We finished the coffee between us. I peeled a banana and waited for the DeSoto to approach us, but it just kept following, staying way back.

"We should do something," I said and dropped the banana skin into the sack.

"Like what?" Johnnie responded with an uptick in her voice.

"I don't know. Something."

"Well, we have the Louisville Slugger. Why don't I pull off and you go back and knock them silly?"

I laughed. "Yeah, I can just envision me doing that."

"So, keep going?"

"What are they doing?"

"Nothing, just burning gas."

"Okay, keep going. Maybe look for a place to pull off where there are other people."

"Michael, look out there. There's nothing, just flat land, no human life, and just more highway. Sure, a few cars and trucks pass by, but—"

"What's that?" I sat up straight. "Coming up there, on the right. That tall thing."

"I don't know. Wait, that's one them, whata they call it? A grain elevator. That's what it is. Seen them out in eastern Oregon too. Wheat storage."

I pounded a hand on the dashboard. "Okay, pull off there. There's likely people around a place that size. Slow down and drive in."

She squirmed in the seat and leaned forward. As we got nearer, she slowed, found the exit road off the highway, and drove in, creating a cloud of gravel dust; the coach jounced over some railroad tracks adjacent to the elevator. I looked back and saw the DeSoto drop back before pulling off onto the highway shoulder and stopping. Johnnie idled closer and pulled up to a building that looked like an office next to the elevator silos. An International pickup was parked by the office, but there was no sign of life. She put the transmission in neutral and leaned back and heaved a sigh. After a moment she looked around, back the way we'd come in.

"They're still out there," I said.

Chapter Fifteen,

After we had been sitting in the Meteor, engine idling for a few minutes, a stocky man wearing Levis and a red and black plaid shirt came out of the elevator office building and stood staring at us. We laughed, and Johnnie declared that we were making his day. Finally, I got out, waved, and walked toward him.

"Hello there," I said, offering him my best smile. He nodded and shoved his hands into the pockets of his denims. "I know," I said, "a little unnerving to look out your window and see that a hearse has just pulled up."

He smiled with unease. "Yeah. A bit startling."

"No reason to worry," I said. "We just pulled off to stretch our legs. Not a lot of places to do that out here."

"Nope." He pulled on the bill of his cap with a Massey-Ferguson logo stitched on it. "One thing we have in these parts is lots of space. On top of that, this is our dead time of year here at the co-op." He looked at the coach. "Where you headed?"

He listened attentively as I gave him the gist of what we were up to. He shook his head smiling, looked toward the coach once more, and wished us well. I asked if we might use his restroom; he agreed. Johnnie went first, and while she was gone, I asked the man if he recognized the car parked out on the highway. I raised my arm and pointed at the Desoto so they'd see me gesturing. He studied the vehicle but then shook his head; he did not recognize the car. He asked why I wanted to know.

"Well," I answered, "that car has been following us for some time. Never passing or turning off, just staying behind us. Now they've stopped when we have and seem to be waiting for us." He looked at the car and back to me. "I know, sounding a little paranoid. But in our circumstance, transporting human remains across country, we have encountered the curious. Not sure what they're up to but it makes us a little nervous." I didn't reveal our earlier exchange with the miscreants.

He looked at the DeSoto once more. "Do you want me to call the sheriff? It'll take a while to get a deputy out here, but if you want I can do it."

"No, it will probably be okay, could be just some curious folks."

When Johnnie came out, I took my turn at the restroom. Upon my return, the co-op manager said he was closing for the day and offered to follow us for a few miles as he was heading our direction as well. We accepted, and he kept his pickup between us and the DeSoto, though it continued to follow. After about ten miles, the man flashed his lights, and the pickup pulled off onto another road. We were alone again, and the purple car was still trailing us.

"Damn," Johnnie said after the co-op manager left us. "Bold as brass. Looka that, they're coming right up on us. And flashing their headlights."

"They're making a point." My stomach was churning. "Trying to intimidate us. We have to do something."

"Like what?"

"Where are we?"

"Coming up on a town called McPherson. We can stop there for lunch, but I was planning on doing that in Salina."

"How much farther...to Salina?"

"I don't know for sure, maybe forty more miles."

"Keep going. Once we pass through McPherson and have clear road ahead, look for a wide spot and pull off."

"Then what?"

"Where's the bat?"

"It's under the seat, my side."

I found it and held it in my lap and gripped the tapered end.

"What are you thinking? Not you and those two." She chuckled and shook her head.

I ran my hands over the finished wood. "Johnnie, I do not want them on our tail any longer."

"Yes, but they are...Michael, you can't take them on."

"Don't think I'm scary enough? Me and the bat?"

She grinned and checked the rearview mirror again. "Scary? That's not what I'm thinking. I'm thinking there's two of them, and they're set on making their point. We don't even know if they have weapons."

I gripped the bat harder. "You means guns?"

"Yes."

"Come on, they're just muscle, not gunsels."

She came up behind a Mayflower moving van and settled in at an even speed. I looked over the casket through the rear window; the DeSoto fell back and matched our speed. What were they up to? The moving van lumbered along. Johnnie calmly drove the coach with one hand, and the burgundy DeSoto hung back about ten car lengths. I massaged the slugger and grew impatient. This pursuit had to end somehow—and in our favor; still, I felt nervous electricity across my shoulders.

We'd traveled maybe five miles from McPherson when I thunked the business end of the bat on the floor. "Okay, pass this truck, and let's look for a place to pull over."

Johnnie continued along behind the van, placing two hands on the wheel and making no move to pass. I hit the floor again; she looked over at me and finally pulled out and accelerated past the truck. She settled back into her lane and maintained passing speed. There was nothing but empty road ahead of us. Shortly, the burgundy car came around the van and fell in behind us again. I stared down the highway and looked for a place to stop. There was nothing for miles; then off in the distance I made out a wide shoulder and told Johnnie to pull off when she got up to that spot. She grunted her displeasure but eased up on the accelerator and drifted off; it looked like an exit onto some ranch property.

"They pulling over?" I asked.

She nodded. "They are indeed. Staying back some, but closer than before."

I lifted the bat. "Okay, here I go. Stay in here." I opened the door and stepped out. Johnnie yelled something, but I couldn't make it out.

I slammed the door when I got out and took off at a fast pace, closing on the DeSoto as quickly as I could. I didn't want to give them the time to consider what I might be up to, not imagining me to be any kind of threat. I came up on the driver's side of the car, holding the bat in my right hand, my heart throbbing. The skinny one was at the wheel, not wearing

Summation

his fedora. He looked up at me, wide-eyed, rolled down his window and stared out, uncertainty etched on his face. He opened his thin lips to say something, but I cut him off.

"This is going to stop. Now! You will turn this car around and head back the way you came and never approach us again. You got it?"

"Listen, Bub, don't you give us no guff."

I leaned down, close to his face and shouted, "Shut up!" I was gripping the bat hard. "Do you hear me?"

It was then that the fat man leaned into view from the passenger seat. "Tough guy, huh? May I remind you, sir, we have a job to do, and until we conclude what we've been paid to do, we will be in your shadow."

"That's it, is it?"

"Yes, that's it."

I stood up straight, my ears ringing, and said as calmly as I could muster, "Well, this is our answer." Just then I felt the draft of a big truck as it rumbled by; I didn't give a damn.

I stepped back and brought the bat down against the windshield. I missed the visor and hit the glass full force. It was a two-piece windshield, split down the middle; the bat hit the driver's side, and the laminated glass sagged in and fractured into a spiderweb of cracks. When the driver uttered some colorful profanities and emerged from the car, I turned my attention to the headlights and obliterated their lenses in two swings of the bat. By that time the skinny guy was coming at me, but my adrenaline was on full force. He was carrying a tire iron, ready to wreck my body. My timing was surprisingly accurate; at that moment I could do no wrong. My retaliation was not to be denied. I cocked the bat, breathing heavily, and whirled around, striking the driver's left knee. The Louisville Slugger gave no quarter. The man's scream pierced the air and caused me to step back as he fell to the ground writhing. When I looked into the car where the big man sat and made a move in his direction, he raised two hands in submission. I took a couple of steps his way. Again he waved his hands and shook his head.

I walked back to where the driver lay on the ground holding onto his knee and moaning. He looked up at me, his eyes ablaze, and cursed me. I had no sympathy. Before leaving them, I walked to the passenger side of the DeSoto and peered in. The window was down. The heavy man looked up at me; his face held the expression of one defeated. It was strange, me being at such a juncture. I held the bat out of sight and leaned forward.

"I suppose," I said, "that you and your colleague could regroup and come after us again. You planning on that?"

The man's face was florid, and he appeared dismayed. "No," he answered.

"And tell Ripley that if I see you or anyone else like you, I will return to Pine Bluff with my bat and visit him personally. Will you do that, please."

The man nodded.

"You know, none of this was a necessary. I had no intention of sharing what I know about Ripley with anyone. No reason to."

The man sighed. "I wouldn't know."

"Believe me. Sorry for your car and your partner's injury. All avoidable." I stood up, leaned the bat on my shoulder. "We'll be leaving now. And whoever shows up to help you, even the sheriff, I wouldn't suggest blaming us. You had this coming. Agreed?"

He nodded again and drew a fleshy hand across his face. "Agreed."

When I turned, Johnnie was standing at the rear of the coach. She was holding the big metal flashlight and smiling.

Once we were back in the coach, Johnnie said nothing, just pulled back out onto the highway and accelerated away from the scene of the confrontation. For some reason, I held onto the bat and stared straight down the road which stretched out before us, an unending band of tar and rock. There was no traffic coming our way to interfere with the sight. I sat up straight, my breathing tight and shallow, and considered what has just happened. It had happened. I knew that, but still it seemed imagined. When I lifted a hand to rub my face, it quivered. I held it out and looked at my trembling fingers. I laughed in a voice that wasn't mine. Well, it was, but I couldn't stop laughing until I had to gasp for air.

"Michael?" Johnnie glanced over before looking back to the road.

"Yeah, I'm okay, I think." I looked at her. "That…what happened really happened, didn't it?"

She grinned. "It did! My god, Michael, I couldn't believe my eyes. You and the bat. Then it was over before I could even get over there. You were something, I tell ya. I had my heavy-duty flashlight in case I had to weigh in. But I didn't have to."

I blew out a grunting breath and laughed hard once more; tears ran down my cheeks. "Dang fool. I was a dang fool. Wasn't I...a dang fool?"

"Yeah, when you bombed out the door, I was thinking more like idiot, if you want to know."

I wiped the wetness off my face. "To tell the truth, it's all a blur. Are they following us again?"

"No, Michael. They couldn't be. You blinded them. No, I figure they're still sitting there by the side of the road wondering what happened."

"Okay." I put the bat back under the seat and leaned back.

I dozed off and didn't come to until Johnnie gently poked my left shoulder. "We're here, in Salina," she said. "Hungry?"

I thought on that. "I just checked, and my stomach thinks my throat's been cut," I said, knuckling my eyes. "Yes, I'm hungry." I sat up. "What's that odor? Smells like food. I must be hallucinating."

"No, it's food," she said. "A sackful of burgers from Cozy Inn Hamburgers, just across the street there. That's how they do it, by the sack. They're small, so I got six of 'em. That, a couple of Cokes, and a wad of paper napkins. We'll eat on the go. We're running way behind time. Three hours and more to go before we reach Colby."

"Colby."

"Yeah. Need to keep pushing. No rest for the wicked, and you were wicked."

I smiled, reached into the bag, and pulled out a hamburger; the first bite was juicy and laced with lots of onion. Johnnie reminded me there was a church key in the glove box; I used it to pry the caps off of the Cokes. We gassed up at a Flying A then juggled food and soda while she drove. I cleaned up afterward, filling the paper sack with greasy napkins and empty bottles. The coach's interior was permeated with the smell onions. I hoped that my father, who had hated onions, had taken note.

Chapter Sixteen,

We passed the Colby city limits at 5:38—a good two hours behind Johnnie's schedule. With dusk approaching, we had limited time to locate our beds, store the coach, and find local cuisine before dark. Johnnie drove straight down the main street and pulled to a stop in front of a new car showroom. Fluorescent lights shined down on the latest model of a Nash automobile.

"What's this?" I asked.

"We'll bed the coach here for the night. The local funeral home has no room for us, so he shunted us off to this auto dealer."

Right then there was a tap on my side window. A smiling middle-aged man with big teeth and thick gold-rimmed glasses was peering in. I cranked the window down and did my best to return a smile as good as I was getting.

"Good evening," the man said in a salesman's voice. He reached a hand in; I shook it and felt a lumpy gold ring in my grasp. "Richard Hill," he said. "Welcome to Colby. My pleasure to provide accommodations for your beautiful hearse tonight right here at Hill Motors. Harvey over at the funeral parlor, he told me about your journey. Quite something I must say." I merely nodded.

Johnnie followed instructions and drove around behind the dealership, where he waved her into the empty body shop bay. With the coach nestled in, we made our way back through a small showroom where Mr. Hill paused to extoll the virtues of a willow green Nash Ambassador with Air-flex suspension and Pinin Farina Italian design. He would make me a special deal, if I was interested.

He generously drove us to our motel, chatting all the way—seemed like a lonely fellow. He delivered us to the front door of the Curve-In Court & Barber Shop, tapped his horn, and drove away. Colby was turning out to be a most interesting stop. We checked in with the host, one Cecil Nibbs: skinny, arms covered in thick black hair and a scalp with nary a strand.

Cecil gave us the keys for two stucco cottages built in a boxy Spanish style. The rooms smelled of pine cleaner and cigarette smoke—a familiar pungent combination. When we asked where we could eat, Cecil chuckled and let it be known that all of the town's eateries were closed down by four o'clock weekdays. The only place left was the bowling alley, where the diner served food as long as the alley was open. It was only a few blocks, so we walked and entered a square, uninspiring building with a red neon sign on the roof reading Colby Bow; the L was dark. A cacophony of rolling balls and crashing pins serenaded our ears when we entered.

We sat on spinner stools. The middle-aged waitress behind the counter wore a tired face, skin dehydrated by too many cigarettes, and lank brown hair. But she smiled at us anyway and took our orders for deluxe burger baskets while the sounds of league bowling night reverberated in the background. The burgers came. We had vanilla shakes with them and listened to the waitress brag that the alley was closing for a week to install new automatic pinsetter machinery. No more human pinsetters. We smiled, enjoyed the burgers, and returned to Curve-In Court and our fragrant rooms.

Johnnie brought what was left of her bottle of Old Crow to my room and poured us short shots in bathroom sink glasses. I promised myself restraint and sipped modestly. I had propped myself up on the bed while Johnnie claimed a small armed chair covered in ugly yellow mustard upholstery.

"How are you after the DeSoto fight?" she said after a sip of whiskey.

"Fight? Was that a fight? You know, I was never a fighter. Or much of an athlete. Never recorded a truly heroic physical deed in my life."

"I don't know about that, but what you did to those guys was pretty gutsy."

"I was terrified right down to my toenails."

"Really nervy then, taking them on when you were scared to death."

"Acted on rage. No prize for that. Blew right by my fears. But I'm still seeing them in my head. Beyond that, I'm pretty okay. Now it's back on track."

"Yeah, back on track. You know, your dad's carcass may be all fixed up in a Hawaiian shirt, festive like, but it's over and done for him. Can't be messing with you now. Thought this was a journey of obligation not absolution."

Somehow she had ripened from chauffeur to tour guide and now counselor.

"Big words now. You know what they mean?"

"Go to hell," she said.

"There's a thought."

"Dang, Michael, you're just a delivery boy. You've got no call to carry your old man's garbage from place to place and wear it like a hair shirt."

So there I was, sprawled out on a lumpy bed in a disinfected motel room in a place called Colby, somewhere in Kansas. My father's remains were parked in an automobile dealership body shop, and my square-shouldered blonde driver with undisciplined hair was taking me to task. She sat forward and leaned on her thighs, looked over at me, and clasped her hands together.

"Something more on your mind?" I said.

"This trip, it's crazy," she said and shook her head.

I reached back and rearranged two flat lifeless pillows and stretched out on the bed. "It is that for sure."

She chuffed out a laugh. "For us, me and my dad, it was just a contract for Pete's sake. All business. I made the arrangements, showed up at the airport to meet this spit-and-polish business type guy—you. We picked up the remains and set off on a set schedule. All professional and thorough."

"Okay."

"You, the methodical son, as I saw it, doing what you'd agreed to, and I the licensed mortician fulfilling the bargain as agreed to and paid for. All business."

"Again true."

"Then." She raised her hands. "Then right outa the box you get punched in the face. Very first stop."

"Didn't hurt too bad."

"Still and all, it was a warning sign. Then came Pine Bluff and that Ripley guy. Nasty, what he did. And then he sent the thugs."

I knuckled my eyes and nodded. "Yeah, I hadn't figured on that."

"But you read those letters. You knew."

"Sure, but all I imagined was introducing myself, handing off the letter, and making a polite exit."

Summation

"Oh, come on. We drive up outa the blue—in a hearse, with a body on board. You shove one of them letters in their face and don't expect any kickback?"

"Okay, I should have been more aware. I wasn't. So what?"

"So what? We've only made three stops, and things are turning ugly"

I didn't say anything, just stared over at her. I kept my mouth shut for a change. I was considering that reality when there came a knock at the door. It was the motel manager—and barber. He stood in the doorway and peered in past me at Johnnie, gave her a wave, and told me that I could have a hair trim tomorrow if I wanted. Came with the room. I thanked him and said I'd think about it. He didn't offer the same to Johnnie. When he'd gone, I laughed out loud—a free haircut. Johnnie didn't share my amusement; I suspected she was still thinking on turning ugly.

I sat on the edge of the bed, hands on my knees. "So, okay," I said. "Not sure if I'd call it ugly, but different than I expected, yeah."

She stood and walked to the window, pulled the curtain aside, and looked out. She turned back and looked at me. "You know, this is gonna keep on happening. Boulder. The next stop, whoever the person is there, will they be glad to see you? When they get their letter?"

I met her gaze and recalled the name of the woman I would see in Colorado.

Jasmine was her name, and no, she would not be glad to see me. I shook my head.

Johnnie came over to me and looked down into my eyes. "Do you love your wife?" she asked. "Nadine, do you love her?"

Chapter Seventeen,

Those words, that question, rang in my ears as if I had just fallen on my head. She stood as still as a manikin; one eye twitched. The question wasn't wrong, in way it wasn't even out of line, but it was one of those moments when you don't know the truth. Not totally anyway. I was struck dumb. I knew the answer I should give, even the answer I wanted to give. But why had she asked it?

"What the hell? Why would you ask such a question?"

"Just thinking, with all this going on. A simple question. Isn't it?"

I huffed out a snarky laugh. "No."

"Can't every husband or wife be able to answer it in one word?"

"Marriage, it can be…well, it's a trial—right from the start, even before the start."

"Yes, but do you or don't you?"

My eyes were watering. I waved her off, bristling; she kept looking at me in spite of my scowl. "All right," I said. "It gets underway when that first wave of desire hits you, all wrapped up in fascination. For a man it's when you can't take your eyes off of a certain woman. From there you become infatuated with each other, never wanting to be apart."

"Then what?"

"I guess that's when the in-love part enters the picture. After that, you convince yourselves you can spend your lives together."

"Can?"

"Okay, want to."

"Then what?"

"Come off it, Johnnie. It's time we got some sleep." When she just kept looking at me, I said louder than I should have, "Okay! We got married, had regular sex, and have lived happily ever after. That what you wanted to hear?"

"What was it like? Being with a woman other than your own wife?"

My head jerked back, a hoarse laugh erupted from my throat. I clapped my hands together. "Damnation! Enough. No more probing my life."

Her face viewed me sadly. "I was only wondering."

"Wondering?"

She was still standing; I was still seated on the bed. She stepped back and said, "Yeah. Curious. About, you know, intimacy."

Intimacy. I said the word in my head and wanted to laugh but then saw the expression in Johnnie's eyes. She was beseeching me to respond, to open the door on the province of enticement, of the attraction and fulfillment of conjoining with someone. How could I not respond?

"Being with someone other than my wife was both exhilarating and despicable. Both at once. Do you understand how that could be?"

She folded her arms beneath her breasts and looked down. "No."

Then it was clear. This woman, this curiously unique woman, had not yet engaged in intimacy. She was indeed merely curious—and yet harboring a yearning to be wanted in that way. Now what?

"Maria, I told you of her. My involvement with her is not something I'm proud of," I said. "Nadine is so much the better person in our marriage."

She bit on her lower lip and looked at me again. "But, the involvement… with the other woman, was it still…?"

"Seductive? Yes, of course it was. But I regret it to this day. Now let's get some shut-eye."

"All right." I heard the disappointment in her voice. "But I need to use the bathroom before I go."

I waved a hand and flopped back on the bed. Almost instantly my eyes closed. I'm not sure how long I was out before I heard Johnnie clear her throat. I blinked and rubbed my eyes before rising up on one elbow, prepared to tell her goodnight before she headed to her own room. Instead, there she stood at the foot of the bed, stark naked. I heard my own gasp as I was driven up into a sitting position.

"Johnnie, what are you doing?" I couldn't help it. I saw her. My eyes were on her nudity. My brain took in her pale skin, wide shoulders, stocky build, and small breasts. She was motionless, hands at her sides, eyes wide, watching my reaction and chewing on her lower lip some more.

When I turned away and got off the bed, she said, "Are you okay?"

I shook my head. "No, I'm not okay. Get your clothes back on," I said, not looking at her, waving an arm away.

"I wanted you to see my body."

"What?"

"I've never been seen by a man. Not this way."

I turned around to look into her face. There was no falsehood, no devilry, in those eyes. I felt tears forming. Her honest face, with its square jaw and arresting nose, was imploring me to accept her. I wanted to just hold her and sob. Sadness filled my chest. I couldn't speak.

"Michael," she said when I didn't respond. "I want you to to look at me like this. To see me and touch me…in those places."

I was frozen in place, not turning away, not ogling, just feeling stranded and unable to address the sympathy swimming in my head. "Johnnie," I said on a weak breath, "I can't. We mustn't."

I could see the humiliation in her face. She just looked at me, one hand running fingers through her hair, and seemed at a loss of what to do. A gauzy image of Maria entered my head in that moment. I had seen her body all of those years ago and as much as humanly possible had tried to erase all recall of that time. But the long-ago, delight of Nadine and I enjoying our youthful bodies remained with me. Then again, there had been the inevitable ebbing of our physical selves as the years had passed. I doubted that either of us could remember the last time we had looked upon our bodies with desire. This was crazy.

There we stood, each of us unmoving, fearful of the moment. Somewhere a car door slammed, then another. Voices rose, and a door closed on an adjoining cottage. The distraction gave us a brief reprieve. I inhaled.

"Never?"

A self-conscious smile appeared on her mouth. She drew her lips in and moved her head slowly side to side.

"Why now?"

"Because…I need to know."

I hesitated. "Know what?"

"That I," she raised a hand to her mouth, "that I am not repulsive." She began to cry and then to sob.

I was frozen in place for a long moment. She cried then I went to her, held her, and waited for her to calm. When she did, I stepped back, my hands on her shoulders, and looked into her eyes. She sniffed and gave up a little laugh. I smiled back and asked what she wanted. She told me in a soft uncertain voice. And so I touched her the ways she wished, gently, not grossly, and assured her she was not repulsive, that her skin was lovely and her body desirable. She wanted me to lie with her on the bed, just to be close. I didn't remove my clothes, just held her. We slept until around midnight, when she roused, dressed, and left for her room. I didn't really sleep after that.

The next morning, when I stepped out of my cottage, Johnnie was already waiting outside. She turned toward me, no expression on her face, pointed down the street, and set off in long strides toward a small cafe. There was a nip in the air at that early hour. I wished for a coat but accepted the chill and followed along, keeping pace as if I were her underling. Inside the steamy little eatery, among a mix of locals, we took an open booth and ordered basic breakfasts. While waiting, Johnnie unfolded her road map and began running a finger along the route she'd be taking. Nothing was said about the night before. It would take maybe five to six hours to reach our destination—a reasonable day for once.

After breakfast we returned to the Curve-In Court & Barber Shop, where I checked us out and consented to a quick hair trim. I leaned back in the barber chair while Cecil Nibbs wrapped tissue around my neck and spread the cape over me. He chatted amiably about nothing and snipped around my ears and neck; I listened patiently, but my mind was on the miles that lay ahead and how Johnnie and I could possibly pass the time in view of the previous evening's awkwardness.

I tipped the barber; then we carried our bags to the Nash dealership, where a curious body shop crew stood by and watched as Johnnie slowly eased the Meteor out of the garage into the cool March sunlight. I opened a side door to corroborate the presence of my father one more time, patted the casket, and loaded our luggage. Richard Hill was standing behind me when I closed the coach door, having come out to see us off; he brandished another big-toothed smile and waved heartily as we departed. Yes indeed, Colby was an interesting little town.

We were about ten miles out when Johnnie finally spoke, saying, "I hate myself for that." She gripped the steering wheel with both hands.

I looked over at her. She stared straight down the highway, her mouth a tight line. "You shouldn't," I said.

She coughed out a mocking laugh. "I humiliated myself."

The road map lay on the seat between us. I picked it up and pretended to be tracing our route. I didn't know how to respond to such self-reproach, so I said nothing. It was then that I felt the coach begin to accelerate; the engine noise rose as it strained against the vehicle's weight. I stared ahead waiting for Johnnie to ease off, but she didn't.

"Johnnie," I said as calmly as I could but with my eyes widening.

The speedometer needle continued to sweep to the right. A truck could be seen in the distance; we were gaining on it—rapidly. The coach body began to shudder. The trailer of the semi grew nearer.

"That's enough," I said. This time my voice was not calm. She continued to press down on the accelerator. "Damn it, Johnnie, stop this!"

Then we were right there behind the truck, the signage on its tailgate, Ringsby Freight Lines, suddenly big and bold. I yelled something indecipherable just before Johnnie veered into the oncoming lane and flashed by the tractor and trailer; mercifully there was no traffic coming our way. I had just an instant to glimpse the bright orange cab of the semi, laboring up the small grade, the black of its exhaust spewing out. I never really saw the driver, just felt two wide eyes meeting mine in return. Johnnie veered the coach back into our lane, struggled for a moment to keep control, and then I felt the vehicle's forward trajectory begin to slow.

Maybe half a mile down the road, Johnnie decelerated enough to pull off onto a wide gravel turnout; she pumped the brakes and brought the coach to a skidding stop. A cloud of dust billowed over the coach as she turned the ignition off with a flip of the wrist and got out just as the Ringsby truck passed us; the driver yanked on the lanyard of his air horn, giving us several indignant blasts. She gave the noise no mind and strode off in a determined gait. I stepped out of the coach and watched her walk away.

When she gave no sign of stopping or turning back, I sat back inside with the door open, legs sticking out and my feet planted on the gravel of the turnout.

Through the windshield I saw her pause at the end of the turnout, face the barbed wire fence that paralleled the highway, and stare off across the adjacent field. There was nothing to see, just acres of plowed field. A short time had passed when a police car, coming from the opposite direction, pulled off the highway and pulled up beside the coach. A square-shouldered officer, tall and thin, eased out of his Kansas Highway Patrol car and sauntered over to the coach. He was clad right out of the manual on proper patrolman attire: dark blue twill uniform pants, a billed cap with a medallion above the brim, and a traditional Sam Browne belt across his chest.

I got out and walked around to where he stood examining the coach. "Officer," I said.

He nodded. "Had a chat with a trucker back down the road at a fuel stop. Said he'd had a near death experience with a hearse." He chuckled. "An appropriate reference it seems. Anyhow, fella told me this hearse was traveling at excessive speed and scared the bejesus out of him. Might that be you?"

I conjured up a smile. "Not many other funeral coaches out on the road, I would venture. In fact, we did pass a big truck a bit ago before pulling over here to stretch our legs. Truck was hauling up a slight grade, so it may have seemed we were going faster when we passed him." I was fudging the truth, but he seemed to buy it.

The patrolman stepped over to the coach and tried to peer in, but the side curtain blocked his view, so he stepped back. "Where you headed?"

"Right now we're on the way to Boulder, in Colorado. That's our next stop anyway."

He nodded and noticed Johnnie walking up. "Oregon plates, I see. Would you mind filling me in on your itinerary?"

So I did while Johnnie stood by the nose of the coach, her right hand-gripping the hood ornament. She let me do the explaining. When I'd finished, the man looked at his watch, tipped his head toward Johnnie, and wished us a safe journey. She waited until the patrol car had gone before coming around and getting back behind the wheel, where she sat staring ahead, waiting for me to get in. I scooted in over the upholstery nap and opened the glove box once more.

"Here, read this," I said, handing her the Boulder letter.

After an inert moment, she eyeballed the envelope in my hand and finally took it from me. She spread the letter across the horn ring of the steering wheel and tilted her head slightly forward. When she'd finished, she looked out through the windshield then back down at the letter and seemed to read part of it again.

"He was a bastard."

I shrugged. "Could be, and was more than once."

"Could be?" She waved the letter. "Your mother, she aware of this?"

I took in a slow breath. "You mean any more than Nadine was of my transgressions? I don't know. I hope not."

Handing the letter back, she added, "But you fessed up."

I smiled with no humor. "That make me a better man?"

She turned the key in the ignition and brought the big engine to life, dropped the transmission into gear, and eased forward. Once she'd checked the side mirror, we were back on the highway; there was no traffic in either direction. I put away the letter and settled in. Several oncoming cars sent sharp windshield reflections of the cool sunlight into my eyes. We each pulled down our visor.

"Maybe not," she said. I blinked and looked over at her. "Maybe not a better man," she said, "but not a scoundrel. Not like what's in that letter."

What could I say to that? I kept my arms folded and looked out at the dry grassland, scrub brush, and passing parade of fence posts and barbed wire.

"After all," she said, "I have some firsthand proof now, don't I?"

"That's proof of nothing."

Chapter Eighteen.

She had no response to my refutation. I left it there. Comparing my father's behavior to my own was a waste of time. He no longer had a voice in the debate, so I left it hanging. We spoke no more of it right then and soon came upon the tiny town of Flagler, where we pulled off, found the local eatery, had their corned beef hash special, and returned to the highway. Johnnie was committed to driving straight through to Boulder. The quiet between us remained.

After few miles, I broke the silence. "You know," I said staring straight ahead, "it's weird, this cockamamie journey. Like you said, a crazy trip."

She kept her hands at ten and two and slowed behind a flatbed farm truck carrying a mountain of burlap feed sacks. "That right? Like me getting naked, exposing my pathetic self-image? That kind of weird?"

I winced. "Okay," I responded carefully. "But no, it's because I was certain this would all be a cakewalk. Just a cross-country jaunt. Then right from the start this damnable road trip reached out and shook the bejesus out of my ego."

"It's a trick, Michael. A game. We've been suckered."

I hadn't thought of it that way, but of course it had been a game from the beginning. From that time on my father's patio in Jupiter, he'd created a method not only to make amends but to get even—maybe even with me too.

"Don't you see? And part of the game is messing us over. Hell, your dad, he had it all planned out all along and..." Her voice faded.

"And what?" I asked.

She turned her head toward me for a quick eye-to-eye look. "Whata you think? He's got us going back through stuff, digging in our own dirt."

"Come on, he didn't know about you, who you'd be."

"Doesn't matter. He knew someone would be driving. And whatever you'd be going through would spill over onto whoever was at the wheel. Plus, you and the driver would sure enough end up talking about everything that's rolled out. Not only am I soaking it all in, I'm taking a dip back into my own missteps. Same as you. Part of the plan, I tell you."

"Have it figured out, do you?"

She gave me a small smile. "I do."

We crossed the Boulder city limits right around four o'clock. I looked for the city limits sign: Boulder's population was just under 20,000 but was living larger, more energetic than even larger cities we gone through. The address on the envelope took us downtown in the midst of businesses and traffic, in fact, to Foley's Department Store, a big square building rising at least five stories. Johnnie circled the block twice before we decided there was no easy place to park a funeral coach; instead we went on to our scheduled parking place for the night.

Maples Mortuary was housed in a white Victorian-style house with a huge wraparound porch, two stories, and a peaked roofline. Towering sugar maples stood regally on each corner of a wide front yard surrounded by an iron picket fence. Johnnie maneuvered the coach down a side street and pulled into a paved lot behind the building; the lot was large enough to accommodate vehicles for a big funeral but was empty. She parked next to a white ambulance. Beyond that, a man wearing coveralls was washing a funeral coach with a wool mitt and hose. He dropped the mitt into a bucket, turned off the nozzle, and came over when we stepped out.

He was young and slim and wore a wide smile. He made points by wiping his hands on his legs before reaching out to shake Johnnie's hand rather than mine.

"You the folks from Oregon?" he said on a soft voice. His smile revealed one of his front incisors was set askew.

Johnnie let him hold onto her hand a tad longer and returned his smile.

"Indeed we are," she said, pulling her hand away. "I'm Jonalynn Gates." She used her actual name. "With Gates & Collier Funeral Home in Portland. And this is our client, Michael Sanborn."

The man stepped toward me and extended a large, still moist hand. "A pleasure, Mr. Sanborn. I'm Toby Ellis."

"Thank you for letting us park the couch here overnight," I offered.

"Not my doing at all." He grinned more. "That was Mr. Keller's invitation. I was just told to watch out for you and help you in any way I can. And here you are. What can I do for you?"

He agreed to drive us to Gilpin's Inn to check in and leave our luggage, then dropped us off downtown in front of Foley's Department Store. It was after six o'clock by then, but the store was still open and alive with shoppers. Toby agreed to pick us up the next morning at eight o'clock and drove away, leaving us to find out if our next letter designee was somewhere within the walls of the big structure. We pushed through a bank of glass doors and were immediately confronted by bright fluorescent lighting and the smells of new merchandise, not dissimilar from experiencing the smell of a new car.

We approached a sales counter where a young clerk smiled at us over a glass case filled with small leather goods. She eagerly offered to help us and only dimmed her smile when I asked the floor for the beauty salon instead of showing interest in gloves. We took an elevator to the fifth floor and emerged into a mixture of bedspreads, draperies, fabrics, and linens. The salon was in a far corner.

The pungent, almost medicinal, aroma announced the beauty salon before we actually entered. There was a long wall of chairs, basins, hair dryers, and mirrors where the beauticians were all wearing the same burgundy dresses with white collars. Most of them stood behind a customer whose hair was being cut, trimmed, or permed. I asked one of the women if Jasmine Karras was available. She had already gone for the day. I took a chance and pleaded my case to be given her phone number due to a death in the family. Not a lie, just not her family.

I found a bank of pay phones on the mezzanine and made the call. On the third ring, a raspy male voice answered. I asked for Jasmine, and whoever it was set the receiver down with a clunk and called out her name. I heard a female voice ask Who is it? The response was No idea. I waited, listening in on the general ambient sounds of motion and ruffling of a newspaper perhaps.

And then she was on the line. "Yes?"

"Is this Jasmine Karras?"

"Yes. Who is this?" The voice rode the timbre of fatigue.

"Miss Karras, my name is Michael Sanborn. You don't know me, but you knew my father." Silence on the line. "Randolph Sanborn." More silence. "In Portland. In Oregon."

"I know," she said. After hesitating, she asked, "Why are you calling me?"

"You see, my father passed away recently."

"I see. And what has that got to do with me—your father dying?"

Her alto voice had taken on a decided edge. I knew why, of course. I'd read the letter often enough. "I have something for you...from him. I'd like to deliver it to you...in person if I may."

"What?"

"I'm here, in Boulder. Would it be possible to visit you briefly?"

She made a sound, sort of like a laugh, an incredulous laugh. "What is it?"

"A letter. To you. From him."

"A letter?" I waited. "We're just sitting down to eat dinner," she said.

"I could come by later, when it's convenient for you."

"Convenient? This, this whatever it is, will not be convenient."

"I won't take much of your time...it's just that I promised him to do this."

Chapter Nineteen,

She wavered but ultimately gave me her address and suggested I come by at eight o'clock. We found a diner just a block from Foley's Department Store, ate quickly, and took a cab back to Gilpin's Inn, where I freshened up. The same cab returned to pick us up. The driver knew right where the mortuary was; in fact he had attended a funeral there a month ago—fellow cabby, heart attack. He clucked his regrets, let us off, and drove away in a clash of gears.

Toby Ellis answered when Johnnie rang the night bell and gave us general directions to the street where Jasmine Karras lived.

The Maxwell Avenue address was a two-story boxy apartment building with a hipped roof, a large wrap-around porch, and typical clapboard siding; a porch swing hung inertly on link chains. Johnnie eased the coach up the gravel drive next to the building and parked behind a faded blue Chevy coupe. She killed the ignition, and we sat in the dark for a moment before I turned on the interior light and reached into the glove box for the letter. I smoothed the envelope between my hands and stepped out.

"Here we go again."

"I'll be here."

"Yeah, don't leave me. Please."

I clumped up a rise of worn wooden steps onto the porch and faced a span of four black metal mailboxes attached to the wall. Under a dim porch light I saw that J. Karras was in apartment four. I pressed the doorbell button beneath that box and stood back, hands at my side, envelope held between the fingers and thumb of my right hand. When the door opened, I put on a protective smile. She was tall. Her hair was shoulder length. Her face, even in the dim light, was slender with nice cheekbones and penetrating eyes. She was silhouetted with a hall light behind her and stood quite still.

"So," she said on the same low voice I'd heard over the phone, "here you are."

"Yes," I answered, on a smile, "here I am."

"Not much resemblance, actually."

"More of my mother, I guess."

"Good for you."

When I chose to not respond to that, she asked me in. As we climbed a short flight of stairs, a mixture of cooking odors emanated from the aggregate of apartments—overwhelmingly onion and garlic; she commented offhandedly about her neighbors' cooking. At the top of the stairs there were two doors on the landing. She entered the one on the right with the ease of knowing one's own space and left the door open for me to follow her in. I closed the door quietly and noted at once how neat and tidy the small apartment was; there was no cooking odor. The very next thing noted was the sound of a hacking cough; it belonged to the wreck of a man sitting in a weathered leather chair and holding a handkerchief up to his mouth.

Jasmine went to his side and placed a hand on his right shoulder. She patted him and said, "This is my friend Walter. He's not well."

"Obviously," the man said and cracked a dry-lipped smile. He waved the hand holding the handkerchief. "Walter Eldridge. And you are?"

"Michael. Sanborn."

He nodded then went off on another coughing jag and waved a hand by way of apology. We waited for him to regain some control. He looked to be maybe seventy but was probably younger. His arms protruding from a short-sleeved shirt were thin and scrawny, his skin was pale, papery dry, and his face drawn, nearly skeletal. We stared at one another; it was as uncomfortable to observe a person in his state as it had been seeing my father in his waning days.

He blew his nose. "It's a heart thing," he said finally. "Dang pump is getting ready to quit on me."

"Walter," Jasmine broke in, "you've had a good week."

The man tried to scoot up in his chair. Couldn't. "My cheer leader," he said and smiled up at her. She leaned down to lift his legs onto a leather ottoman.

"You take a nap while I talk with Michael. We'll go into the other room."

We walked through a curved archway into a very tiny space that had a table that might serve two. We sat on straight slat-backed wooden chairs. If they'd actually had the meal she had spoken of, there was no evidence of it. I positioned myself on the chair and held the envelope in one hand under the table.

"His heart is failing." She clasped her hands together on the table top. "Not sure how much longer he has."

When she fell silent, I spoke. "A friend, you said."

Her expression was now one of annoyance.

"I'm sorry. Just interested."

She hesitated. In the full light, I saw that her hair was a light brunette. Her eyes were brown, and her expression determined. I suspected that she was in her mid-fifties.

"Walter worked at Foley's," she said. "I work there in the salon. That's where I know him from. He was head custodian. Literally made the store run. When his health failed him, I took him in. I had to—we all adored the man. So here he is. And he's dying."

"That's terrible. Sorry."

She grimaced. "Well, that's the way it is. You said a letter."

I brought the envelope up and placed it on the table. "Yes."

"To me. From Randolph." When I nodded, she said, "Why would I want that? Do you know about me and your father?"

I offered her a weak smile. "Only what I read in the letter."

Her eyes bored into mine. "You read the letter?"

"I did. Read it, and you'll understand." I held it out. "Please."

She waited, looked at the envelope in my extended hand, and reluctantly took it from me. Her name and address were typed on the front. She studied it then said, "That's the store address. He knew then. That I was still in the same business." She looked away from me then held the envelope out. "Take it. I can't do this. I want nothing from him, certainly not some dead man's words."

"I can understand. Like I said, I did read the letter. I'm merely fulfilling a pledge I made to him to deliver the letters."

"Letters? There are others?"

"Yes. If you read what he's written, you'll know."

"I'll know. What if I don't want to know?"

I shrugged. "Up to you. Tear it up. Throw it away. Then again, there's nothing more he can do to you."

Finally, she lifted the flap, took the letter out, spread it open, and held it out, squinting. After a moment she gave me a little smile and said she needed her eyeglasses and went to get them. I waited patiently until she returned, propped plastic rimmed frames on her nose, and began to read. The time it took for a recipient to read my father's words had become a time when I held my breath and waited them out.

RANDOLPH E. SANBORN
FLORHAVEN ESTATES
JUPITER, FLORIDA

February 1952

Jasmine Karras
1900 28th St
Boulder, Colorado

Dear Jasmine,

It's been some time now. You've moved on, my wife has passed, and now I have died. My son, Michael, whom you've just met, is fulfilling a bargain he struck with me back when he came to see me in Florida where I had retired. He came to be with me as I endured the insufferable cancer that was eating away at my lungs. He agreed under the duress of my pleading to shepherd my remains back home to Portland. On the trip he was to deliver letters to a number of people who had been a significant presence in my life. And so here he is in Boulder to see you. Michael has brought me here so I can, posthumously, thank you and at the same time fall on my sword of bitter regret.

For God's sake, Jasmine, what a mess I made of your life. The first day I came into the Olds & King salon to have you cut my hair, I was captivated. I couldn't help it. The despicable part was my persistence until you submitted to my advances. The drinks, then the hotel rooms. I invaded your life and tried to make it mine and wouldn't let you go. Damn, the threats, the bullying. I was contemptible.

And worst of all, you had to escape to rid yourself of my obscene hold on your life. That has torn at me ever since. Being forced to leave the city you loved and abandon the many people who revered you for what you did better than anyone, what an awful price. Jasmine, I know I do not deserve your forgiveness, but at least realize that I left this world knowing the wrong I did to you and that it made me less of the man I wanted to be.

May you enjoy the rest of your life,

Randolph

After reading it, she placed the letter on the table and examined it as one would a bizarre photograph. After maybe a full minute, she laid an open palm on the page and with the opposite hand removed her glasses. She was quiet; in the other room we could hear Walter having another vicious round of coughing. She raised her head, all attention going to the sick man until he stopped.

"What does he mean," she said, "shepherd my remains back home?"
"Outside. There's a funeral coach."
Her eyes grew wide, and her mouth fell slightly open. "Truly?"
"That's the way he wanted it."
"And you agreed to this?"
We studied one another. I said, "He was dying."

She looked down at the letter again and nodded. "So was Walter. I understand that part." She raised her eyes to mine again. "I don't want him to die alone. Did you...love him—your father? Or care if he died alone?"

Those questions hit me in a strange way. My ears rang from the impact. I had not thought about my father dying alone. But he had been alone. Alone except for a small band of unrelated retirees. Besides, no, I hadn't cared.

I paused and considered my answer. "He was my father," I answered. "Did I love him?" I paused again. "I loved my mother, but Dad, we shared a long-held sense of indifference. We really just tolerated each other. I'm carrying out this crazy scheme of his because I am in control. He's dead and has no say—about anything. At least it started out that way."

"And?"

I looked at her hand as it rested atop the letter. Her fingers were long and slender, her nails finely trimmed, painted in pale pink. I felt a strange smile ease onto my face. "It was to be a tightly planned itinerary, seven pauses en route, pass off the envelopes, back home in two weeks. An outlandishly long trip, but that would be it. Only it hasn't been that simple."

"I imagine not. The loss of a parent is tough no matter what."

"No. That's not it. I hadn't imagined that I would be personally disturbed by the recipients' responses to the letters. I'd read them all, of course. My father had me read them so I knew what he was asking of me. But I didn't take much in, just read them and agreed to do what he asked. After that, when the call came telling me of his death, I would just get it over with." I straightened up against the chair back and folded my arms.

She tilted her head. "Disturbed?"

It was then that I truly noted her eyes, uniquely penetrating; but just then they'd softened, focused on me with what seemed to be empathy, even sadness. I had expected only anger or resentment and was moved by her soft appeal to my expression of doubt. How should I answer her one-word question?

I gave a little laugh and said, "Never mind, it's just been another long day. Thanks for letting us drop by this late." I leaned forward, elbows on the table. "Would you like to see the coach...his presence?"

She remained calm and considered my question. "Perhaps," she answered. "But not just yet. I'm not sure you've given me the answer to my question: Why have you been disturbed? By the responses to Randolph's letters."

Summation

"Really, it's nothing."

She was poised to respond when Walter erupted with another cascade of coughing. It went on until she rose and disappeared into the living room. I listened to the man's torturous coughs and lamented his dismal prognosis. When the coughs had subsided, I could hear Jasmine's calming voice and his guttural response. Shortly, she returned and sat across from me again. Her face was etched with the worry she felt for her friend. She apologized.

"No need for apologies. I should leave now. You can see the coach if you wish, but really I should go."

She inhaled, smiled a bit, and raised a hand. "Walter is okay for the time being. And I'm still curious about your being disturbed, as you put it."

We shared a long moment of silence while we exchanged eye contact. I was drawn to the intent of her question. Instead, I asked the other question, the one I had to ask, "Were you fond of my father?"

Her brows raised a bit; then she lowered her gaze and knitted her fingers on the tabletop. I saw her lips tighten. She didn't look up until I took in a deep breath. When she did, her eyes brimmed, and her mouth was crimped in a sad smile.

"I mean the letter alludes to some level of intimacy." I said. "Isn't that so?"

She brought a hand to her mouth and pressed fingertips into her eyes as tears formed.

"Watcha doin' to her?" Walter's voice barked behind me. He had staggered from his chair to the dining room archway and was leaning there, gripping a bentwood cane. "Leave her be!" he gasped.

"Walter." Jasmine sat up. "It's okay. Go back to your chair."

"I know what this's about," the man said, his voice reduced to nothing more than a whisper. "Yeah, she told me about it. About yer old man." He tried to point the cane at me but faltered.

Jasmine rose, went to his side, and took him by an elbow. She held on and guided him back into the other room. I could hear Walter's mutterings and her pacifying purr. She returned, stood by her chair and studied me, then dropped down onto the seat.

"He's agitated," she said.

"Did he really do that to you, my dad? What he insinuates in the letter?" She just looked at me. I raised my voice a bit. "Well, did he? Come on now."

She flinched then came back at me. "Yes! Yes, yes, yes—he did that to me."

Damn! I mean, I'd read the letter—more than once—thought it was disgraceful, but I hadn't gone beyond that. My father actually forcing himself onto this woman, seducing her, insistent, he admitted. With my mother in the background, he was violating this woman against her will. And he died knowing I would meet her, that I would see the person he took advantage of and violated. Violated until she had to run from him.

Chapter Twenty,

I don't know how much time elapsed while I sat slumped over, elbows on the table, my mind creating an imagined version of my father's prurient behavior. It seemed unfeasible that the man I knew to be without charm, lacking in personal appeal, dull as a fence post, could have been the perpetrator of such unwanted pursuit.

"Are you okay?" she said at last.

I sat up. She was watching me, her eyes still moist, her face a tapestry of concern. I pushed out a breath. "Hell no. I'm not okay. How can I be, knowing what I now know? You asked why I was disturbed. I am disturbed because every stop I've made with my goddamned father's dead body has shown me the dark side of a life I only knew in the abstract. A life I assumed to be as irrelevant as the dandelions growing in our yard."

Jasmine's smile was not warm this time; she was calm, but something cold had claimed her now. "He has manipulated you too, hasn't he? His own son. But I can't feel sorry for you, not in the least. You're spending a mere two weeks on this journey. I was manipulated too, but for much longer. I was debased and subjected to his obsessive need to dominate me—that was your father."

"Why did you allow it? Why didn't you force him out of your life? Shove him away. Were you intrigued or even addicted to being mistreated?"

She looked at me as one would a fool. "You don't understand, do you? It was enticing at first to be sought after. Yes, intriguing even. Your father was no Tyrone Power, but to be found attractive, maybe even alluring to an intelligent man...it was seductive. I allowed things to happen until I was unable to resist. It did become an addiction."

I reached up to my cheek and fingered the stubble from another day's growth. Both anger and regret were written on her face. What could I say to that? Nothing.

"Yes," she said finally, "I was complicit and allowed it all to happen. I found his advances captivating in the beginning. I was as pathetic as he was predatory. So I ran from him to escape those dark times and tried to reclaim my life."

"Did you? Reclaim your life."

"No. Never. I searched for a way out. I haunted the library everyday, reading the want ads in every out-of-town newspaper. I considered several positions, none equal to what I had at Olds & King, so never applied. Then I saw a help wanted ad in the Boulder Daily Camera newspaper seeking a veteran hair stylist for the new Foley's Department Store beauty salon. They listened to my credentials and hired me over the phone. I left Portland literally in the dead of night and never looked back. I've been here for seven years."

"Not the same then?"

She shook her head. "The people are good, and the company, but in Portland I had my own clientele. I had a reputation. I was somebody. Here I'm a senior stylist and have a reasonable following of customers, but I'm not Jasmine of Olds & King. I'm not her anymore."

"You miss it then?"

Her smile was charitable. "Of course. I think about those fine times in Portland most everyday. Pitiable, don't you think?"

"Do you think he meant it, this apology of his?"

She looked down the letter again. "Not for a minute. Or he would have done it back then, when he knew I was suffering. Your father had an empty soul. I'm ashamed that I feel some degree of pleasure knowing that he lived his last moments alone and died as a man in exile. It was evil what he did to me, and vile."

I had nothing say to that, except, "I get it."

"Do you?"

"As much as I can." I reached my arms up and stretched them above my head. "Anyway, I know that something has been taken away from me in all of this."

"What?"

"My aloof sense that I'm certain where I'm headed in my life. That is gone now. I had it all figured out, but then I didn't even think that I had to have it figured it out. After all, I am who I am—what more needs to be tended to?"

"Do you do this at each stop...when you deliver a letter? Have this kind of self-revelation?"

"No," I said. "It's been gradual. A rolling thing. Like this. Here, with you, another layer has been skinned off. Any more insights, and in the end I will be a mere shadow of who I thought myself to be. Then what?"

"Maybe, you and I, maybe we'll get past this onto something else."

"Like what?"

She smiled and held up her hands. "No idea. But when I got up this morning, I never imagined seeing you today. Nor going back over that despicable part of my life. And yet, here we are, peeling off the scabs and looking ahead—maybe? Me, I can stay right where I am, with that part of my life officially over, literally dead, and forget it."

"And me?"

"All roses. You get to start over, if you want."

"Ha." I thought of Nadine and my career and wondered. "Not easy to change gears at my age."

She smiled. "Not so. You have more years than I do." She pushed her chair back and stood. "Come on, let's go out so I can visit Randolph one last time."

I smelled tobacco smoke as we emerged onto the porch of the apartment house. There sat Johnnie on the porch swing with a cigarette between her lips; an old man with brown leathery skin and bushy gray hair sat next to her brandishing a curved stem pipe and chattering away.

"...and we buried him two days later in a snow storm."

Johnnie saw me, drew on her smoke, exhaled, and stood up. The old guy swiveled his head, stuck this pipe stem in his mouth, and stood as well. The swing shivered and quickly stalled.

"All done?" Johnnie asked. She held the cigarette down and away from her body.

"Just about," I said. "This is Jasmine Karras. Jasmine, Johnnie Gates, my matchless road engineer and partner."

They nodded to each other. Jasmine saw the coach, looked at me, shook her head in disbelief, and took a couple of steps toward the porch railing where she stood unmoving. Even though I knew her story, I wondered what was going through her mind just then.

"Ain't that something," the man said. He let a whiff of tobacco smoke escape as he spoke. "Hazel, my wife, she sends me outside to smoke, so when I came out here and saw that there hearse I dang near collapsed. Figured someone in the place here had, you know…died."

Jasmine turned back. "Ivan," she said, "would you please leave us for now. We need some privacy. Okay?"

He nodded his head submissively, raised his pipe in the air, and disappeared back into the building. Jasmine stepped forward and stared down. Beneath the porch light's glow sat the coach, dignified and aloof. She stood that way for a very long moment before turning around and tipping her head to me. I waited for her approach and followed her down the stairs to the coach. Johnnie stood behind me awaiting some sort of decision. Jasmine stepped forward and placed an open palm on the cool metal of the vehicle.

"All right," she said.

I signaled Johnnie. She flipped her cigarette away and moved past me to open the side door of the coach and swung it back as far as it would go. The interior light reflected once more on the metal box. Jasmine stood transfixed until, surprisingly, she approached the open doorway, hesitated, then leaned forward and rested the fingers of her right hand on the casket.

"Jasmine," I interrupted, "do you want to see him?"

That idea seemed to startle her. She stood up, still looking in. "No. I couldn't. Please, no."

After Johnnie shut the door, we all stood calmly in the gravel driveway, the coolness of the hour enveloping us. Did she have more to say? No, nor did I. I reached out to shake her hand; instead she came to me and gave me a firm hug. I held onto her as well until we let go and looked at each other with shared empathy. She squeezed my arm and walked away, up the stairs and into the building. She didn't look back.

Letter number four had been delivered.

We sat in the coach for several minutes, Johnnie letting me adjust to the moment.

"Different then," she said after a minute or so.

I thought on that and responded to the obvious. "Yes."

"Bad. Better?"

I looked out through the driver's side window, saw the dim glow of the porch light. "Sad, but a better outcome…for both of us."

Johnnie inserted the key into the ignition, held on before turning it, and said, "I wondered. Took longer than the others. What was different?"

I knuckled my eyes. "Different? It wasn't all one-sided this time."

"Meaning?"

"I lost some skin too. I've felt that way at each stop, but this time it was more revelatory."

"Big word. Like you learning more or something?"

"Yeah, that's it…about myself."

"How much more of this you gonna take?"

I considered the next letter and felt a chill. "Not sure. But a guy named Clyde is next in our line of fire." In Clovis, New Mexico, I would deliver an ominous message.

She cranked the Meteor engine to life, and we returned to Maples Mortuary, where Toby Ellis was awaiting our return. Johnnie parked the coach for the night; then Toby drove us back to the motel. He had a toothy smile which he shared mostly with Johnnie. We accepted his animated invitation to meet us for breakfast then take us back to the coach.

Johnnie watched Toby Ellis drive away and commented that she liked Maples Mortuary. "That place, the building and the trees, felt like home. You know."

Just then, four people, two couples, walked by on the sidewalk, enjoying themselves, their voices an animated chorus.

"Happy people," I said, "with nary a clue of what we're up to."

"But then, what do we know of them? The troubles they may have: can't pay their bills, marriage problems, alcoholic father—name it. Let alone the dark sides of their own lives."

"You could be right, I guess."

She looked after the group. "I am right. I've seen it. When it comes time for a family to bury one of its own, the arguments, the accusations, the crying over wrongs shared by the deceased's kin. I've witnessed some damned unpleasant stuff."

Her face had taken on the look of a frozen pork chop. "Just part of the business, I guess."

"My dad, he's like a priest. The shameful things he knows but never talks about. And you wouldn't believe the women who come on to my widower father, even before their husband's in the ground."

I couldn't imagine a woman whose husband had just died approaching another man with salacious intent, especially the undertaker. I knew without question that my mother had never cheated on my father, even though the two men in her life had two-timed the women committed to us. Damn, I had to call Nadine. After Johnnie had gone to her room, I dialed.

Nadine answered after several rings and accepted my collect call. Since it was late, she asked if everything was okay.

"Things are fine," I said. "Just wanted to check in and hear your voice. Sorry if I woke you."

She cleared her throat and said, "That's okay. Where are you?"

"Still in Boulder, but we leave in the morning and head to Clovis, New Mexico. Letter number five coming up. Won't be long now, back in Portland soon."

She didn't respond for a moment before saying, "Sam Painmayer called today. He was a bit prickly wondering when you'd be back at your desk. Seems whatever timber deal you've been working on is on the cusp. Maybe you'd best give him a call and reassure him."

"I will. We have the deal tied down. Earnest money's been paid. Not to worry. How you doing?"

"I'm all right, doing regular things regularly. You know how it goes."

I inhaled. "No, I really don't know."

She hesitated, then said, "Why are you calling really, Michael?"

I held the receiver to my right ear, as I sat on the edge of the bed in another carbon copy motel room, and absorbed her silent waiting. "We made our fourth delivery today. To a woman named Jasmine Karras."

"Not the Jasmine. Of the Olds & King Salon?"

"That's the one."

"My heavens. What does she have to do with all of this? She's been gone for years. I used to go to her myself."

Reluctantly, I told her the story. She listened without comment except for an occasional hum in response to a particular revelation. I left out the words evil and vile, though they fit.

"Despicable. So that's why you called?" she said after I'd finished.

"Yes."

"But for what reason?"

I fingered the phone cord. "Reason?" So I told her, like I'd told Jasmine Karras, that a piece of me had been peeled back with every letter delivered. "Nadine, I'm so wanting this thing to be over and done. To be back home with you. To be better at living my life. Better for you."

"My, my. That could've come right out of How to Win Friends and Influence People."

I stood. "Come on, Nadine, I'm serious."

"Maybe you are. Maybe so. But whatever your intent, it's overdue. And now you expect me to fall back in love with you, is that it? To be bewitched by your sudden transformation? Fall on my knees?"

I couldn't speak. I set the receiver down and wondered, just wondered.

Chapter Twenty One.

There, in that stuffy motel room, I continued to wonder why—but of course I knew. My father had orchestrated me being dragged through the muck of his life. And once his indecency had been exposed, my own offenses had shoved their way in, and my need to atone along with it. But to what end? Nadine wouldn't throw me a ticker tape parade to celebrate my supposed reconditioned life. Any reclamation would take more than declaring to her that I was now ready to be a better man.

I spent the night atop a rock-hard mattress trying to rid my head of troubling images. I failed and got up when it was still dark outside. Took a quick shower, rubbed my skin dry and red on a scratchy towel, shaved and dressed in chinos and a long-sleeved plaid shirt. I needed a laundry, but at that moment my mind had sprinted forward to a town in New Mexico and letter number five.

I had taken the envelope from the glove box the night before and now read those five paragraphs again. The message hadn't changed. It still gave me chills. Around six thirty I slipped out of my room and rapped a knuckle on Johnnie's door. I felt the nip in the air and noted that the rosy edges of sunrise promised a nice day. A man and woman with two fussing children emerged from a room down the way and hustled suitcases out to an idling station wagon. The scene was still in full swing when Johnnie popped her door open. She was dressed and ready to go; her yellow hair was tied back. I held the envelope up, and she stepped back to let me into the room.

"Read this," I said. "I want your opinion before we get underway."

She took the envelope from me, curiosity in her eyes, and sat in the room's only chair. "Okay," she said after reading the letter to Clyde Stone. "Whata ya want to know?"

"Your reaction?"

She refolded the letter and handed it back to me. "Spooky. You think it's true?"

"Could be. Probably is. The thing is, what to do with it."

She stretched her legs out and folded her arms. "Meaning what?"

"Meaning do I deliver it or not? Ever since I first read it, I've been uneasy about knocking on that guy's door. The most alarming letter of them all—I think."

"Even more than that Ripley scumbag?"

I nodded. "Yeah. More."

"Agreed." She bit her lower lip. "Ripley, he sent those thugs after us. You thinking we'll need a bigger bat?"

"Funny. Do we deliver it or not? I don't want you to be in any danger—either of us for that matter."

She stood, pulled at the cuffs of her white shirt. "Why not just mail it? Send it from here then step on the gas for Reno. Your dad's not gonna know."

"Let's think on it. We'll both decide."

Toby Ellis, wearing the broad grin of a vacuum cleaner salesman, was waiting when we came out. He drove us to a place called Errol's where we enjoyed his suggested sheepherder's breakfast; it would be our last real meal for the day. While we ate, Toby questioned us about the trip and what was next, but mostly he wanted to know about Johnnie and her life back in Portland. She was hesitant about how to respond to such attention, an abnormal experience in her life—being interesting.

We ended breakfast as soon as possible, retrieved the coach, gassed up, and began again. For the first few miles we debated over the letter yet to be delivered. Our decision? The letter would be personally handed over in Clovis as scheduled; we'd face any risks that might arise then. A drive straight through would take an entire day of hard driving. Johnnie held the accelerator down; the engine cooperated.

After eight days on the road, I could still recall my wife's face—but I had to think on it. In the interim, new faces, the ones squaring with each letter, had intervened and taken up prevailing space. Each day had become a ritual of miles and road-weary bodies. We were a door-to-door delivery service that never left its consignment. And every time, I looked into a set of eyes I'd never seen before. Thus, visions of home and other clear memories were temporarily shoved aside.

It was well past ten o'clock when Johnnie idled by the Clovis city limits; she decided to bypass the local mortuary due to the hour and apologize to them later. She roused the night clerk at La Contenta Courts & Lodge and got the keys to our reserved rooms. The coach fit snugly in one of the garages built into the long gangly structure with one double garage between every two rooms. Johnnie backed the vehicle in so that only its nose could be seen, locked it up, and came into my room with the remnants of road food we'd acquired en route. We sat at small table, finished what was left of two dry turkey sandwiches, washed them down from a half-bottle of leftover V8 juice, and shared Hydrox cookies. Sumptuous.

Johnnie dusted cookie crumbs off her hands, crumpled up the paper wrappings, and tossed it all in a wastebasket. "Now what?" she said.

I looked at my wristwatch. "Get some sleep. I'll make contact in the morning. Try to set up a time to meet with our Mr. Stone."

"You think he will? Meet with you?"

I smiled and pulled on an earlobe. "Depends on how I handle it, I guess. Though I have a feeling that this time will be different."

She grinned. "You know, I've been thinking. You and me, we woulda never had this crazy journey together if your old man had just had his body shipped home. Or if my dad was the driver instead of me, and even better, what if we'd been born to other people or in another country?"

I couldn't help but laugh.

"Don't you ever think of things like that? The whys of life?"

"Oh sure, but never much farther than a curious moment. Rudimentary thoughts is all."

"Like?"

"Oh, I don't know, like why I wasn't chosen for something over someone else. I always wondered why Harvey Schultz made the junior varsity basketball team and I didn't. Ridiculous, but painful at the time."

"Uh-huh." She studied me. "Okay, being a teenager was a bitch. But I'm thinking like now when we're older, and have lived beyond baby steps and pimples. Once in awhile I get up in the morning, facing another day of the same thing, and wonder."

"What?"

"Like I said, why I am who I am and what else I could have been."

"And this trip, it causes you to have such thoughts?"

She stood, stretched her arms above her head, and sat back down. "Been thinking as the miles rolled by, sure. About how weird it is…what we're doing. And not just you and me but all these people your dad has sicced us on. Just think on it, Michael, how their lives woulda been a whole lot different if they'd never met him."

"Mostly for the better, I'm thinking. I'm sorry you've ended up in the middle of all this."

She startled me when she clapped her hands together. "Not me. Wouldn't have missed this even if I'd known ahead of time. Most fascinating experience I've ever had."

We talked about it, who we were and why, until the premise had more or less run its course, then laughed it off as an odd but fascinating discourse and turned in.

The sun was up by the time I'd risen, showered, dressed, and stepped out of my room. Johnnie was already outside, leaning against the hood of the coach still parked in the garage, engaged in a conversation with a tall lanky character with thick black hair, long neck, and hunched-over shoulders. He was gesticulating and pointing his right arm and a big knuckled finger in the direction of the highway.

When I approached, he smiled. "Morning, sir. I was just telling the lady here I don't think we've ever had a hearse stay overnight before. I understand that you're on the way to Orey-gone." He tilted his head toward the coach. "Taking someone home?"

"My father."

He looked toward the coach then back to me and bobbed his head. "All righty then, good luck to ya. Hope you enjoy your stay. Not like there's a lot to do here, except you know I hear'd about that guy Add-a-lee's, he's coming here. Down to the train station. You know, the one running to be president, Stevenson his name is I think. Personally, I like Ike, but I'm still planning on going down there just to see the guy. Add-a-lee, what a name."

We thanked him, asked where we could get breakfast, and returned to our rooms to pack up. I placed a call to my boss Sam Painmayer and re-assured him again that the timber deal in play was solid and would hold until I returned.

Then it was time to make contact with Clyde Stone. I found a number for Farm Bureau Insurance in the yellow pages. Their ad featured a smiling man wearing a cowboy hat: William "Billy" Smith, senior agent and manager.

Billy actually answered the phone. "This is Billy. What can I do for you?"

I hesitated. He said hello like nobody was on the line. "I'm calling for Clyde Stone," I said.

"Clyde? Lemme see. Clyde here?" he called out, his mouth away from the receiver. "What? Oh yeah." He spoke directly into the receiver again. "Yeah, I forgot. He isn't in the office on Thursdays. Anything I can do for you or leave a message?"

I took in a shallow breath. "Uh, no. I'm a...friend passing through town and was hoping to see him. You know how I can contact him?"

"Yeah, well maybe. Who'd you say you were again?"

"A friend just traveling through. From Portland where he used to live. In Oregon?"

"Sure. Yeah, he mentions that part of the country every now and then. Let's see, I can give you his phone number and address. He lives outside of town out to Farwell."

"Farwell?"

"Yeah, Farwell, Texas, just across the border. Not far, about ten miles or so. Just head west outa town. Doesn't take any time at all."

I wrote down the numbers and thanked the man; he knew not what he was putting on his colleague. I placed my bag back in the coach and rested a flattened hand on the casket, an unmoving presence that was causing so much turbulence in an unsuspecting collection of lives. Johnnie took the time to wipe a film of dust off the Meteor with the soft cloth she kept just for that purpose, then drove us off to the local diner recommended by the motel manager. Another day, another greasy spoon. We sat at the counter of the Hi-Way Cafe & Depot, ordered the usual breakfast fare amid customers who were both locals grabbing a bite and passengers waiting for the next bus.

By the time we'd finished off our food, a Greyhound Scenicruiser had arrived, and a large-bodied driver was loading baggage into the belly of the vehicle. The Meteor was parked a block up the street from the bus. Not unpredictably, a couple of adolescent boys were giggling and trying to see in through the closed curtains. When we walked up, a woman's voice rose, scolding the boys to Get on away from there now. Most everyone else just stared as we got into the vehicle most knew was for carrying dead bodies. No one spoke or moved, nor did we smile or nod.

Johnnie gripped the steering wheel and chuckled. "Crazy kids."

"Boys being boys," I said.

"Heard that one over a hundred times. Such baloney."

"What about your brother? Danny, right?"

She ran her hands through her hair before answering. "Yeah. Danny, he's different. He's grown now, at least physically. But he'll always be a child." She looked out at the side mirror. "Hell, I'd love it if he would do stupid boy stuff like those kids. He's trapped in the body of a man and the mind of a seven-year-old."

"Sorry."

"Yeah, well, the sorry part is long past. Now it's just Dad and me making sure he's safe, fed, and loved." She looked over and gave me a simple smile. "I never asked—you have brothers or sisters?"

It was like being handed a View-Master with a photo disk of the past, except that the scene I wanted wasn't there; the photo I wanted to see had never been developed. "I did," was my response. "A brother. At least that is what I was told when I was old enough to comprehend the story."

"What's that mean?"

"Six or seven years before I was born, my mother delivered a stillborn baby boy. They had picked the name of David if the baby turned out to be a boy. Angela, I think, if a girl. For the rest of my mother's life, David was ever-present. Whether on the anniversary of his delivery, or in thoughts of who he might have become when she looked at me. In some ways, she had more passion for his nonexistence than for my actual presence. That was the way it felt, true or not."

Johnnie, her hands resting on the steering wheel, let my screed quietly dissipate, then said, "Jeez, I've been living just like that but from the other side of the nickel. Your nonexistent David, that's Danny in my life. My dad loves me, I know that, but his passion is for Danny. I'm just his parental partner. We have been raising and taking care of Danny together all these years, but I've lived in a support role. Not many hugs for me."

Right then the Greyhound Scenicruiser surged past us, a blue cloud of diesel fumes spewing in its wake. We watched it pass and let the familial trauma drift.

Chapter Twenty Two,

We drove directly west out of Clovis to Farwell over the border. I decided against calling Clyde Stone beforehand. After passing through the blip of the town of Texico on the New Mexico side, one mile later we were across the border into Texas. The highway turned into Avenue A when we entered Farwell, which then intersected with a run of numerical streets. It didn't take long to find fourth street. Johnnie hung a right and drove along a street of modest to dilapidated dwellings, brown grass, and few trees.

"So the address is what again?" Johnnie said.

"Seven ten."

"Not far. Ready?"

I took in a breath. "Let's do it."

We continued slowly down fourth street. After two blocks, the housing improved. We passed several newer single-story ranch style structures. But when we finally came up on seven ten, we discovered a large two-story house obviously built in the last century. A big yard hosted at least six mature live oak trees. There was a long dirt and gravel drive leading back behind the house. A relatively new green Chevrolet pickup was parked down the lane, where I saw a man wearing a broad-brimmed straw hat wrestling a rototiller through a swath of a garden patch. It had to be Clyde Stone.

Johnnie idled the coach down the lane and stopped a good measure from the pickup. We sat there watching the man finish the row he was on, then stop, release the clutch, and swing the machine around, ready to make another pass. It was then that he saw the Meteor. For a moment he stood stark still before leaning over to turn off the pulsating engine and remove his leather gloves. He kept his eyes on us and walked over the pulverized soil, slapping his gloves against a leg. Johnnie and I stepped out of the coach and waited by the nose of the vehicle.

He was square-shouldered, not much of a gut, wore a tan canvas shirt and Levis over high-top boots with leather laces. Had a face that made me think of the movie actor Sterling Hayden: square tapered jaw, deep-set dark brown eyes, thick eyebrows, and a long, determined nose. As he drew near, I felt a flutter in my stomach and wondered again what the hell I was doing there. I stood as straight and confidently as I could and gripped the letter between the fingers and thumb of my right hand.

After passing the pickup, he paused and examined the coach. "This can't be good news," he said in a husky voice tinged with sarcasm. "Am I dead and don't know it?"

"Nothing like that," I said. "Are you Clyde Stone?"

He nodded and removed his straw hat, revealing a crown of thinning brown hair. "That I am. You're not selling burial plots, are you?"

I smiled and wondered if his humor would be sustained after he read the letter. Glancing at Johnnie, I said, "This is Jonalynn Gates, and I'm Michael Sanborn."

"Okay. What's this all about?"

"It will take some explaining," I answered.

He looked directly into my eyes and wiped a hand across the perspiration on his forehead. "All right. How about we go sit in the shade then. Over there, where those chairs are under the trees."

As we walked, I commented on his garden plot. He looked back over his shoulder and alleged that gardening was both a passion and a pain. After the three of us had settled into weathered Adirondack chairs, Stone cleared his throat expectantly and looked between us—waiting for the shoe to drop.

"As I said, Mr. Stone, my name is Michael Sanborn." I rearranged my rear end in the chair and added, "I'm the son of Randolph Sanborn."

At first, Stone's eyes flashed open wide; then he closed them and lowered his chin. When he looked back up at me, his glib sense of humor had been replaced with a sardonic smile. "Been a long time since I've heard that name." He looked first at me then at Johnnie. "He's a bastard, you know."

I hesitated, my mouth dry. Finally, after long moments where nothing more was said, I spoke. "Yes, he's in there. I'm taking him home...to Portland."

Stone leaned forward on his knees and looked long and deliberately at the Meteor. "And on your way, you just happened to pass through Farwell, Texas, the leading boondocks tourist venue if there ever was one. How'd you find me anyway?"

"Billy Smith. In Clovis."

"The agency," he responded. "But why Clovis in the first place?"

"I have something for you," I said. "A letter. It will give you full details of why we're here."

"A letter." He leaned back in the chair. "Let me guess. It's from him, your old man."

"That's right."

"Unbelievable." He slapped the leather gloves on the arm of the chair. "Why in hell would he write me a letter after all this time?"

"Like I say, it's all there in the letter...his message to you." I held up the envelope as I'd done every other time. And like those before him, Stone eyed what I was holding with skepticism etched on his face.

No one spoke; it was an awkward silence. I lowered the envelope into my lap and waited. "It's to you, personally," I said after his nonresponse.

"I get that, damn it. But why should I even bother? I've got work to do." He gestured out to where the rototiller sat. After a long pause he said, "You knew your father...you knew what he was like?"

I shrugged. "Mostly. Maybe not from your perspective."

"Why would I want to accept anything he'd written to me?"

The twinge in my chest caused me to sit up more and take in a breath. Of course I knew my father, and now I knew even more about his life and his failings. But I'd also read the letter he'd written to Clyde Stone. I didn't answer his question, just raised the letter again.

"Up to you," I said.

At that point Johnnie pushed herself up out of the chair and wandered over to the coach. Once there she opened the driver's door and sat sideways on the seat, leaving the door open and her feet dangling out. She looked over to where Stone and I sat; we were looking back, her movement being a mild distraction from the tenseness of the moment.

Stone turned his eyes from Johnnie back to me. He lowered his voice so only I could hear. "What are you up to? It's been a decade since I cleared out of Portland, and today, out of the blue, you and that woman drive up in a bloody hearse. I'm holding down a job in to-hell-and-gone Clovis, New Mexico, a thousand and a half miles from Portland, living on a piece of land in nowhere Texas and...why are you here?" He leaned forward. "Why?"

I was feeling apprehensive. Stone was physically fit for a man I assumed was in his fifties, with the build of a person who could likely handle himself, as well as manhandle a big rototiller. In an attempt to appear calm, I looked back into the man's eyes and tried to show no emotion. He squinted and waited for my response.

"It's in the letter." I held it up again.

"Give it to me," he said, reaching out.

He took it, saw his name typed on the outside of the envelope and my hand scribbling of his Farwell address, then opened the flap. He pulled the letter out, looked at me first, and unfolded it. Here's what he read:

RANDOLPH E. SANBORN
FLORHAVEN ESTATES
JUPITER, FLORIDA

```
                                            February 1952

Clyde Stone
Clovis Farm Bureau Insurance
330 Main Street
Clovis, New Mexico

Clyde,

You may not remember much about me, but you know
who I am, or was. You see, I died recently, lung
cancer. Foul way to go. From my son Michael, who
has parked me somewhere nearby, you've been in-
formed of what he is up to, transporting my body
back to our old stomping grounds. The thing is, I
asked him to make several stops along the way, and
here we are in Clovis, to see you.
```

I knew you were in Clovis because way back when, after you left Portland, I received a call from the Clovis Farm Bureau Insurance Agency there wanting a reference. I gave them an adequate rundown of your experience, and maybe that helped you get the job. Anyway you're still there, at least you were when I called the agency before my demise.

So, why make this effort to visit you after all this time, especially as a cadaver? After all, we were never chummy at Natron Insurance. In underwriting, you had your desk, I had my office, and we rarely had contact. But then, you know very well why I've shown up, don't you? Give you chills maybe? It should, you evil bastard.

Nancy Beeman was a lovely woman, adored by her co-workers, loved to flirt with the men and they with her. As a divorced woman she was free to do that. But she never took to you, did she? And she fought back, didn't she, on that August night in 1943, when you strangled her. Oh, I know, the police never had any leads or suspects, and the case turned cold. You were in the clear, but still you left town.

I made an effort to interact with the staff about the loss of Nancy. My rather strained attempts were accepted warmly enough, until I approached you. When I lamented Nancy's murder, you wouldn't look at me. The first time you just grabbed your coat and left for the day. My suspicions were born at that moment. So, I made it a habit to drop by to chat and always mention Nancy. You never responded. But your demeanor turned more sullen. Those deep-set dark eyes of yours radiated fury. So, I knew Clyde. I knew you were the one who did it. Damn you! There's nothing to be done now, but I couldn't let you live out your life thinking no one suspected your heinous act.

May you suffer in Hades,
Randolph

I watched as Clyde Stone read, saw his eyebrows arch up partway down the page—must have been with the mention of the woman's name. He paused and looked to the side before continuing to read. I waited for him to get to the sentence where my farther blatantly accused him of murder. Curiosity coupled with foreboding raced through my mind. When he finished reading, he held the page out in one hand and studied it. Both of my hands were gripping the wide arms of the Adirondack chair as I poised for fight or flight. Stone did the predictable and scanned the letter once more, his brow furrowed. When finished, he slumped back in his chair then leaned forward and stood abruptly.

"My god!" he roared and stepped toward me. I drew back in my chair and held my breath. He waved the letter in my face. "This…this is outrageous! A scurrilous accusation!"

I sat glued to my chair and stared up into the man's glowering face. He stood still, breathing hard, and looked again at the letter. After turning in a circle, he focused his attention back on me. His face had flattened into a cold mask.

"Oh, I get it," he said after standing like a pillar. "You want something."

I took in a breath and swallowed my apprehension. "What? No, I don't want anything from you."

"Money? You want money, is that it? For this trash?" He waved the paper at me like a thesis with a failing grade. "Extortion, is it?"

I was shaking my head. "No!" I complained.

"You want something. Otherwise why would you be here?" He came closer and leaned down close to my face. His jaw muscles flexed as he bit down in rage.

When I shook my head, he reached down, grabbed the chair arms, lifted the Adirondack up and pushed it over backwards with me in it. I ended up on my back, seated in the chair as if it was upright. Adrenaline kicked in. I scrambled away, rolled over, and pushed up onto my feet. By that time, Johnnie had raced over from the coach, carrying the Louisville Slugger. The three of us stood in a cluster; I was panting from the shock,

Johnnie stood poised with the bat, but Stone suddenly dropped his arms and seemed to relent. I waved Johnnie off. She nodded at me and motioned with her head in the direction of the house.

I turned my body, keeping Stone in my peripheral vision, and saw a person walking toward us, apparently coming from the house. It was a woman. She seemed quite small, walking assuredly across the yard until she drew near; then she slowed and looked at Stone. She was decidedly younger than he. Her expression was one of curiosity. Stone raised a hand for her to stop. She did, stood straight, and waited.

Stone looked at me then dragged his right hand across his chin. His eyes locked onto mine, and he stepped forward to my left side. "You know," he whispered into my ear, "I left that job in Portland and a nice house in the Laurelhurst neighborhood, because of your old man's torment, and ended up way out here in nowhere land. I had to literally start over. It was like coming out of a long tunnel into a totally different country. I didn't know anybody. I didn't know the local lore or terminology. Came to work, went home, ate alone, slept and went to work again." He glanced toward the woman. "I still have that reasonable job, but now I have someone sharing my life."

I looked over at the petite woman, who still stood quietly watching the scene. "Seems nice," I said in a feeble attempt to diffuse the moment.

"That's Lucille, my wife. She's from here." He gave her a little wave but still held up a hand to keep her where she was. "We've been married for three years. So you see, it took me a good stretch of living in this place to find the one person who wanted me."

He stuck a forefinger into my chest and held it there. It didn't feel good, but I stood stark still like it was inconsequential. "Good for you," I said.

Stone pushed his finger even harder. I finally shoved his hand down and stepped back. But he moved toward me and spoke in my ear again. "No, not good because now, while I have the semblance of a life, here you show up carting your father's rotting body into my world. You give me a letter from his dead hand accusing me of committing an abomination."

I swallowed some saliva and took a risk. "It's not true then, what he wrote?"

The squint he gave me forced his eyelids into the thinnest of slits. "It makes no difference. You have no way of proving his contemptible allegation, and I have no way of refuting it." He took in a breath and said,

"But let me tell you this, Mr. Sanborn, offspring of that vile piece of flotsam: if you tell my wife of this scurrilous accusation…in any way, I will hurt you." His finger found my chest again.

I stepped back and slapped his hand away. Johnnie came forward a step or two. I patted the air so she knew to stay back. "Listen, Stone," I said, "I don't know if you did strangle that woman or not. Frankly, yours was the one letter of all in my possession that I most didn't want to deliver. I have no control over your conscience, nor do I want to accuse you of something I cannot prove. I'm only here to fulfill my father's wishes. It was obviously his intent to let you know what he believed to be true and, if so, for you to suffer his wrath in absentia. That's all I have to say on the matter. We will be leaving now. Give your wife our apologies for not having the time to meet her personally."

I nodded at Johnnie, and we walked to the coach. She put the bat beneath the seat. Clyde Stone watched us walk away, picked up the letter from the ground where it had fallen, and shoved it into his shirt pocket. He didn't make a move to follow me or call out. His wife slowly made her way to his side and put her arm through his. I could see her mouth move as she was evidently asking him what had just happened. His shrug indicated he was probably giving her a sanitized version of why a hearse was on their property and who those people were. I would have loved to have heard his explanation.

I stood next to the coach and looked across the hood at Stone and his wife, both of them staring back at us. After a minute or so, I opened the door and slid onto the seat, looked out to where Stone's rototiller sat waiting to gnaw into the raw Texas dirt again, and let go with a big sigh. Johnnie slowly backed the coach down the drive.

Chapter Twenty Three.

Johnnie drove us back into Clovis to do the usual: eat, gas up, and check the coach's vitals before moving on to Reno. First we wolfed down burgers, fries, and Cokes at Blake's Lotaburger, then filled a sack with food for the road at a nearby grocery. We were at a Phillips 66 station getting the tank filled when a pickup pulled in behind the coach; its engine clattered to a stop. The driver was Clyde Stone in his green Chevy. The attendant washing our windshield while the tank filled waved Stone forward to the next pump. He ignored the directive and sat unmoving, one hand on the steering wheel. Johnnie and I had been standing beside the coach chatting about the road ahead when Stone drove up.

"Maybe I should get the bat," Johnnie said.

I shook my head slightly. "No, let's see what he wants first. Could be he's just here to buy gas."

She chuckled. "Oh sure. And those thugs Ripley what's-his-name sent after us just wanted to be our pen pals."

While the service station attendant topped off the gas tank, checked the oil and tire pressure, Stone sat in his truck. When we were ready to go, I sauntered back and looked in as he sat immobile with his left arm resting on the edge of the open window.

"Mr. Stone," I said, "you here to fill your tank?"

"I forgot something," he responded.

"That being?"

"I didn't see it."

"You mean the casket?"

"I need to see it. To close this thing off."

I studied his square face, saw the determination, and nodded. "Okay. That's fair. Now?"

He looked confused. "No, not here. Let me think. Okay, there's a Baptist church down the way about a mile. There's a big parking lot. I'll meet you there."

"All right. We're nearly done here. See you in a few minutes." With that, Stone ground the starter and drove off.

The lot was empty except for a Plymouth sedan parked near the entrance to the church and Stone's pickup. He had positioned the truck to the far end of the parking lot, facing forward as if for an easy departure. He was sitting on the left front fender when we arrived. Johnnie drove up and parked about a car length away from the pickup. I asked her to stay where she was and to forget the bat. She muttered her grudging consent and held her place while I got out and approached Stone.

He slid off the fender. "He's really in there? His body?"

"He is," I said. "You want to see the casket, is that it?"

He twisted his head around as if searching for anyone who might be watching. "Yeah," he finally agreed. "Need to see the box that bastard's in."

I ignored his comment and tapped the roof of the coach. Johnnie cracked her door ajar, and I asked her to open the coach's left side door. Stone and I stood back while she got out and eyeballed the two of us before swinging the door wide open. Stone stood unmoving when he saw the casket.

After a long moment, he moved forward, peered in, then reached out to place an open hand on the gunmetal gray casket. I was taken in by witnessing the man's passive observation when a ball peen hammer suddenly appeared in his right hand. He was swinging it before I caught on to what he was up to. He'd leaned in and lambasted the casket with a resounding blow. I grabbed onto him when he reared back to strike again and tried to swing him around.

He was strong and easily pulled loose from my grasp, wielding the hammer once again. I had stumbled back but managed to wobble forward and grab for the arm holding the hammer. Again he shook me loose, and I dropped to one knee. His arm was cocked for another strike when Johnnie came at the man, bat in hand, and drove the business end into Stone's kidney. She amazed me. He groaned, faltered, then turned and with his hammer knocked the bat out of her hands. It clattered and spun around on the asphalt paving.

I fumbled around and scooped it up. "Stop!" I yelled, holding the bat in a hitter's stance. "Damn you, Stone, I swear I'll knock your head off. Get back!" I spoke more aggressively than I truly felt; my hands trembled as I gripped the tapered end of that hunk of ash.

He lowered the arm carrying the hammer. "The bastard," he groaned.

"The hammer!" I shouted, "Drop the damn hammer."

After looking at the tool in his hand, he reluctantly let it drop at his feet. He glowered at me for a moment then looked inside the coach. We could all see the pronounced dimple on the lid directly above where my father's head was most assuredly positioned.

"Tough guy, huh?" Stone turned and kicked the hammer away.

I leaned on the bat and waited for my breathing to level off. "What the hell were you doing? Are you insane?"

Stone turned square around and faced me. "Maybe. Maybe so, but then aren't we all a little nuts?"

Johnnie leaned over and picked up the hammer. I relaxed some with us holding all the weapons. "Now what?" I asked. "You get whatever it is out of your system?"

He grimaced a brittle smile. "Never. If I had my way I'd drag his corpse behind my truck until there would be nothing left but a bit of bone and sinew."

The thought of such an image paralyzed me. Johnnie gave out with a disgusted grunt and walked forward to close the coach door. When the latch clicked, she turned toward me and bounced the hammer in her hands. "We done?"

I ignored her comment and instead studied the square-shouldered man and tried to balance Stone's alleged heinous act against his vitriol for my father.

"Maybe my father is not the one to be dragged down the road." I had no idea how he would react, but I had to say it.

He looked over his shoulder, saw the coach door was closed, glanced at Johnnie, then turned to me. His expression was indecipherable, neither angry nor bemused, but still chilling. "Are you threatening me? You gonna hold that lying letter over my head?" He took one step forward, his hands clenched at his sides. "What are you going to do with it?"

"Nothing. I gave it to you. It's yours."

He smirked. "You think I just fell off the turnip truck? You have a copy."

"I do. That's right. So what?"

He raised his fists over his head and roared, "I made a life! I have a life! And now you've ruined it. He's ruined it, your loathsome old man." He took two strides toward me. "Now what do I do?"

I cringed. Should I have felt the guilt that was running through my brain? I looked to Johnnie. There must have been pleading in my face. She smiled sweetly and shrugged.

"Go on living it," I said. "I guess."

"You guess." A harsh laugh came from Stone. He hugged himself, leaned back slightly, and said, "Live my life on a guess? Knowing that out there somewhere you'll still have a dead man's accusation that labels me a bad man."

I hesitated and swallowed the real words: strangled, murdered. "Bad. Is that the real word?"

Stone squinted at me then sank down in a squat, shook his head, and picked up a pebble off the pavement. He bounced it in his hand and tossed it out a few feet. "That real word, as you put it, was written down by a man who knew he was gonna die before I'd see it on that piece of paper. Cowardly."

"Not if it's true."

He sat back on his rump. "I already told you it's not true. You can't prove anything, and neither can I. So whata we gonna do?"

I fingered the knob of the bat. "Look, Stone, I've done what I came to do—deliver that damn letter. Now, we're leaving this place and have a very long drive to Reno. It's done...over."

"The copy. I want it."

I froze. Waited a moment, then I lied. "I don't have it with me."

"That true? I doubt it."

"What difference does it make? What could I do with it?"

He pushed up from the pavement and brushed his pants off. "Show it to people I know. Ruin things."

"Who?"

He knuckled his eyes. "Lucille. You'd ruin what I have with her. And my job. Billy, you'd tell him."

"Stone, that's nonsense. I don't know your wife or Billy. I was just a voice on the phone. Now we're leaving. Go on back home, crank up your rototiller, and get that garden planted."

He stepped forward. I held up a hand. "Your life—go take care of it."

The three of us stood stark still. The only sounds right then were of vehicles passing by out on the street. After a couple of long minutes, Stone took in a deep breath, patted the air with both hands, and nodded his head in agreement. He looked around as if taking inventory before walking to his pickup and driving away. I waited, holding the bat in both hands until I heard the pickup out on the road run through the gears, the sound of Clyde Stone returning to his made-up life.

Johnnie and I, we sat in the coach for a spell, our doors open as the March breeze passed through while we processed what had just happened. Maybe ten minutes passed before Johnnie pulled out her road map, unfolded it, and checked the route we were to take.

"Well," she said after folding the map again. "Is that the worst we'll face? If not, give me a heads up now. I'm adding that hammer to our weapon cache."

I pulled my door closed with a click of the latch and rolled the window down. "We'll be fine…I think. My old man threw a stick of dynamite into his more or less ordinary life and left us to absorb the concussion, damn his dead hide."

"Fine, you think? He's intent on you not spreading the word about him having done someone in."

"Yeah. Let's get moving."

She pulled her door closed and turned the ignition key. "We're not hard to find. I mean, we do stand out."

"Meaning?"

"Easy to track us down if a person had a mind to. Like before."

"Naw, he's headed back to his garden."

We had just passed through an unincorporated village name of Saint Vrain, about half an hour out of Clovis, when Johnnie said, "Told ya."

I leaned over to look out my sideview mirror. There it was, the green pickup closing the distance between us. "How long has he been back there?"

"Just caught sight of him. Shall I just keep on going?"

"Damn. No, pull off."

She eased off the highway into the parking lot of a farm supply store. A couple of pickups and a flatbed truck were parked by the front of the business. She parked where it was most vacant, and I got out as she was rolling to a stop. I hesitated to take the bat when she held it out but relented and carried it with me. Stone paused at the entrance to the lot then coasted in and parked several car lengths away. I didn't wait. He was emerging from the truck when I approached at a fast clip. He held up, standing behind the partially open door. I raised the bat.

"Damn it, Stone," I said at the top of my voice. "What the hell are you doing?"

He stood behind the door, his hands gripping the frame. "Told you, the letter, your copy, I want it."

"I told you, I don't have it, not with me," I lied again. There was a carbon copy in my suitcase.

"Sure you do."

"And if I do? What then?"

He stepped away from the truck and shut the door. "I'll take it from you."

"Like I said before, are you insane? Get in your pickup and get outa here."

"No."

I stepped closer, the bat in my right hand, held down against my leg. "Think for a minute, will you? I could have ten copies of that letter."

"But you don't. I want it. I can't be thinking about you and that letter every day of my life from now on. Give it to me." He came toward me.

I lifted the bat up. "Stop right there. With or without the letter, I could still pass the accusation on to your wife or your boss. Anybody, if I wanted to. But I won't. In my gut, do I think you killed that woman? Maybe. And if you did, you are one heinous human being. But what the hell do I know for sure? Nothing." I moved forward and raised the bat higher. He retreated a couple of steps. "So what's it gonna be?"

He looked past me, and I sensed that Johnnie was back there causing him to hesitate. A couple of men came out of the farm store, paused, and looked over at our strange scene. One of them laughed before they climbed into the flatbed truck. Stone saw them.

"Yes, witnesses," I said. "You want to get into it with witnesses?"

Summation

Stone watched the truck drive away, thought about it, turned and went back to the pickup. "All right. This is over," he said and opened the door.

I moved closer. "Good. We're on our way. You won't ever hear from me—ever. But if we see you behind us again, the first thing I will do is pull off the road and call your boss, Billy. And next Lucille. Do you understand?"

He hesitated with one foot on the ground and one entering the pickup. We shared hard stares before he nodded and slid back into the pickup. He leaned over the steering wheel, head down, before cranking the engine on. He didn't look our way when he reversed course, got back onto the highway, and accelerated back the way he'd come; I stood listening until the whine of the pickup's engine faded.

Chapter Twenty Four.

I handed the bat to Johnnie and got into the coach. She slipped the weapon beneath the seat and scooted in behind the wheel. "Were you really gonna take a swing at him?"

My burst of laughter was muffled in the upholstered compartment. "Hell, if I'd tried that he would have ripped it out of my hands and beat me bloody." I held out flattened hands; they quivered slightly.

"Dang it," she laughed. "This just gets crazier. Can that be?"

"Don't know."

"Offer still stands: drive on through to Portland."

There were moments when I was ready to do that. But the sixth letter was the one I most wanted to deliver. "Reno. Let's do it."

She reached over and gripped my arm. "First, what say we take a look at your father? That one hammer blow didn't do him any damage, but can't hurt to take a look."

In a desolate wide spot we opened my father's casket to see how he fared after being peened. He looked spiffy enough to attend a patio party. Johnnie cinched the lid back down. It was just past noon.

I settled in, closed the door, and said, "I feel as if I'm on a leave of absence, like my time in the Navy. When I was on furlough, back on home ground, I still felt like a drifter navigating unfamiliar terrain. I'm feeling nomadic now."

"Same here."

"I'm not sure if that feeling will pass once we return."

"Guess we'll find out." She turned the key in the ignition; the throb of reciprocating pistons returned.

She reached into our road food sack, ripped opened a cellophane package of Hydrox, put a cookie in her mouth, and drove out of the farm store parking lot. We had to cover twelve hundred miles of blacktop ranging from smooth aggregate-and-tar to choppy pavement, rough road, and potholes. Eisenhower's campaign proclamation that he intended to tackle the nation's appalling highways was of no value to us right then.

The Meteor's midway layover would be in Gallup. We stopped for food and gas in Albuquerque and drifted into Gallup just after eight o'clock. The Wyngarde Mortuary was just off Route 66 on Coal Avenue; it was a flat-roofed stucco building with an adobe look to it. Two flagpoles stood out front with small floodlights illuminating the American and New Mexico flags. It was well past sunset when Johnnie eased the coach to the rear of the building and parked near a three-bay garage. I exited the coach and was leaning against a fender flexing my back when a spotlight mounted on the garage lit up; a rear door to the mortuary opened, and an elderly man stepped out. He was slightly bent, wore a dark suit and a tie, was bald with white hair on the sides, and wore aviator-style glasses. Walking unevenly, he approached us wearing a wide grin fronted by square teeth the color of aged ivory.

"And here you are." His voice had the tonal qualities of a preacher. "You must be Miss Gates." She nodded. "And you are the client, I assume." When I shook his long-fingered hand, the skin felt smoother and younger than expected. "I'm Ishmael Wyngarde, but folks just call me Wyn."

"Michael Sanborn."

"And I'm Jonalynn, but I go by Johnnie."

"Good to have you here. My, my your coach is a real beauty. A Meteor. Cadillac Meteor Landau."

Johnnie smiled. "She could use a wash job. Any chance I could use your hose tomorrow?"

"Most assuredly. Most assuredly. I bet you folks are hungry."

"We had a late lunch. We'll be fine."

"Nonsense. Nothing worse than being road hungry. I live right here at the mortuary, so I insist you join me for a bite." He struck off, leaning forward as his curved back allowed. "You see," he said as we walked, "I'm a widower, so it's convenient to live where the action is. A local woman, Sofia, she takes care of me." He laughed. "Without her, I'd be at sea. She made up a batch of her special turkey sandwiches."

We entered through a rear door and were enveloped in the airborne residue of flowers past and the staleness of space that only awakened when people congregated for the sorriest of reasons. In Wyngarde's apartment kitchen, we sat at a small table covered with a blue and white checked tablecloth and ate Sofia's delectable turkey sandwiches along with long-necked bottles of Schlitz.

"So, Michael," Wyngarde said, "You're taking your father back home."

"I am."

"Florida to Portland?" I nodded again. "A lotta miles." He smiled. "There's a story there. Tell me all about it."

By the time we'd eaten and finished the beers, I'd told Wyngarde the story. He never took his eyes off mine. After we'd finished, he daubed mayonnaise from his lips, turned to Johnnie, and smiled.

"A most fascinating tale. I've experienced a few myself. My daddy, he opened the first mortuary here in Gallup in 1922. Town had grown blisteringly from 1910 to 1920. He saw the need. Wyngarde's has been in business for thirty years. My son Charles and I run the place now." He leaned back on the legs of his chair. "We've buried murderers, those murdered, and Madam Ida—our most fascinating client. She operated the Desert Pearl, a noted brothel. When she died, her funeral was spectacular. Story is that half the male population in town turned out. That was in 1927. Was like Mardi Gras."

"My dad and you would have a grand time trading war stories," Johnnie said.

"'Spect so. Still, this pilgrimage of yours is unique."

"More like a back breaker," I said. "On that note, I think it best we get on to our motel for the night. Been a long day."

"Surely," Wyngarde said. "Just so you know, we do have a service tomorrow. A young boy. Polio victim." He waved a hand to dismiss the subject. "You're staying at the Log Cabin Lodge, right? I'll run you over there." On the way, while he chattered incessantly, my mind was distracted by thought of the boy who died from polio and of David, the brother born with no heartbeat. Both lives were never to be lived.

When alone in a log cabin replica room, I phoned Nadine. We exchanged the usual pleasantries; then at her request I roughly estimated when we'd be back in Portland. Her voice had an edge to it. The tension was sharpening between us. Something was different. I had fully intended to deliver my father and his letters and return home unchanged. That idea was no longer in play. I had a growing sense that seeing my wife again would be as if meeting a distant cousin, one who knew bad things about me. How would I face her? What would it be like to touch her, hold her, be intimate with her again?

Those things were in my head when Johnnie rapped on the door and entered carrying a fresh bottle of Old Crow. I looked at her and thought thank god. She waggled the bottle. I nodded. I didn't know where she had gotten a new bottle, and I didn't care. She removed the cork and set the bottle on the room's small pine table by the window. I appropriated two glasses from the bathroom; we sat at the table and toasted one another. Then we were quiet.

"I needed that," I said then.

She merely nodded. "How about a fire?" The fireplace was made of field stones with a red brick fire box. Attached to the wooden mantel was a printed card advising how to use the damper properly and to enjoy the fragrance and warmth from the local piñon pine logs. Soon she had a bright fire going. We enjoyed a second pour of bourbon and let the fire do the talking for a time.

"I called my dad," she said, breaking the calm. "Filled him in."

"How was that?"

She chuckled. "Fine, but I left out the part about our latest go-round with that Clyde person. Guesstimated on when we might hit Portland. Just routine. You call Nadine?"

"I did." She stared at me, waiting. "Touched base. Played nice and told her I'd be back soon. I left out the fracas too."

"Looking forward to being back?"

I was staring into the fire. "Not sure, guess so."

She held the bottle up again. I didn't resist. "Yeah, it's been a helluva trip, but I'm ready to be done. Sleep in my own bed, see Danny and Dad, get back in the groove."

The fire popped, sending an ember out onto the rough cut carpet. I jumped up and kicked it back onto the hearth. "I want that part too," I said. "The comforts and the familiar. But the rest of it...I'm not sure... what that will be like."

"What's that mean: The rest of it?"

I returned to my chair and stretched my legs out. "That'd be my marriage and my job, but mainly my marriage." When I looked over, her eyes were large and fixed on me; she didn't blink. "I know, what else is there? Everything else is just on the edges."

"I suppose." She rose, crossed to the fireplace, and added another log. Flames surged up as the fire bit into fresh fuel. She turned where she stood and stared back at me. "We've been through it, haven't we now? You and me, but mostly you. Hell's bells, meeting those people and facing up to 'em with your old man stretched out in a box?"

"It's my failings," I went on. She stood with her back to the fire and just listened. "The ones I'd packed away."

"I know, you keep harping on that ," she said. "But your father, there's the bad stuff."

"Maybe. That's not what I'm referring to when I say the rest of it. What I'm struggling with is that after I'm home, what then? All of that baggage will still be stowed away."

"You're just tired. I know I am. Once we're back home, we'll settle right back into our usual routines."

I considered her opinion. "No. Not like it was."

"Michael, come on."

"No...I've been processing this for a lot of miles, and I'm very sure that I don't want to be the same guy."

She stood fast, unmoving. "To not want to be yourself, that is something. Can anyone do that? Not be themselves?"

"Don't know. Never tried it."

She returned to sit at the table but didn't offer to pour more bourbon. "And Nadine?" she asked boldly.

I leaned back, my glass empty. "And that's the real question. The worst question. I don't deserve her, never have."

"I doubt that's true." She spoke in my favor but without knowing.

"Oh, but it is."

Chapter Twenty Five,

We talked more that night, or rather Johnnie listened to my regrets and how the trip had worked its trickery. Until near midnight, she sat across the table from me, took in my rambling without reacting, with no sign of skepticism or tedium. Eventually my soliloquy wore us both down, and we parted after setting a time to meet for yet another breakfast on the road. After her departure, I stood before the fading bed of coals and revisited how she had become more than a teamster; she was my alter ego, my accomplice and my sympathizer. It seemed I'd come to need her empathy more than her driving skills.

I was in the Log Cabin Cafe around seven-thirty the next morning already consuming hotcakes and coffee when Johnnie sat across from me and snagged a menu. We shared subdued morning greetings; she chose eggs and bacon with coffee. While she doctored her coffee, I offered an apology for my nonstop dialogue over whiskey and a fire the night before. She shrugged.

When the waitress came by to warm up our coffee, I asked about getting a cab. She pointed toward the counter and said, There's Darby. She drifted over that way and spoke to a middled-aged fellow with a full head of black hair and a broad nose. The only cab driver in Gallup gave me the high sign. By the time we'd eaten and gone to our rooms, Darby's Taxi, a yellow Chrysler Windsor, was idling outside. Within minutes we were deposited behind Wyngarde's Mortuary. Darby took his fare and drove away with nary a side long glance at the funeral home.

The garage door shielding the Meteor was already open, and a coil of rubber hose, a bucket, a nozzle, and wash mitt had been left for Johnnie to use. She backed the coach out and set about washing the vehicle. After a minute or two of moral support, I entered the mortuary and found Ishmael Wyngarde rearranging rows of white wicker chairs in the chapel. I thanked him for his hospitality then asked permission to look in on the young polio victim. After a moment, he nodded and led me to a viewing room. Once there he hesitated, studied me briefly, then left me alone.

A white, child-sized casket, its lid propped open, rested on a raised platform; white crepe plush fabric adorned the edge of the funerary box. I stepped forward, hands hanging loosely at my sides. The child's body was small and pale and fragile looking; his hands had been crossed, and he was dressed in a small gray suit, white dress shirt, and blue tie. I wondered if he had ever worn a suit in life. From Wyngarde, I knew the boy had been only six years old; he seemed smaller than that. In the stillness, he appeared to only be at rest, his blonde hair combed and lips lightly rouged. I was drawn to look upon the deceased child because of the imagined characterization of the brother I never knew. There was no likeness, nothing in his frozen face that reminded me of anyone, certainly not the David I never knew, nor any resemblance of my parents. I had not expected that, of course, but to look on the boy's body was to imagine in some small way what my brother might have looked like at that age.

Wyngarde returned. The parents were there to visit their child. I left quickly. Outside, I stood watching Johnnie as she dried the coach with her chamois skin. She glanced at me and twisted water from the soft leather square; she had no idea what I was feeling right then.

Shortly after gassing up we were on the road. Johnnie had calculated we had just north of 900 more miles to go before I could deliver the sixth letter; that meant another stop and another rented bed before reaching Reno.

We had gone maybe ten miles, just passed a tiny township named Defiance, when Johnnie spoke. "So?"

"What?"

"Why'd you go back inside, at the mortuary? To say goodbye to Wyn?"

"To see the child."

She kept looking down the road. "Why?"

"I wondered is all. What a child that age would look like."

"You mean deceased?"

"Not that really, but…just wondering if my brother would have looked similar at that age."

"And what was that like?"

"Intrusive. Disturbing to see. A small child as if sleeping but with no semblance of life. It was strange to take in…that he had been alive only days ago."

"The first time I saw a dead child," she said, "was in my father's prep room. A wee toddler, a little girl, lying still, like napping. But there were wounds. She'd been hit by a car. I've never forgotten."

I could only nod. "David. He never was, yet has always been. My mother, she could never let him go. She spoke of him randomly as if he had lived."

She nodded. "You told me about that."

I heard her but went on. "She kept the hospital's ink imprint of his baby feet in a frame that hung in my parent's bedroom. That little boy back there, he's not alive, but he'll be a shadow presence in that family—always. But at least he actually existed."

Johnnie turned her head to look at me. "Is that how you feel?"

"I lived it. For a long time, I lived it. But time passed, and I must have figured that David's ghost had gone away. Until I saw the boy in the casket, I was sure David had gone away…but guess he never did. I know my mom loved me, but she was also attached to her child who never was."

Johnnie pushed the cigarette lighter in on the dashboard and one-handed a Lucky Strike out of her pack. I watched her push the wing window out and light up when the hot-tipped lighter popped back out—a set of practiced maneuvers with no reduction in her driving ability. She exhaled her first puff in a stream out through pursed lips. A moment later she began to chuckle.

"You know, it just keeps unraveling, doesn't it?" She held the cigarette next to the vent window and bobbed her head. "I mean the both of us. It's like we've been locked in this moving crypt and told to reveal the most disturbing parts of our lives to each other."

"Guess so."

"No guessing, it's happening."

The miles droned on. But we spoke only of the road, the next meal stop, or the need to refuel—nothing more of shared regrets. Not right then anyway. Our next layover was Henderson, Nevada, just south of Las Vegas. There was one funeral home in the small town, Penwell Mortuary, where we would park the coach overnight for a ten dollar fee. We arrived late. A sour-faced, exceedingly tall man took the money and begrudgingly drove us a couple of miles to the Cozy-Up Inn, another unremarkable structure of boxy rooms, no charm and the familiar stale aroma of previous guests' smoking blended with the flat smell of space more vacant than lived in.

When Johnnie appeared at my room with the half-full bottle of Old Crow, I had no objections. We sat quietly, she in a weary upholstered chair and me on the bed, and toasted yet another day. I waved Johnnie off when she raised the bottle for a second round and instead reached into my suitcase where I'd put the sixth envelope; this time I'd be handing it off to an uncle I'd never met.

I held the envelope up for Johnnie to see, pulled out the paper, unfolded it, and read the first three words to myself: This is painful. That letter wasn't like the others because it carried sibling baggage. I handed it to Johnnie. She set her glass down, gave me a questioning look, and began to read. I watched her reactions: raised eyebrows, lips drawn in, finally a twitch of her shoulders.

"Family," she said and flat-handed the page on the table. "My dad once told me that he seldom met a family that wasn't carrying around a backwash of stuff never to be forgotten nor forgiven. He's refereed a goodly number of funeral-day feuds."

My mother's funeral had actually been a serene gathering, modestly attended. Since my parents had cut the cord from their lives in Portland, many personal connections had faded away. If my father's brother Charlie had showed up, he would have stood out—but he wasn't among those in attendance at the River View Cemetery chapel when Melba Sue Sanborn was remembered. There'd been little reason for a funeral-day feud. The entire observance had cleared out well short of an hour. My father, Nadine, and I were the only ones present at the graveside to witness Mom's casket laid to rest.

The next day, I drove Dad to the airport, and it was over; my mother was gone and would be little remembered, I am ashamed to say. Right then, with Johnnie watching me, I thought of the brother I never knew and imagined that he and Mom might have somehow found each other, depending on one's beliefs. That also reminded me that among the family artifacts Dad sent to me from Florida had been that framed impression of tiny baby feet. What had I done with it?

Johnnie refolded the letter. "Like I told you five hundred miles ago, this has been a god-damned set up. He could've handled his own dirty laundry before he kicked the bucket. Cowardly." She tossed the letter at me. "He's been manipulating you."

I caught the page in mid-flight. "So you say," I said.

She scoffed. "I do say." She batted the air with an open hand. "You've as much as said you're gonna change your life after this."

"Just thinking out loud."

"Okay then, tell me, were you planning on rearranging your life before you climbed aboard back in Jupiter? Never mind, the answer is no. More than no: not on your life, I'd bet."

"Okay." I slipped the letter back into its envelope. "What about you? Outside of navigating and making various reservations, what's your beef?"

She shook her head. "You can ask that?"

We sat looking at each other. I knew, of course, what she meant, that she'd driven every mile, been present at every letter delivery, endured the reactions from borderline violence to deep emotion. "You've been with me at every stop. Seen it all. And I'm grateful."

"Damn you!" She leaned forward, placed her hands on her knees, extended her strong neck, and said, "My chauffeuring is the least of it, the very least, Michael."

"What are you saying?"

"Get a grip, that's what. I'm not some mechanical device. Sure, I've watched you endure layer after layer of your self-esteem being peeled off your hide. But I have lost some skin too."

I stood up from the bed and walked over to the side table, where I poured myself another finger of whiskey and downed it. As it burned its way down, I looked into her angry eyes. "You're right," I said, turning the empty glass in my hand. "I owe you. I don't mean to make light of your part in all of this. Besides, you wielded the bat when needed," I laughed. "Can't forget that."

"I'll be rid of this sideshow once we're back home. But still it won't really be over for me then either. This trip will leave scar tissue." Her eyes stayed on me. Then she stood, picked up the bottle and left.

Chapter Twenty Six.

I dozed that night. First I was too warm, so I threw off the blankets. Then I was too cool. It went like that until there was a rap on the door early the next morning. I sat up as if on a spring, waited out those first foggy moments, then pulled on my pants. It was Johnnie. She was fully dressed, smoking a cigarette; the coach was parked behind her. She'd evidently gotten up early and walked to the mortuary. I stood there bare chested wondering what the heck?

"Best we get going," she said. "I'll wait while you cover up. We can catch breakfast on the way. Found a place." I looked at my watch—6:35.

It was just another hash house, place called Buddy's. We ate quickly, had our waitress fill paper cups of coffee to take with us, then gassed up at an Esso. Overnight a gas war had begun. The price per gallon had dropped from 27 cents to 14 cents. Johnnie topped off the tank for two bucks and headed north. It would be another long day. I considered how to broach the topic again, of skin lost, but couldn't. I settled back and unfolded the Las Vegas Review-Journal I'd plucked out of a newspaper rack at the gas station. The lead story was that on April 22 the U.S. Government would detonate a another nuclear bomb at Yucca Flat.

"They're going to blow up Nevada," I said. "Again."

"Whata you mean?"

"Government's going to detonate an atomic bomb." I held up the paper. "At that place, Yucca Flat. Another test."

She glanced over. "Scary. That radiation is hair-raising stuff."

"Agreed."

"Fortunately, we'll be long gone by the time they flip the switch."

I rolled the paper, lay it on the seat between us, and looked out at the desert terrain we were passing as we neared Las Vegas. I cranked down my window a few inches and inhaled the cooler air that came in. Then we were passing through Las Vegas. We didn't intend to stop to take in any of the city's attractions; however, Fremont Street was a sight. Even in daylight the Las Vegas Strip's array of neon signs was something.

The mobile sign of a huge cowboy stood high above the Pioneer Club, his hat and body outlined in neon tubes, his left arm slowly moving in an exaggerated wave. The array went on from one casino to another: the 49er Club, the Golden Nugget, the 4 Queens. Reader boards boasted famous performers from Nat King Cole to Frank Sinatra. After several miles, we flushed the intensity and pushed ahead on U.S. 95.

"Quite a show," I said.

"Not my kinda thing," she responded.

I let it pass. "What's next?"

"Tonopah. There's an old hotel there where we can catch a bite. About noon."

Half of that distance later, we came up on a crossroads called Beatty, which declared itself to be a Gateway to Death Valley. Johnnie pointed to the gas gauge, pulled off, and drove down a dust-blown street with a few parked cars and no people. She pulled up to a gas pump beside a woeful little building posing as a Union 76 station—it had two pumps, one with ethyl one without. A skinny fellow wearing faded bib overalls and a sweat-stained fedora came out through a screen door that slapped back. He stood looking at us. Waited for a moment then walked past the pumps and turned his eyes from the Meteor onto us.

As asked, he filled the tank with ethyl and minutes later we were back on the highway. Beatty's arid little desert junction fell away.

In Tonopah, the main street actually had some life: cars were parked curbside, people could be seen walking about, but still and all, it was another remnant of a prosperous silver mining history long past its peak. A stone-faced concrete structure rose five stories, topped off by two huge signs rising on Erector Set style frames spelling out MIZPAH HOTEL.

"We can eat here," Johnnie said. She circled the block and parked up next to the curb on a side street.

Upon exiting the coach, I was hit by air so lacking in moisture that I worked to draw in a clear breath. A small dust devil appeared out on the street and swirled a mixture of grit and dust around us. We made for the hotel and burst through the big wooden double doors into the lobby laughing and coughing. A young woman who stood behind the registration counter smiled.

"Restaurant," Johnnie croaked.

The woman raised an arm and aimed a forefinger. The Pittman Cafe was a throwback to earlier times: rustic high-back wooden chairs, plank flooring, round marble-topped tables, and brass light fixtures. We each chose their special, a beef brisket sandwich, and ate in relative silence.

Once lunch was consumed, I went looking for a pay phone and placed a call home. Nadine accepted my call. I started to fill her in on trip details, but she cut me off.

"Michael, stop and listen, please," she said forcefully. "I received a strange phone call today." I heard her inhale. "It was a man, asking for you. Strange."

"Who was he?"

"He wouldn't say...even when I asked."

My mind buzzed with unease. "What did he want?"

"That's the thing," she said. "He didn't want anything, not really. When I told him you were out of town, he said I know. Weird."

My mind whirled as a tall man wearing Levi's and cowboy boots walked across the lobby. I closed the accordion door on the phone booth. "And he wouldn't say who he was?"

"No. Just that he had a message for you. It was unsettling. He said something like, Tell him I know where he lives now. That's it."

My mind raced. It had to be one of them. I fingered the coiled telephone cord and watched through the booth glass door as the man in the Levi's left the hotel. Nadine was saying something, but I wasn't taking it in.

"What?"

"I asked who do you think he was, and what did he mean?"

"It's a long story."

"That means you know who he was?"

"Possibly. What was his voice like?"

"Just a regular voice, like I said. Maybe deeper than yours."

I knew. "Okay."

"So you know who it was?"

"Maybe."

"It has something to do with this trip, isn't that so? One of the people you visited?"

"I'll have to think on it. Right now, we need to get back on the road. I'll call you again when we get to Reno. My Uncle Charlie's next."

She hesitated. "That ought to be interesting. When did you last see him?"

"I don't even know him. Nadine, if that character calls again, just hang up. Promise me."

She willingly agreed. When I returned to the table, Johnnie was having a second cup of coffee. I eased into my chair and told her about Nadine's unnerving phone call. Her eyes widened. She set her cup down.

Summation

Chapter Twenty Seven,

After a moment of silent assessment, we concurred that it had to be Clyde Stone: the deep voice, the threatening words. It wasn't Ripley Miller; his voice was thin and reedy. Plus he had others do his dirty work. It was Stone. I dropped a couple bills on the table; we drove on.

After we'd gotten clear of Tonopah, Johnnie said, "You think he'll act on it, his warning? Stone?"

"Maybe. He wants to hang on to the life he's orchestrated for himself. Sees me as potentially putting the kibosh to all that."

"He could be violent…I think."

That thought gave me pause. "I doubt it," I said as if I knew what the man was capable of. "If I turned up dead, you'd turn him in, wouldn't you?"

"Not funny. Besides, he'd need to get rid of both of us."

More than I wished to consider. The highway yellow line wavered in my line of vision. But what if he showed up at the house and confronted Nadine, threatened her? The thought ran cold through me.

"Let's get on to my Uncle Charlie and hand off letter number six. Then we can put the pedal down for home."

"Okay. But in the meantime you got a guy suspected of murder maybe bird-dogging us."

"A bluff, I wager. Scare tactic to keep me from making a couple of phone calls, which I never intended to make anyway. Like I told him, I have no proof that he killed that woman."

"Okay then, why'd he do this, threaten you, if he's not guilty?"

"Maybe he is."

She grunted and pulled on the steering wheel. "That really helps. I'll be keeping the bat close."

I jabbed her lightly on the shoulder and laughed. "How long until we hit Reno?"

"It'll be awhile. Six o'clock or so."

After a road-weary sigh, I thought of Charlie's letter and wondered just how I was going to face an estranged family member.

I was roused from dozing when a sudden downpour hit and pounded on the coach's windshield. Johnnie had the wipers on full bore. The force of the rain caused her to slow the vehicle and fall back from several cars in front of us, which had likewise reduced their speed. Then, just as soon as it had begun, the rain was over, and blue sky shone again. A few miles on, Johnnie pulled off the highway onto a crossroad called Yerington and found another gas station. The spring cloudburst that had been so thunderous had all but dissipated in the dry air; only steam rising off the street's asphalt gave evidence of the deluge. The attendant, visibly unnerved by fueling a hearse, topped off the tank and watched askance while I shoved coins into a vending machine and extracted two bottles of Coke.

Johnnie emerged from the restroom, the attendant gave a final swipe at the windshield, and we left that place as if it had never existed. We sucked down our sodas, and I wished that the miles ahead would magically disappear. They didn't. But by the time we cut beneath the arching neon sign declaring RENO: The Biggest Little City in the World, it was just shy of six o'clock, and twilight was drawing its curtain. Johnnie easily found the Farris Motel on fourth street. We checked in, stowed our luggage, and I made the call.

The woman who answered spoke in a manner of someone who was used to getting calls and sounded neither curious nor suspicious. When I asked for Charles, she calmly said he wasn't home from the job site yet. She expected him anytime, saying he'd better because dinner was getting cold. I agreed to call back in fifteen minutes, set the receiver in the phone cradle, and considered the calm voice I'd never heard before; I knew her name to be Alma, but that was all.

When I called back, a man I assumed to be my uncle answered. His voice, did it sound familiar, like my father's? Could be. But maybe I just wanted it to. "I'm glad to connect with you," I said.

"That right?" It sounded like he was chewing on something. "Who's this?"

"You sitting down?"

He huffed a chuckle. "I am."

"This is Michael, your nephew. Michael Sanborn."

After a pause. "You don't say."

"Yes." I gauged his lackluster response then said, "Would it be all right if I dropped by in a while?"

"Now? Tonight?"

"Yes."

"So you're here, in Reno?"

"That's right. Passing through."

I could hear him speaking quietly to his wife before saying, "That'd be okay I guess. When?"

"Say an hour? Need to get a bite. You still live at 836 South Arlington Avenue?"

He did. I agreed to arrive around seven thirty. Johnnie and I grabbed burgers at the Hay Lift Cafe and by a quarter after seven, wearing the most presentable of my road-weary clothes, we were en route to meet a man I'd only heard of. More than previous recipients, I was worried that my uncle and aunt would be horrified over what I was bringing to their doorstep. How toxic would be the baggage between the brothers from Springfield?

The house, a two-story structure covered with a gambrel roof, sat on a large lot with a manicured front lawn and three elm trees adorning the parking strip. A Dodge pickup sat in the driveway with Sanborn Builders painted on the door. I asked Johnnie to park so the coach wasn't directly in front of the house. I felt like I was about to walk into a police station and admit to a crime. After a moment of doubt, I approached the front door and levered an attached brass knocker. It seemed a very long moment before the door opened. He was stocky, somewhat shorter than I was, with thinning gray hair, bushy eyebrows, possessing a replica of my father's sharp nose. He wore a duck cloth work shirt, weathered denims, and dusty boots—evidently right off the job. He stood erect, square shouldered, and wore flat expression over pale blue eyes. We studied each other.

"So here you are," he said finally, with less enthusiasm than a truant officer. The tone of his voice seemed to have a Sanborn timbre. He stepped back and gestured for me to follow him in; thus he didn't catch sight of the coach. We stood in a small foyer, he with his hands on his hips, me clutching the letter in my right hand.

"Well, best you come on in." He ushered me into a large living room where a short woman stood, hands clasped at her waist, boasting a nice smile and an even set of white teeth. She was handsome, slender, wearing a gingham red and white checked house dress, cinched at the waist, and nicely styled auburn hair. Her smile was welcoming.

"Alma, this is him. Michael. Randolph's boy."

We nodded and acknowledged each other while Charlie stood in place, hands jammed into his back pockets, obviously uncertain of what to do next. Finally he pulled his hands out and brushed them together. "We could sit down." He waved me into a large leather armchair; they sat across from me on a plush sofa, a spacious dining area spread out behind them. Charlie stared at me. "Not seeing much of your old man in your face," he said.

"Really? You resemble him to me, especially your nose."

"Makes me feel real special having his schnoz. So tell me, what are you doing knocking on my door? Business trip? Vacation? I know you didn't come all this way to call on your all but forgotten uncle."

"But I did...come to see you."

His smile was forced. "Really? And to what purpose?" When Alma placed a hand on his arms, he shook it off.

"Family business."

Charlie was puzzled but kept his tight smile in place. "Family business. Don't you know, we don't have a family. We have blood lines but sure as hell no family. Tell me, did your dad send you?"

I took in a breath and let it out slowly. "Yes...he did."

Charlie's eyebrows rose. "Gutless ass. Couldn't carry his own water."

"May I fill in the gaps for you?"

He turned to his wife and grimaced; she smiled and patted his arm. "Oh, what the hell." He waved a thick paw at me.

"Well, Mom passed, but you knew that." He nodded. I held my breath before saying, "And now...Dad has died, but you likely heard that too."

He flopped back on the sofa, his face slack. "No. Died? No. How in hell would I have heard that? We've been alienated...for a very long time." He closed his eyes then opened them and looked at me. "When?"

Alma was watching me, sympathy written on her face. We gave each other low-level smiles. "He and Mom moved to Jupiter, Florida, a few years ago."

"Yeah, I knew that much through the family grapevine. Then I heard about Melba passing from a distant cousin."

I hesitated, covered my nerves with a small cough, before going on. "Dad died a little over a week ago in Jupiter. Of cancer."

"Oh, my," Alma said.

My uncle was studying me, gripping his thighs. "So, why on earth would you be here, in Reno? Now? Thinking I'd be all broke up?"

There it was. Facing family was different. Not like going eye-to-eye with edgy strangers. My gut had predicted that handing one of my father's letters to a blood relation would test the limits of his scheme. I would see. "I have something for you," I answered.

Charlie gave me an inquisitive appraisal then leaned back and folded his arms. "That a fact? Not my birthday."

I smiled. "I wouldn't know. It's a letter. To you." I saw him catch sight of the envelope I'd slipped into my shirt pocket. "From Dad...from Randolph."

Strangely, neither of them reacted—no facial changes, no vocal murmurs.

Finally, Charlie inhaled and let it out slowly. "A letter. You came all this way to deliver a letter from my brother...my now dead brother? The bastard."

I took the envelope out and held it up. "There's more to it than that. Best you read this first."

I waited him out. Alma sat quietly and waited along with me. Eventually, Charlie leaned forward, his forehead creased in a band of wrinkles.

"This letter, have you read it?" I nodded. He nodded back. "And you think I ought to read it?"

"Not for me to say."

He heaved a sigh and came over to me. I handed it to him. They sat on the sofa and read the letter together. I sank back in the chair and tried become invisible while I replayed the letter in my head:

RANDOLPH E. SANBORN
FLORHAVEN ESTATES
JUPITER, FLORIDA

February 1952

Charles Sanborn
836 South Arlington Avenue
Reno, Nevada

Dear Charlie,

This is painful. By now I assume you know that I have died from the cancer brought on by too many years of smoking at my desk. Not sure if Michael gave you a heads-up about me being delivered to your doorstep in my present state, but here I am. Must seem almost creepy for the hearse carrying your brother's dead body to be sitting outside. I coerced your nephew into this, driving me back home via a meandering route, making pre-planned stops along the way. And Reno is our sixth of seven. Howdy, brother.

Charlie, not long after my sweet Melba left me, I took note of being totally alone for the first time. The void was beyond anything I'd felt before. And then cancer invaded my body. As I have related to others along the route, I was drawn to take stock of my life. And, no surprise to you, I came up wanting. I'd worked my way up in the business world, but there was little else to applaud, especially how I had treated you.

As I said, this is painful. While the radiation and new drugs they used were sucking the life out of me, I had time, focused time, to think and remember.

Like when my kid brother, from Springfield, came to Portland, back around 1912 as I recall, to get my help in finding a job, a start in life. Instead of helping, I told you, "I made my own way, you can do the same." I dumped you, shoved you away. I could have helped, but my ego overrode family and compassion. What an ass. And you were not alone. This journey is awash with my failings, but forsaking you was the worst.

I know you were successful as a carpenter, builder, and now have your own construction company, no thanks to me. You didn't require my approval, now or ever. I just need you to know, as I pass this way for the only and last time, that I knew. I knew what I'd done and all the while lacked the moral courage to seek your forgiveness. In the grip of dying, please know that our alienation was a lump of pain in my gut. I'm sorry.

With belated love,
Randolph

Within moments of beginning to read, Charlie sat up quickly, like on a spring, and looked at me, eyes wide. I bobbed my head, assuring him that the funeral coach was indeed out front. Alma gripped his forearm, gently restraining him; they finished reading, after which they sat in stunned silence. When he could stand it no longer, my uncle got up and strode to the front door. I followed and stood behind him on the stoop; it took him a moment to spot the coach.

He turned to me. "Unbelievable." He spoke on a hoarse breath. He looked back and drew Alma to him with an arm around her shoulders. We stood there, the three of us, just staring at the black hearse, its chrome grill gleaming beneath a street lamp. "Now what?" he asked.

"That's up to you," I answered.

Chapter Twenty Eight,

My uncle suddenly wrapped his arms around himself and stared back to where the coach was parked. I raised a hand and motioned for Johnnie to drive forward. When the coach was directly in front of the house, she turned off the engine. The three of us stood silently in the cool evening air beneath the yellow glow of the porch light.

"Who is that?" Charlie asked after a moment. "The person driving? Your wife?"

"No, that's Johnnie," I said. "Jonalynn Gates. She's from the funeral home in Portland. Dad contracted with them to transport his remains back home."

"Remains," he said softly. "What a dreadful word. He's really in there?"

"Yes, he is."

He shuddered and turned to me. "And you've done this how many times?"

"Six, counting you. One more to go."

My uncle stared at me and moved his head up and down, letting me know he understood. "Am I supposed to do something? How does this go?"

"There's nothing to do in particular. Do you want to view the casket or see...?"

"Gad no." He looked at Alma, visibly unnerved. "Why would I do that after all this time. Alma, should I?"

"I don't know," Alma responded. "Maybe put it to rest."

My uncle sagged down and sat on the top step. From there he stared out at the long, black vehicle parked at the curb. "Put it to rest," he muttered. "No, I can't do it...see him, give him the satisfaction."

I placed a hand on his back. "You know, I'm curious to know the story. To get acquainted."

His shoulders hunched beneath my hand. He pushed up on his legs, stood and turned to look at me. I could see the moistness in his eyes. "It's not a good story. It's like he wrote in the letter. No warm family tale for you, Michael. The bastard."

"Still, I'd like to know."

Alma reached out for her husband, took an arm, and guided him back inside. As we passed, she whispered for me to invite the driver to join us. I gestured to Johnnie. Once we were all in the house, I introduced the couple to Johnnie; they quietly acknowledged each other, and then we stood in a cluster, no one sure what to do next. A ringing phone provided a momentary reprieve. Alma hustled off toward the sound, and we waited. Charlie stood with his hands in his pockets and looked down as Alma's voice filtered in from another room.

Shortly she returned, the trace of a smile on her face. "That was Oscar, Charlie." To us she said, "He's our neighbor across the street. He saw the hearse and was concerned. I think he thought you'd died, Honey."

"Some days it feels like I have. Besides, he's always wanted my DeWalt table saw."

"Charlie!" Alma said on a suppressed laugh. "What a horrible thing to say."

My uncle waved her off and walked away down the hall. In the kitchen she brewed coffee. By the time the percolator had begun to gurgle, my uncle had reappeared holding a small envelope.

"Coffee's almost ready," Alma said, "and there are oatmeal and molasses cookies."

Charlie held the envelope in two hands. "I don't care about coffee and cookies. Michael. I have something I want to show you." We sat at an oaken kitchen table on spindle-backed wooden chairs.

My uncle rested his elbows on the table top and withdrew a photograph from the envelope. "This," he said, holding it up and looking at me, "this is the only picture I have from my early childhood."

Alma and Johnnie brought over a tray of cookies and coffee; my uncle ignored the food. He finally put the picture down and slid it over to me. It had plainly been taken long ago. It was a small black-and-white print with a crease across one corner, faded with age. There were three children in the frame, two boys and a little girl.

"Who are they?" I asked.

"Us," he said. "We kids." He pointed. "That's me, there's Randy and Ruthie, our little sister, in that tall wooden chair. My dad built that."

The scene was of a kitchen. The children were seated at a wooden table, apparently having breakfast. To the side was a large Superior cookstove with bright nickel trim; a stovepipe ran up the wall to the flue outlet. A speckled gray enamel kettle sat on the stove top. It was an eerie photograph with trappings from another era but seeming to be in real time, with the children at table ready to eat.

"When was that?" I asked.

"I know exactly when it was. Look on the back—someone wrote down the date, August 19, 1897. Looks like my mother's hand. That was my birthday. I would have just turned four. That means Ruthie was only two, Randy at least ten, close as I can figure." I'd never heard my dad called Randy.

In the picture, the two younger children were watching their big brother pour what could have been orange juice from a bulbous glass pitcher into small glasses.

"My folks had a photographer friend who had one of the new Kodak folding pocket cameras of that time. That's how we got this picture."

Charlie took the photo when I handed it back and studied it again.

"Remarkable," I said. "A look back, frozen in time."

He shook his head and dropped an open palm on the table. "I looked up to him. We both did, Ruthie and I. He was our hero, our guide, our protector." He ran a hand over the photo as if dusting away old memories. When he fell quiet, I picked up the cup of coffee at my elbow and sipped; it had already cooled. None of us spoke. The cookies sat untouched.

Then he spoke, seemingly to himself. "Our dad, he was a faller in the woods. After that, he worked at the Booth-Kelly lumber mill. He provided for us, but he was one mean son-of-a-bitch. He expected Randy would follow him into lumbering or logging, but my brother wasn't ever going to do that. Dad, he would knock him around some, to convince his eldest to do what he wanted. But Randy, he'd just let his bruises heal and stick to his plan. After three years of high school, he escaped and left Springfield for good."

He looked at me and said, "So you see, that's why he was my hero."

"What about the letter?" I said. "There truth to it?"

He laid his forearms on the table. "Hell yes! Why do you think he conned you into driving to heck and gone and just happened to work in a side trip to Reno? Painful. He wrote that it was painful for him to dredge up that old shit." He looked at the picture once again.

"You know," he went on, "when we kids were growing up, there was Ruthie and me, us being the little ones, and then there was Randy. We were six years apart, him and me. How about you? You have an older brother or sister?"

"I'm an only child."

"Really." He looked curious. "Guess I shoulda known that."

"I would've had an older brother. David. But he was stillborn, about six years before I came along."

"Well, that's something now. Isn't it? Something else I didn't know of."

We locked eyes. "I heard about him, about David, all my life, the big brother I never knew."

My uncle finally reached out for a cookie. He took a bite, chewed, and said, "A big brother. How'd your parents handle that?"

"Not well. Mom held onto the memory tightly. Dad did the opposite. He ignored that there had ever been a lost child."

Charlie took another bite of oats and molasses. "Sounds like him." He drank cold coffee. "Were you close. You and your dad?"

I pushed my coffee cup away. "No. We weren't. Close."

"And yet here you are delivering his letters, being his messenger boy. For what reason?"

"I've asked myself that at every stop from Florida to Kansas and all the rest. And Johnnie here, she's endured it right along with me, and she's not even related. Right, Johnnie?"

Her face reddened. "Part of the job."

Charlie gave her an incurious look; her role in all of this was of no interest to him. "So why do it, this long journey?"

"A dying man's wish."

"But you say you weren't close. Me either," his voice faltered.

"Was it about what he said in the letter?"

"The letter. Where is it?" He looked around, felt his shirt pocket, and discovered it in his back pocket. He opened it up again, laid it on the table, and ran a finger down the page. "There," he said, "right there, he says: after your repeated pleas…You see, I'd asked him to help me get a job, but he cut me off with, here," he placed a forefinger down, "he says…I made my my own way, you can do the same. Like he said, he dumped me. He did! God damn him."

"Charlie." Alma's voice broke in. "Ancient history. Best to leave it there, don't you think?"

Anger came from his eyes on ice chips. "No, I don't think. It's been in me all these years, right here." He stabbed a finger into his stomach. "Oh, I've tried, tricked myself into thinking it was gone…didn't matter anymore. But now, out of the blue, a blood relation appears, carting around my brother's cadaver. Michael, you may be the one to truly understand what I've been harboring. I have had a rage in me for lo these many years. It's ridden in my gut like an abscess."

He held up the letter. "And even in death he's sticking it to me. Like he wants a posthumous medal of valor for owning up. What's he say, oh yes, that he lacked moral courage to beg for forgiveness."

Charlie drank from his cup and looked straight ahead, not at anyone or anything, just stared as eyes can do with no focus. I chose that moment to see if I could learn more about this man, of whom I knew virtually nothing. "Uncle Charlie," I began. He looked at me with an expression as if that was the first time he had ever been addressed as Uncle. "Was it like in the letter—what he admitted— is that what really caused the split between you and Dad?"

Chapter Twenty Nine.

Charlie considered my question. He looked over at Alma. Her face had taken on deeper lines of concern. His smile was one one of resignation.

"Cornered me, didn't you?"

I raised my hands as if surrendering. "No. It's just that…well, I'm here. After all this time. I've known of you, but the cloud of alienation was always there, hovering in the background."

My uncle nodded and maintained his cheerless smile. "I understand. Where to begin?"

Johnnie rose and leaned over to whisper in my ear. I nodded, and she went to call the funeral home; we'd be later than expected.

Charlie and I sat at the table. The photograph was still in front of us. I slid it over to look at again and marveled at seeing my father as a boy—portrayed in the leaden gray of another time. I didn't recognize him, of course, no hint of the man I'd known.

When I looked up, Charlie had his eyes on me. "I can't see my dad in that picture. Do you?"

"Oh, sure. But then I would. I watched him every day, didn't I? As he grew from a boy into a teenager and then a young man, I was following along even as a tyke—I saw it all. Hell, I adored it all. That is until…"

Right then, Johnnie re-emerged, caught my eye, and signaled we were okay with the funeral home.

I took my eyes off the photo. "Until?" I replayed his last word.

He blinked, nodded to himself: "I was sixteen when my dad died on the job at the mill. A joyous day in May. His brutality would no longer torment our lives. Mom married again. Thomas Killian. He owned a hardware store in Springfield, a decent man. He was my opportunity to move on like Randy.

"Mr. Killian, he bought me a ticket to Portland on the Southern Pacific and shoved a hundred dollars into my hand to get started on. Lotta money in those days.

"Randy was working at Olds, Wortman & King Department Store in Portland. I found him there selling men's clothing. He was dressed like a real swell: black suit with a vest, watch chain and fob, striped tie, high-collared white shirt, shiny black shoes.

"When he caught sight of me with my mouth gaping open, hanging onto my pasteboard suitcase, his jaw dropped. I'm sure I looked like a real hick. He dragged me aside and snarled in my ear, What the hell are you doing here? No hug, no smile, none of that." Charlie massaged his hands like he was washing them. "He just walked away, left me standing there, red-faced; he adjusted the knot of his tie and smiled at some guy looking at socks."

I leaned forward a bit. "What happened after that?"

He stared straight ahead. "First, I bunked at the YMCA and explored the city. Portland was booming. It had more than doubled in size in the decade before. After a couple of fruitless weeks looking for work, I went back to see him. He gave me the bum's rush again but agreed to meet me after work at a nearby cafe. He bought me a bowl of soup and a roll and while I ate ordered me to quit coming around. To make my own way like he had. He bragged that he was going to business college. That he planned on getting into banking, which he did. Told me to get lost...I never saw him again. That what you wanted to know?"

"No," I responded. "No...I wanted to know your story is all. Of what happened...between you and Dad."

He nodded, massaged his forehead, and exchanged a smile with Alma. "So now you know. To survive, I held lots of low-level jobs doing back-breaking work. For the next thirty years, I worked as a carpenter's apprentice, became a journeyman, met Alma, fell in love, and she agreed to marry me. Foolish girl."

The look between them was warm and genuine. When was the last time Nadine and I had shared feelings like that or exchanged a loving glance between us? I couldn't recall.

"How'd you end up here, in Reno?"

"The war. There was a demand for carpenters to build barracks at U.S. Army airfields in Nevada. Alma and I packed all we had into our old Dodge and gingerly drove down here with the kids. We had three of them by then, two boys and a girl. After the war I worked constructing houses for returning vets. Eventually started my own construction business. Timing was right, business was good, so here we are."

"You know something?" I said. "If not for Dad's letter, you and I would likely have never laid eyes on one another."

"Maybe," he responded.

"Maybe we owe him that much? Introducing us to each other—at last?"

His eyes widened, almost in alarm. "He has no credit coming, no honor in this moment. With time running out, he found a way to torture his victims one more time. And he made you his hatchet man."

"I know. I've been drawn in to revisiting some of my own wrongs, the part of me that is: like father, like son."

He shook his head. "Damn, planned it all out, didn't he? You've figured that out, haven't you? Why not just drive home?"

"We had an agreement. On top of that, I wanted to meet up with you, the blood kin I'd only ever heard of. That would be something, I figured."

His eyes fixed on mine. "Something."

We sat quietly, each of us with his own thoughts. The photograph was still on the table, I picked it up again, studied it one more time.

"This has been a special time for me," I said. "But I should be going."

My uncle stared at me. "Wait," he said when I stood and looked at Johnnie. "I need to finish this. May I see?"

"If you want."

When we all exited the house, Johnnie walked straight out to the coach and opened the side door, exposing the casket. My uncle stood beside me, shoulder to shoulder, and didn't move. After a quiet moment, I turned to him. His head was tipped slightly forward. His face was expressionless.

"Would you like to get closer?" I asked.

There was a pause while he considered. "Yes."

"All right." I gestured with my right arm and took a step down from the porch.

He followed my lead. Johnnie stood to the side. He peered in at the receptacle containing his brother: his hero, one-time protector and guardian. After a bit he stepped back and turned around to find his wife. Alma mustered a smile for her husband, accepting whatever he wanted to do at that moment.

He stepped off the curb right up to the open door and leaned in. After a moment of hesitation, he reached out and placed an open palm against the smooth metal of the casket. Less than a minute passed before he stepped back and rose up.

"It has a dent," he said.

"There was a dispute. One of the recipients found fault in the content of his letter."

A flat smile crossed his lips. "No wonder."

"Are you okay now?"

He stood still. "No. I want to see him."

"Charlie." Alma spoke in a tone of admonition.

He waved a hand at her and nodded his wish to continue. I looked at Johnnie. She reached into the coach, retrieved the casket key, inserted it, and turned. When she looked back, our eyes met, and she knew to lift the lid. Then, for the first time, an actual relation other than me approached my father's body and peered in; this time brother to brother. Charlie remained poised above the casket for some time, unmoving, just looking.

Eventually he stepped back. "He's dressed for a party."

"That's the way he wanted it."

"Bastard. Couldn't even take his own death seriously. All show."

"Maybe."

"Doesn't look like him, not really."

"Been a long time."

He took in a deep breath and looked back at Alma, a smile on his face. "You know, I'm glad this happened. Just look at him, a dead slab of flesh and bone. Nothing more to fear or hate." He looked at me then Johnnie and said, "You can go now. You've done your duty. It's over, and I'm glad of it." He reached out a thick workman's hand, and we gripped.

"It has been special to meet you," I said.

Summation

"Same for me, Michael. Same for me. Here." He stepped closer and put his muscled arms around me. I hugged him back. It felt surreal.

I said goodbye, and watched as they walked back up to the porch. Just before they went inside, my uncle dropped to one knee and began to sob. Alma put an arm across his back and stroked. She looked back at me. Neither of us said a word. Johnnie closed up the coach, and we left as quietly as we had arrived.

Chapter Thirty,

Johnnie found the funeral Home in the center of town. The night attendant, a middle-aged woman, she showed us to a garage and called us a cab. We stood outside our rooms in the chilly night air, the exhaust of the cab floating about us; it was over, the sibling exchange. We didn't speak of it, just agreed to another early breakfast. Even though it was after eleven, I checked in with Nadine. Clyde Stone was in my head.

The phone rang at least five times before she answered, her voice soft with sleep. "Yes. Who is it?"

"Me."

"Michael?"

"Sorry to wake you, but I need to know. Have you heard anything more from the ominous caller?"

"Not a word."

"Did he ask when I'd be back in Portland?"

There was a pause. "Let me think. No. He just delivered that message, the one about knowing where you live. When will you be home, by the way?"

"Soon. I just got back to the motel after a visit with my Uncle Charlie."

"My, my. How'd that go?"

"It ran from delightful to tense and sad. I'll tell you all about it when I see you. We leave first thing after breakfast and head straight for Portland with just one more night on the road."

"Over and done then?"

"Except for delivering one last letter in Portland—the seventh. After that, over and done with but for burying Dad next to Mom, and then…"

When I hesitated, she said, and then? "You and me," I answered, "we'll need time to catch up and talk about the future."

I could hear her yawn. "The future? What about the future?"

"This trip, Nadine, it's changed my thinking about what lies ahead. In a different way."

She wasn't groggy anymore. "You're confusing me."

"Never mind, go back to sleep. I'll call you tomorrow from wherever we stop for the night."

"How am I supposed to sleep with talk about the future in my head?"

"I was just rambling. I'll call you tomorrow."

She hummed. We shared a couple of calming words and rang off.

I was packed and ready by six-thirty—ready to get the damned trip over with. After a routine breakfast and a taxi ride to the funeral home, I paid the storage fee, and we were gassing up by eight o'clock. I made a quick visit to an adjacent diner, had the Thermos topped off, and we were on the highway.

The plan was to stop for the night in Klamath Falls just inside the Oregon border. It was Sunday, March 23. It would be just short of two weeks by the time we were back in Portland—seemed longer, another lifetime in a way. In addition, I would be returning with a different mindset than when I'd left. It would be as if I was a kid again coming home after summer camp and feeling out of place by being back home. But as Nadine had asked: Then what?

As Johnnie pushed the coach through the flat arid terrain, past scattered rocky mesas, scrub brush, and lumpy dry hills, I pictured the green canopy of trees that enveloped Portland; it would be good to be back in that environment again.

We were passing an Old Dominion freight liner when Johnnie broke the silence. "So, your uncle, how was that for you?"

"You were there."

"Yeah, but I was just an observer. Not kinfolk."

"My uncle, he cried for his brother, the brother he had hated. I haven't, not yet. Cried for my father."

"Will you?"

"Hearing of his death was a gut check, but there's been nothing more. So, no, there'll be no tears. Time to get this over with. Don't you think?"

"This snakebite of a trip? Am I glad it's near over? Mostly. But not totally. You must be relieved though."

I pinched my nose and squinted out through the windshield. "Guess so."

"This here's been the weirdest happening in my life. But I wouldn't have missed it."

I looked over at her. "Jonalynn Gates, damn! You are bold as brass and fearless. Frankly, this trip has been a head shot for me. But you saw me through all of it."

She shook her head. "I was just the navigator, but you had to face the music. I mean, you read them letters. You had to know there'd sure enough be some bad reactions to what he wrote, your dad."

"I was too detached to think that way. Never imagined my old man's deviousness would drag me back through my own back water."

"We'll be back soon. You can sleep it off."

"Don't think so."

"And why not?"

"For one thing, we're not done yet. There's one more letter to deliver. And we still have to put him in the ground."

"Already arranged. A graveside service and a burial next to your mother. What else?"

I let out a short breath. "There are other things to sort through."

"Hey lookie there," she broke in, "just when I was getting hungry, we got us a stop-for-a-minute place."

There were just four buildings: a tiny post office, a one-bay volunteer fire department, a boarded-up building, and a general store with a gas pump; the sign also said Food. We had just stumbled into Madeline, California, population not noted. The general store, likely built in the late 1800s, had a Western movie false front and a well-worn wooden porch with posted signs touting Old Gold cigarettes and Sky Chief gas.

We left the coach out front, entered the store through a complaining screen door, and inhaled musty air. We didn't see him at first; then he rose up from behind an ancient glass-encased counter. I say rose up, but it was more like a slow eruption. The man looked to be in his sixties and had enough flesh and bone to make two strong men. He was bearded, had shaggy hair, and wore very thick smudged glasses.

He leaned muscular slab hands on the counter and in a voice out of a barrel said, "What can I do for you?"

"Well," I began, "a couple of things. First we'd like a bite to eat, and next we'll be needing a toilet."

He nodded his big head and looked between us. "That a hearse you drove up in?"

"It is," I answered. "We're transporting a body back home. To Portland."

He nodded again. "Interesting. Had a fella in here an hour or so ago asking if I'd seen a hearse go by."

My throat constricted. I turned my head toward Johnnie; she squinted. "You don't say." I tried to sound calm. "What did he look like?"

The man studied both of us for a moment. "Stocky. Serious. Baseball cap. Other'n that one question, didn't say much. After I filled his pickup with gas, he left. Headed north."

"The pickup, what was it?"

The big man cleared his throat. "Chevy. Green Chevy." When I didn't respond, he asked, "That ring a bell?"

I just shrugged. "Maybe."

"Okay. Well, if you're still interested, I can rustle up something for you to eat. My menu's limited though. I serve one thing, my NCO burger, which you can wash down with a bottle of Schlitz or a Royal Crown Cola. I'll add a slice of American on that burger if you like. That's it."

"Sounds good. What's the NCO stand for?"

He finally showed us a smile. "That'd be because of the railroad we're famous for. The Nevada, California, and Oregon Railway. Madeline here was an important stop back when this place was all promise." He paused. "As far as the toilet, ya go out around the building. You'll see the door with John painted on it in blue letters. When yer done, hold the pull chain down until it's done flushing. It'll quit on ya if you don't."

"Thanks. We'll take two NCOs then, with the cheese, right?" Johnnie nodded, and we agreed on having a beer to go with it.

"Weather's not bad right now. You might like eating outside. I got a table out back, but watch for splinters when you sit down."

We both used the toilet and stood out behind the store waiting until the man brought out the burgers and beers; neither of us commented on the green pickup until then. We sat at the weathered picnic table; splinters were indeed a threat. The cool sun and slight breeze allowed us to enjoy the cheesy burgers and the beer in the outdoor calm of Madeline.

"It's him, isn't it?" Johnnie said, lifting her burger out of a wicker basket lined with wax paper. "Clyde Stone. He's following us."

I chewed on a mouthful of ground beef and cheese, took a swig of Schlitz, and nodded. "Who else could it be?"

"Right. But what's he up to?"

"Damned if I know."

"What if he's lying in wait for us? Might have a gun."

I wiped my mouth with a paper napkin. "For now, he's out ahead of us. So we're likely overthinking this."

"Oh really? Why else would the guy drive all this way, trailing after us, if he isn't up to something? My gawd your father has put us in the crosshairs again! And all we have is that dang bat."

"Let's just keep driving."

We finished our burgers and beers and walked back to the coach. The big man came out on the store's porch and watched the hearse recede into the distance. Klamath Falls was less than three hours away. Where was Clyde Stone? Was he really pursuing us or just on the same road? Yeah, dumb assumption.

Chapter Thirty One.

Half an hour later, we passed through Alturas, cutting across the northeast corner of California on the way into Oregon. We had both been scanning the roadside and checking the side mirrors but saw nothing of Stone's truck. My heart skipped a beat when a pickup with oxidized green paint pulled out of a service station ahead of us, but it was sagging on its springs under a huge load of firewood.

After gassing up, we headed northwest on Route 139, hoping to reach Klamath Falls and drop off the coach by mid-afternoon, then have a quick dinner and be locked into our motel rooms by dark. I couldn't fathom why Clyde Stone was tracking us. I thought we were done. In spite of my father's allegation, I had no evidence that he had taken Nancy Beeman's life, nor could he prove that he hadn't. On that point, we agreed. But there had to be something else on his mind. I recalled his words in that Clovis farm store parking lot when he declared: This is over. Evidently not.

When Johnnie cruised into Klamath Falls, she quickly located the Bennett Mortuary, our final host stop for the Meteor, where we passed off the coach to a young man who drove us to Mann's Motel. Once there we discovered that the town had been invaded by a Future Farmers of America state convention and our two rooms had been reduced to one; we'd have to share. We laughed with relief when we saw that the room had twin beds.

After marking our places by tossing bags on the bed of our choosing, I attempted a collect call to Nadine but got no answer. It was not yet six o'clock. We decided on an early dinner only to find that a small cafe adjacent to the motel was just closing, but we managed to talk the short-order cook into building us a couple of roast beef sandwiches. Along with cold bottles of Hires root beer, we retreated back to the room to dine. I put in a call to Nadine again; this time she answered. I chatted with her briefly while I unwrapped my sandwich, and told her I'd see her tomorrow; I left out any mention of Clyde Stone. When I told her I loved her, she paused before responding with Likewise. We hung up on that note.

Later, after having consumed our fine cuisine, we decided to walk the motel parking lot, stretch our legs—and note if a green pickup was lurking about. It was dark by then, and the temperature was dropping. We strolled around among the cluster of concrete block cottages, all of which were lit up and full of young agriculturists. More than once we were met by teenage boys rushing about between the units, talking and laughing, all wearing dark blue jackets with yellow embroidered patches carrying the FFA logo on it. They were mostly courteous and passed us boring adults swiftly and with no engagement. Why bother?

We saw no sign of Clyde Stone or his pickup. In the quiet of the room, I closed the window curtains and locked the door. We stretched out on the beds, propped up on pillows; I smiled.

"Our final night on the road, it finally comes to this," I said. "Bunk mates."

She harrumphed a laugh. "I promise, I will not get naked in front of you."

"Really? So far that's been the highlight of the trip."

"Humiliating, and you know it."

A clever response was forming when there was a thudding knock on the door. Figuring it was FFA kids choosing the wrong room, I rolled off the bed and opened it. Clyde Stone filled the doorway. He was wearing a red and black checked flannel shirt, an Allis-Chalmers baseball cap shadowed his eyes, and his face was catatonic. When I took a step back, he stepped forward and closed the door behind him. He held a bone-handled hunting knife alongside his right leg. I heard the thump of Johnnie's feet hitting the floor as she got up off the bed, and I sensed her standing off my right shoulder.

I swallowed against the tightness in my chest and pushed out a counterfeit smile. "Stone," I said, my voice not quite failing me. "What are you up to?"

He raised the knife and gestured with it. "Move back. Stand next to her."

I did as he said. Right then a youthful male voice howled outside our room, calling out the name Ronnie! Stone pivoted his head at the sound then turned back, holding the knife out.

He stood still as if he was thinking what to do next. His eyes moved back and forth between us until he said, "Okay, sit on the beds, both of you."

He watched until we were both seated on the ends of the beds before he sat in a side chair and placed his knife on the table. It grew quiet, no sound in the room. We looked at him. He stared at us. Whatever would happen next was up to our uninvited visitor.

"Where's the hearse?" he asked finally.

"You know where it is," I answered. "You followed us from there to here."

He inhaled and took off his cap, which he cupped over the knee of a crossed leg. "So you lock up the dead body wagon every night?"

I planted my hands on my thighs and with more resolve than I felt, challenged, "Come on, Stone, what're you up to? You said you were done with all of this. Coming in here, waving a knife. What's the matter with you?"

He reached for the knife, gripped it, and held it out with the blade pointed up. "Is that what you think? That this is over? Done with?"

"Yes."

He shook his head. "No. The moment you drove that bloody hearse onto my property, there was no way to free me from your old man's allegation."

I matched his head shaking. "We're done with it, we agreed."

He suddenly stood, the cap falling to the floor, and walked over to where I sat. He stuck the tip of the knife against my shirt, into my sternum. My ears rang. I sat up straight but then leaned back away from blade prick.

"It doesn't matter, our agreement. Not a whit."

"Sure it does," I came back.

He pressed the blade point harder. I winced. "She left me." The words came out hoarsely. "Lucille, she moved out, left me. She's gone, you bastard."

"Why?"

He stepped back and lowered his knife hand. "Why?" He laughed a bitter laugh. "Why do you think?"

I let my brain flail around for a moment, then said, "You told her. You told your wife about the letter. Why would…"

"The hell you say!" he bellowed. "I did not."

"Then why did she leave?"

"Because..." He sank to his knees and leaned forward, gripping the knife handle, the blade stuck into the carpet. "Because..." he stammered the words out, "she...she found the letter."

Johnnie and I looked at each other. Neither of us said a word in reaction. We sat unmoving, and waited. While waiting, we once again heard young feet running by our door amidst animated chatter. None of that altered the claustrophobic tension of the room.

After sucking in a gulping sob, Stone dropped the knife, fell back onto his hindquarters, propped himself on outstretched arms, and looked at us. "It was in my shirt pocket...the letter. She found it when she did the laundry."

Again neither of us said a word. Our silence drew a pathetic smile from him.

"I'm sure you're feeling some vindication. Me getting what I had coming, in your minds at least."

I guess I'd been holding my breath, because suddenly I released a burst of air "I don't care what you did or didn't do. I just want you to leave us. Get back in that truck of yours and go. Just go."

He sat up straight, leaned forward over arms folded, still seated on the floor. He ignored my edict. "Lucille, she confronted me the next day, after you'd gone. When I got home from work...from the agency." His voice was dull and speech methodical. "She came at me as soon as I entered the house. Waving the letter. What is this?, she yelled at me. What does it mean? Is this true? She kept screaming and shaking the letter. I reached for her, to hold her, to calm her. She fought me, arms thrashing, clawing at me.

"I had no chance of her listening to me. Letting me explain...to wipe away that monstrous accusation. She was enraged and frightened. I could see the fear in her eyes. Was her husband, the man she slept with, was I a murderer? How do you undo something like that? How could I wipe it away and go back to a clean slate with the one person who had accepted me and wanted to be with me. No questions, just loved me."

I knew I should say nothing. That I should remain quiet and let the man run through his recital uninterrupted. But I spoke anyway—without hesitating. "She left you then, you said. Where did she go?"

He regained his edge. "Where the hell do you think? Back to her family, back to her folks in Clovis. I went there but was literally thrown off the property by Lucille's two brothers. They even followed me home. Came onto my property and faced me down. One of them, the youngest, was carrying a long gun. They threatened me. Warned me that if I tried to make contact with their sister ever again, I would pay a heavy price." He rolled over onto to his side and stood up, gripping the knife by its handle. "So, because of you carrying your dead father into my life, I'm ruined. Everything I had built in that little town, my job, my reputation, my land, and finally the love I'd never known—gone."

I jumped up. "You damn fool, why did you keep that letter? You even hunted us down to get our copy. What were you thinking?"

His face slackened, and a slight, bitter smile formed. "Is that what you think? If I'd only burned the letter, all would be good?"

"Well, wouldn't it?"

He took steps toward me, still holding onto the knife. "No."

"Why not?" It was Johnnie who intervened. She had risen from the bed and asked the question cooly.

Stone turned his gaze onto to her. "Because, my good woman, I did kill Nancy Beeman. His father was right."

Johnnie and I stood frozen in place, processing what had just been said. Of course that made me wonder why he had tracked us down. What were his intentions? It was some time before any of us moved. Finally he went back to the table and sat in the same chair, stretching his legs out.

"I was infatuated with her," he said. "Nancy. And I made every effort to appeal to her, but it never worked. She agreed to a couple of dinners out together, but in the end when I told her of my enamored interest in her, she told me clearly that she did not share those same feelings. Never would. That much was obvious to me.

"It was warm, hot even, the evening I tried one more attempt for her to see things my way. To respond to my desire for her. Yes, I was obsessed." He hesitated, seeming to conjure the memory. "I called on her that night, and right away things went badly. She grew angry. I grew angry. My anger was more intense than hers. Her rejection fueled my rage. I overpowered her and...when I left her apartment, she was dead."

My mouth had gone dry. How does one respond when a person admits to something monstrous? And what was his intention after such an admission? A chill ran across my shoulders. I turned to see how Johnnie was taking things; her eyes were focused squarely on Stone, but outwardly she showed none of the trepidation circling in my head. Again, she amazed me.

I knew there was an endgame. There had to be a purpose to him shadowing us. I swallowed dry spit and said, "Now what?"

He massaged his face with one hand. "My plan was to hunt you down," he said. "and make you pay. I had every intention of…"

"Of what?" I said, my voice hyper, "killing us too?"

"Perhaps."

Chapter Thirty Two,

He had considered it, taking our lives.

But he left us that night without exacting the revenge that had been eating at him. He said nothing more after that word, perhaps—just looked at us in silence, played with the knife, then stood, put his cap back on, and walked out. I followed and stood outside, Johnny beside me; we watched until Stone got into his truck. He sat in the pickup cab for a time before grinding the ignition and letting the engine idle then slowly driving away. Johnnie grabbed my right hand and squeezed it hard while releasing a pent-up grunting breath. Then, of course, we laughed hard, a laugh that replaced the dread holed up in our bodies.

Johnnie still had her bottle with a modest amount of bourbon in it. We would have welcomed an entire bottle right then, but we took solace in the drams we had. The evening passed with us sitting at the table, quietly discussing what had just happened, unsure if there would be more trouble facing us. At one point, Johnnie uttered that she had been wanting that damn bat when Clyde Stone was twirling his knife. Finally, we stretched out on the beds, with the door lock engaged, and fell into our own thoughts. During the night, we took turns using the bathroom, readying ourselves for sleeping—if indeed we could. I doubt that either of us actually did sleep; I didn't, other than dropping off only to then suddenly waken from an abrupt snort and circle my tongue in a dry mouth. Light began to show through the curtains at daybreak. However, by that time we had both been awake for some time; each had showered, gotten dressed, and packed. Thankfully, there was no sign of Clyde Stone's pickup when we stepped outside.

I turned in the key at the motel office; the kid at the counter agreed to call us a cab to arrive in forty-five minutes. We left our bags in his care and walked across to the White Pelican Cafe. The place was busy with travelers and locals. We sat at the only empty table, and before we could even look at the menu a young woman arrived with two cups and a pot of coffee, smiled, filled our mugs, and suggested their cowboy skillet special. We enjoyed the hearty fare and said nothing more about Clyde Stone.

The taxi arrived and delivered us back to the mortuary. Preparations for a funeral later that day were underway, so I respectfully went into the office, expressed our appreciation, paid the agreed storage fee. Johnnie rolled up in the coach. I settled onto the plush seat, leaned back, and sighed. We were on our way. In six hours or so we would be back in Portland, and I would sleep in my own bed again.

We were making good time on the open road, with long straight stretches and light traffic, when we approached the small unincorporated town of Chemult. It was a village we would never forget, because just on the edge of town, at the pullout to a service station and garage, stood a cluster of emergency vehicles. An Oregon State Police patrol car sat near the edge of the highway, along with a local fire truck and a Klamath County Sheriff's car; all were parked with their emergency lights flashing. I was too busy rubber-necking to note the pickup parked off the highway next to the turnoff berm.

Johnnie saw it first. "My god, that's Stone's truck."

"What the hell! This isn't good. Pull off down there in the middle of the block. I'll walk back to see what's happened."

She eased the coach to the edge of the street and let me out. I shrugged into my sport coat against the chill and hiked back down the highway toward the confusion. I wasn't sure what I'd find, but I felt a tremor of foreboding in my gut. I approached the scene, walked up slowly, and stood back from the assemblage of uniformed men conversing among themselves. A gathering of locals was growing; I moved in among them and tried to appear calm and mildly interested. In actuality, I was very nervous.

"Anyone know what happened?" I asked of a skinny fellow wearing oil-stained coveralls that hung loosely on his frame. I thought that he probably worked at the garage.

He glanced at me then back toward the pickup, tossed a spent cigarette on the ground and heeled it. "Yeah, guy killed hisself."

I froze and looked toward the pickup parked sidewise from the road. Then I saw the silhouette of a person through the driver's side window. He was sitting at the steering wheel, upright and unmoving, head down as if napping. At that moment no one was doing anything about the body of Clyde Stone.

The mechanic kept his eyes on the vehicle. "I found him," he said finally. "Was ready to open the garage when I saw that pickup sitting there." He lit another cigarette and tossed the match. "Figured it was somebody waiting for service or gas or something. You know." He paused and took a big drag on his smoke. "So I walked up and knocked a knuckle on the window. Nuthin. Didn't move er nuthin. Thought he was sleeping. I rattled the door handle. Still nuthin. So I tried the door. It opened, and there was blood all over the floorboard. Guy had cut hisself. His wrists. Real deep. Used a big knife. What we call an Arkansas toothpick."

"Are you sure he's dead?" I asked like a fool.

The guy uttered a cackle. "Oh, he's dead all right. Dead as dead can be. I checked for a pulse, and he was cold as a mackerel. Dead? Yeah."

A heavy woman with dark brown mousey hair said, "Why aren't they doing anything about that poor man?"

"Can't," the mechanic said. "Gotta wait for the county coroner."

I attempted to get closer, but the sheriff's deputy waved me away. After standing around for another few minutes, I turned and walked back. Johnnie was standing behind the coach, waiting. I walked up, placed my hands on her shoulders, and gave her the news. She shuddered, stepped away from me, and looked toward the muddle. We stood in place for a while, discussing what we ought to do. We decided nothing we might do would add clarity to Stone's death.

We walked up the street, away from the direction of Stone's pickup, and talked more about the stark occurrence. I thought that I should make a call to someone. Johnnie was against it, but I did it anyway. I found a telephone booth outside the town's grocery store, located the number for Clovis Farm Bureau Insurance in the county phone directory, and spoke urgently with Billy Smith, the agency manager, about what had occurred. After his shocked intake of breath, I suggested that he call the local county sheriff's office on Stone's behalf. When he asked who I was, I merely said that was all I knew and hung up.

When I came back to the coach, Johnnie was still looking back toward the scene. As far as I could tell, nothing had changed. Evidently the coroner had yet to arrive. She asked about the call; I said it went okay. We hung around for a while longer until we saw a white ambulance arrive and pull off. The coroner was on site, so we decided it was time to leave. I went into a cafe next to the grocery store, had them fill the Thermos with coffee, and we left.

We were maybe a mile away from Chemult when Johnnie finally raised the question. "We're guilty, aren't we? Of him killing himself."

"You're not guilty of anything," I said.

"Come on, you know what I mean. If we hadn't delivered that dang letter, had not stopped there, in Farwell, he'd be alive. Still have the life he claimed. You know."

I sipped coffee from a Thermos cup and gave myself a moment to think.

"Guess so. Sure as hell isn't the finest day I've ever had." I looked over at her, driving with one hand, seeing the profile I'd gotten so used to, and felt a pang of regret on her behalf. "Sorry," I said. "For all of this. It's one thing to be the driver, another to be sucked into the tragic consequences of my father's scheme."

I filled a cup for her. She downed the coffee in two swallows and handed it back to me. "Like my dad says, If you're in, you're in. I'm in. Have been since Jupiter. So let's drop all of the baloney about me being a tragic figure in all this. My question is, how will this play out?"

"I don't know. If his wife kept the letter, it might raise some eyebrows. But if she hasn't already, the moment she hears about his death, she'll burn that blasted piece of paper for sure."

"Erase him from her life then?"

"Probably. Still, there'll certainly be talk about town of why her husband committed suicide. I doubt Lucille Stone will be thinking much about us."

"She'll remember us, the funeral coach and all. Don't you think?"

I bit down. "Could be, likely will. But even if she makes any connection, I don't think she'll drag the story out in the open." I massaged the idea. "No, Lucille Stone, or whatever name she'll use, will hole up and avoid any public scrutiny."

Johnnie shook another cigarette out of her pack and punched in the lighter. Once she lit up and blew a stream of smoke toward the open wing window, she said, "Being in this business, we are often privy to the stories of people who lived wasted lives: Those who achieved nothing because they just didn't, and others who had the opportunity but botched it. I see Clyde Stone that way."

"So you're giving us a pass?"

She puffed on her cigarette and hummed. "No. That letter was the spark after all. And we delivered it."

I screwed the cap back on the Thermos and set it on the floorboard. Up ahead the highway ran on, the roadside scenery flashed by, seasoned with the smattering of traffic out ahead and that which dribbled past us in the opposite direction. I thought of what Johnnie had said, and as I'd done after every letter delivered, regretted that I had been the bearer of ill tidings. But then again, we weren't done; letter number seven was in the glove box destined to be delivered to an unsuspecting soul in Portland. How soon could I remove Clyde Stone from my head to do that? Probably never. His saga would be etched in my brain from then on—along with my role in it.

"I wonder," I spoke softly, "how long it takes to expire from cutting yourself like Stone did?"

"Expire? It's okay to say die," she said. "I've seen a few dead folks who killed themselves like that. Depends on how deep..."

"The fellow who found him said the cuts were deep."

"Also depends on finding a person before it's too late. Stone probably sat there in his truck all night."

I nodded. "Must have been awful, sitting there alone, in the dark, feeling your life drain away."

She stubbed out her cigarette in the ashtray. "He was probably unconscious before feeling anything like that."

"Still, imagine his dying thoughts. The one person who loved him for who he was, not only gone from his life, but she had disposed of him as well."

"He paid the price then, didn't he?"

"He did, the bastard."

She looked over at me. "Harsh. By the way, you didn't shave this morning."

"Didn't feel like it." I rubbed at the stubble. "I'll beg forgiveness later."

"Your wife won't care a bit. Just seeing her guy will be enough. Even though you've spent all this time in the company of another woman."

"She knows about that, of course."

She reached out to punch me on the arm. "The taking off my clothes part, we'll be keeping that quiet, right?"

"I don't remember any such thing."

Chapter Thirty Three,

The miles passed. We spoke little; what more was there to say? In between brief moments of dozing, I thought of the trip being on its final leg and of reuniting with Nadine and getting back on the job, back at my desk. Part way, I took another look at the last letter to be delivered, read it for a third or fourth time, was even more dismayed by its content. That moment forced me to recall the image of seeing Clyde Stone sitting cold and dead in his pickup. My father's letter had most assuredly led to Stone taking his life, deserved or not. Every letter had brought about grief, anger, and despair. But I'd lived up to my agreement, had I not? Miserably so.

It was three o'clock by the time we cruised into Biggs Junction, an isolated fuel and food stop that intersected with the Columbia River on the Oregon side. After refueling, we dropped down onto Highway 30 and headed west, cruising along at the edge of the wide river viewing across at the Washington side, seeing the rolling hills, hunched, barren, and brown. We had just entered the monumental Columbia Gorge, 80 miles of road running, as we were, from east to west through dry terrain until merging with green forest and immense basalt cliffs hosting a medley of waterfalls. It felt comforting to sit back, watch the river flow by, and see those hills, with their rolling hulk of earth blanketed by brown grassland across the way. It was all familiar and evidence that our odyssey was winding down.

I was so engaged when Johnnie broke into my reverie. "Read it to me. The letter. The last one."

I studied her determined face before reading my father's final message aloud. The letter, addressed to a Portland woman, was not one of apology;

rather it was another accusation.

When I'd finished, Johnnie's hands were rigidly gripping the steering wheel. "Lordy," she said. "Did your old man know anyone, any human being at all, that he hadn't wronged or who hadn't done something cruel themselves?"

"Seems not." I put the letter away.

We'd gone maybe ten more miles when we came up on one of the most breathtaking points along the Columbia River: Celilo Falls. A magnificent churning waterfall cascaded over basalt cliffs that rose up out of the river itself. From that craggy point, the local native Indian tribes congregated on the rocky shore or stood on precarious wooden platforms built out over the turbulent waters to fish for, net, and spear runs of salmon, an act they had done for over 10,000 years. But soon a bridge and then a dam would be built across the river; the powerful current would slow and rise behind a concrete barrier to submerge Celilo Falls for all time. Sad to think of.

Still, peering out at that terrain I knew so well was calming in spite of the pending ecological tragedy. The bargain I'd struck with my father had nearly been fulfilled. The images from the miles covered and the unique people we'd called on had claimed space in my mind that might fade but never withdraw. Now I had to consider how I would reclaim myself.

"I wish I could talk to my dad," I said suddenly, as we moved past Celilo Falls. "Just for a while. Things I'd like to clear up."

"I've heard that regret before," Johnnie responded. "Usually it's the sons wanting more time. Just give me ten minutes with my old man, five even. What would you say to him?"

I put both palms over my face and scrubbed. "Before this trip, not a thing. Didn't care. But after being suckered into his conspiracy and facing all those people, I'm festering with words I'd like to get out."

"Such as?"

"Such as?" I scooted up in the seat. "Such as?" I repeated. "All right, I wish I could stand nose-to-nose with him, stick a finger in his chest, and yell, what the hell, you bastard! Sucking me into your damn scheme." I stopped the rant and saw a quizzical look on Johnnie's face. "But mostly, why. Why he did it, entangled me the way he did. Sure, I'd read all of those damn letters and was stunned what he'd written but…but the full brunt of them didn't register. The pain and ire they could cause, I didn't suspect the price that might be exacted in the process." I inhaled and went on. "I knew who I was, or thought I knew, had life squared away—now what?"

"So, you and you father never had a face-to-face like that? I know you weren't close, but did you talk? About…about anything: life, feelings?"

"Feelings?" I hummed a laugh. "Nope. No heart-to-heart father-son confessionals. Conversations with my father were really just one-way pronouncements about him: his facts, his criticisms, his achievements, his opinions on anything. Him telling me what he wanted to tell me, perhaps asking me if I'd done something he expected. He never congratulated me for something I accomplished, certainly never asked me how I was or how I felt—never. Certainly never comforted me when it was called for."

"Did he ever say he loved you? Give you a hug or anything? Or did you in return?"

I hesitated, thought backward. "We didn't express ourselves that way. Not our custom. I have no warm memories of him growing up."

"What about your mother?"

"Damn, that's not a fair question, mixing us in with her. Mom was forced into parallel lives between her husband and her son. She loved me totally. I felt that. And I think she mostly cared for my dad. But neither of the men in her life treated her with affection. Oh, I loved her. I just never got around to expressing it. What does that make me?"

"How should I know? I've got my own family issues—as I've told you. After my brother, I'm next in line for whatever warmth is still hanging around."

"My mother," I spoke around her. "She deserved better. Now that I realize what I didn't give her, it's too late. Too damn late."

"How did your mother endure living with your father's indifference?"

"I should know that, shouldn't I? Sure I saw it, didn't like it, but never intervened. Guess I was too caught up in my own war of wills with my old man. Too focused on myself to consider her despair. There it is, my confession."

There was a long moment of quiet between us. When drops of rain began to hit the windshield, she reached for the wiper switch and said, "What about Nadine?"

"What about her?"

"I don't know, guess I'm wondering if she married into the same booby trap."

The rain became a downpour; big drops bounced in front of the coach off the asphalt. I swallowed my chagrin at her heedless remark and watched the wipers fight the cloudburst. By the time we rolled past the town known as The Dalles the rain had subsided, the sun had reappeared, and the roadway had begun to steam. As Johnnie slowed the coach for traffic ahead, I looked out at the river, still considering her blunt assumption, and caught sight of a big ferry, with its pilot house amidships, transporting a covey of cars and one farm truck across to the Washington side. When the bridge went in there'd be no need for ferries.

Facing the side window, I asked, "Why would you say that?"

"What?"

"About Nadine."

When she didn't respond, I turned my head to look at her. She was chewing on her lower lip. "Come on, Michael, I've been with you for all these miles."

"So?"

"You've said stuff...we both have talked about stuff in our lives. Gad, we've kicked your dad down the road like an empty soup can. And he had it coming." She pulled out, drove around an old sedan that was spewing out blue smoke, and passed it. "I told you things, and you did the same."

"Booby trap," I echoed. "So I'm a duplicate of my father?"

"I don't know." She shut off the wipers chattering on dry glass. "Just crossed my mind. Are you?"

I stared out at the river and momentarily became mesmerized by the whitecaps that dotted the water due to the persistent Gorge winds. Nadine. Her maiden name was Colson. I asked her to marry me right after I graduated from college. Her brother and I had been good friends; we met on a double date he'd set up. She was three years younger, cute, laughed at all my jokes, and stared at me wide-eyed—like I was something special.

Thinking back on it, our marriage had been just another scheduled act in my life, but a fairy tale for Nadine—or so I assumed. I see now that I had entered into our marriage as if I were the gift and she my agreed-to duty. I shuddered, thinking of the years of parading around in my arrogance expecting Nadine to bask in my aura and accept my every whim or edict.

"It was an historic day," I said suddenly.

"What's that mean?"

"Nadine and I, we were married on May 28 in 1934. It was in all the papers."

"Your marriage?"

"No. That's the day the Dionne quintuplets were born in Canada. Worldwide news. The first time five babies were born to one woman and all survived."

"Interesting." She didn't sound impressed. "How'd that affect your marriage?"

"Well, it didn't except for the jokes about how many babies were we planning on." I paused and recalled the often-held discussion between Nadine and me about babies. "Nadine did fall into a booby trap in that way at least. She wanted a family. I didn't. It was my decree that we not have children."

Johnnie kept driving, nodded her head, but said nothing.

"Why not?" I said. "Because I didn't want anything interfering."

"With what?"

"Ah, that is the question, isn't it? It is so glaringly clear now. Nothing should interfere with my life—except what I wanted. Our lives have really just been about my life. Just like my mother, Nadine has been part of the background. And having children didn't serve my vanity. That and the ghost of the brother who never was. How's that sound?"

"How should I know?"

I ignored the remark. "Nadine has been present merely to validate my own self-worth. All this time."

"What about her? What has she been doing, you know, with her own life?"

I thumped a closed fist on the dashboard. "That is the question. And guess what?"

"You don't know."

"Correct."

The skies opened up once more as we passed the small town of Hood River. Johnnie had to turn on the wipers again, which evidently gave her time to collect her thoughts. "You've known this for how long?" she said after a bit. "Having no idea of what your wife does with her life would you say?"

"I haven't had her life goals on my mind—ever. And if not for this outlandish trip, my wife's unfulfilled life would not have been a point of discussion. I've been oblivious. "

"Geez, Michael, it's just a trip, a strange trip, but not your life."

"Oh, but it is."

Chapter Thirty Four.

It was in those last miles when settling the score won out. From the very start of the journey, I knew that my father intended me to be maneuvered into comparing my own shortcomings to his; I felt that early, and so acknowledged, but now I conceded—he prevailed. And worst of all was the comparison of our lamentable marriages. My marital alliance stood for everything and for nothing. I said so to my road partner.

"Why am I telling you all of this?" I asked her.

"Because I'm here, there's no one else. You could kill me later. Then no one will ever know."

"Nadine has always been self-assured," I said, ignoring her jibe. "Rather unflappable, to my mind."

"Why? Because she never stood her ground? Did she ever take you on, disagree with you?"

"We've never really had disagreements."

"Really? That can't be true. No disagreements? No arguments?"

I shook my head. "Takes two. Can't remember her taking me to task. Not in all these years."

"Truly amazing, strange even. Even as a kid, I witnessed husband and wife dustups between my folks. My mother would hang back, hold her tongue, sometimes for weeks, months even. Then, when she'd absorbed more than her fair share, she'd stand in front of Dad, stick a finger in his chest, and reclaim her rights." She laughed. "She was as petite as I am not, so it was funny to watch her big man get red and backpedal. Then it would be over. Things would calm until she had to take him to the woodshed again."

"No woodsheds for me. Of course, there should have been. Even so, I probably wouldn't have gotten the point of grievances voiced by Nadine—or understood any criticism directed my way."

The rain was steady now. We were in the green part of the Gorge, with intermittent waterfalls surging off of basalt cliffs. I gazed through the rhythm of the wipers and wondered: would I reconnect with my wife after this misadventure?

When we rolled into Portland, it was right at end of day, under clouds and a steady rain. I directed Johnnie to the Sellwood neighborhood where Nadine and I lived in a two-story foursquare on Sellwood Boulevard. The house stood on a bluff overlooking a wetlands and beyond that the Willamette River and beyond that the lights of the city. It was the house in which I had been raised. Like I said, when they moved to Florida, my parents deeded the place to me. As their only heir, I accepted, and we moved into the house I had been so accustomed to. Of course it had been my decision to sell our house in northwest Portland so I could move back into my boyhood home. Nadine went along with little or no objections, as I recalled. More evidence of my control.

Johnnie parked at the curb and waited, engine running, windshield wipers in motion, while I stepped out of the coach, opened the side door, and reached in to retrieve my bag. I placed a hand on the casket one more time and thought again of the human remnant within. I turned to see that the porch light was on and felt comfort from the familiar illumination cast by the living room lamp. I thought that Nadine would be expecting me. How would it be, seeing her now? Johnnie and I had agreed that we would deliver the last letter the next morning, depending on my making contact with the recipient that evening. And that would be the end of it, except for a perfunctory graveside procedure, placing my father alongside my mother, thus fulfilling the bargain I'd struck.

"Why don't you come meet Nadine?"

"Nah, this is your homecoming. I'll meet her later." She looked at me from behind the steering wheel and smiled. "Go on now. You're getting wet."

I smiled and slapped the coach's rooftop with an open hand. "I'll call as soon as I confirm a time for the last drop-off." We both nodded. "And Johnnie, thanks. For everything. It will seem strange to not have you close at hand."

"I know. Same here. Tomorrow then."

I watched her drive away and kept the coach in sight until it disappeared from view. It was an odd feeling, being separated from the person who'd been my alter ego for the past two weeks. After standing immobile, staring at where the coach had been, getting wet, rain dripping from my brow, I finally took the stairs up to the wide porch and reached for the latch. It was locked. We never locked the door, not in Sellwood. There was a moment of hesitation before I twisted the brass doorbell set in the door. It clanked. I felt like a door-to-door salesman—at my own door.

Then there she was in the doorway, silhouetted by the hall light behind her. The porch light highlighted her face, which after the briefest moment reclaimed the familiarity I knew so well. I actually had a feeling of shyness standing before my own wife. I smiled like a foolish suitor and realized how disheveled I looked in my travel-weary clothes, unshaven, and needing a haircut.

The first thing she said was, "Sorry, I've locked the door ever since you told me that man who called might be dangerous. Is he still threatening you?"

"No." I shook my head. "I'll tell you the whole story later."

She looked up into my face, her eyes slightly widened. Right then I was struck, just looking at her. I'd been re-imagining her face for many miles and was gratified to have my imagery of her validated: her large blue eyes, shoulder-length brown hair, pleasantly shaped nose, lovely mouth, and mostly her warm demeanor. The latter had always been there—if I had taken the time to notice. She was dressed nicely, more so than her daily around the house attire; she was expecting me. I took a moment to actually see what she had on: a pleated beige skirt, a wide brown belt at her narrow waist, and and a soft woolen forest green crewneck sweater.

"What is it?" she asked and looked down at her clothing.

I flushed, feeling embarrassed to be admiring her. "Nothing. I was just noticing how nice you look."

She looked at me as if she couldn't quite make out what I'd just said. Her eyes fluttered for an instant. "Oh, thank you." There was a pause between us. "Well, welcome home." She stepped back, encouraging my entry; an odd gesture in my own home.

I gripped my bag and went into the house I knew so well but where I now strangely felt a visitor. Then the familiar scent of our space made me smile, the comfort of it. I stepped into the living room doorway, looked around at the furniture, and set my bag on the floor. When I turned around, Nadine was standing just behind me, a benign smile on her face. For a moment, I thought How do I do this? Had I ever had such concern before? Never, not even when I was dating this woman, later to become my wife, had I considered how best to be with her, how to treat her. Now after all that had gone through my mind about us during the last two weeks, I was hesitant.

"Nice to be back," I said.

She kept her gentle smile. "You survived."

"Yes, I survived."

"What do you want first? Dinner, a bath, a change of clothes?"

I held my own flat smile. Was this lackluster exchange typical of how we usually conversed? I knew it was. The idea was dispiriting and sadly predictable.

"How about this." I stepped toward her, took hold of her shoulders, pulled her to me, and kissed her mouth gently yet intently and held her in my arms. It was nothing I hadn't done before, but this time I felt something different. I felt something that had been missing for some time—desire for my own wife.

When we stepped back, she looked into my eyes and openly examined me. She tilted her head to the side as if getting a kiss and a hug from me was unexpected. Maybe it was out of the norm; oddly I couldn't say. When was the last time I had kissed her? I could recall giving her a peck on the cheek before I left for the airport to fly to Florida. That was all.

"So," she said, speaking softly. "What now? Food?"

I pulled on my right earlobe, absorbed her tepid reaction, and said, "No."

Chapter Thirty Five,

Nadine paused when I said No. "What then?" she rejoined.

"I can eat and take a bath later. Right now, I'd like for us to talk."

"About the trip?"

"Partly about the trip, but more importantly about us."

Her smile fell away. "Us? What does that mean?"

I gestured, and she followed me into the living room. We sat on the sofa once purchased from Nolf's furniture store in Sellwood because we had liked the plush wine colored fabric and soft cushions. It had been one of the few choices we'd made together. I turned sideways to face her; that maneuver caused a heightening of her wariness.

"I've always liked this sofa," I said.

"Michael, what is it?"

"Nadine, I need to get something off my chest. May I?"

Her blue eyes seemed even bluer. She finally dipped her head, granting me permission to say whatever it was. I ran a hand over my damp hair and began. As I spoke, I could sense that she had no idea where I was going; she sat quietly, her hands resting in her lap. I gambled on how to address this new understanding of how I had squandered my marriage—new to me, probably not her. As my words of stumbling confession came out, her expression went from wondering to anxious. I could see the question in her eyes: What did this mean? What was I getting at?

Was I frightening her? I likely was, but I went on until I said all there was. When I finally stopped, we sat quietly, the only sound being the ticking of my father's old longcase pendulum clock.

"So," I said at last, "that's it...I suppose. Do you understand that I'm asking for your forgiveness? Desperately."

She remained still—staring at me, disbelieving it seemed to me. Maybe not understanding, I wasn't sure. We sat that way, looking at each other; I decided to wait her out, let her respond when she was ready. I swallowed nervously a couple of times. My eyes were blinking too fast. I felt the need to take a deep breath. When she reached out to take hold of my hands, I was near tears brought on by the waiting.

"My," she whispered, "there is much to absorb, isn't there?"

I exhaled. "Do you love me? I've never known for sure. I guess I never needed to know. That's horrible, isn't it?"

"Michael, I am your woman. Your wife. Yes, I love you."

"But do you understand what I've said?"

She smiled. "Of course I do."

"I'm so sorry, Nadine. For the years we've lost. Time lost to you, and the more fulfilled life you could have had."

She sat erect; her smile faded. "Yes, there is that. And I have resented it, many times. But then I went on. What else?"

I grabbed her and clutched her. She was rigid; she did not blend into my embrace. "Why didn't you fight back?"

She pushed away, a small laugh came out. "That is amusing. Can you imagine me speaking my mind to you, Michael? You would have looked at me as if I was an insubordinate employee. You wouldn't have understood, not a word of any assertion I might have made."

"And still you loved me?"

"Mostly. Not always. There were times when I had to fight my way back from my anger to caring for you."

"My god, how have you done it? How would you describe your life?"

"And now we come to it, the nub of our relationship, our marriage. When your husband has to ask you what has your life been like for the past eighteen years, something is amiss."

I shook my head but had no response to that stark reality.

"What now?" she said, changing the subject. "About your father?"

I sniffed and wiped at my nose. "There's one more letter to deliver. Then we'll bury dad and it's over."

"Who's the last letter for?"

I rose and went to my bag and pulled out the envelope, slightly bent, and handed it to her. She slipped a finger under the flap, pulled the letter out, and read it. When she was done, she looked at me.

"Do you know this woman? Katherine Smythe?"

"No. She's just an another recipient, someone else my father had reason to scold on his way out."

"Were all of the letters like this one? Because this accusation is horrid."

"Some were, some weren't—those that weren't were dad seeking forgiveness for acts of his own abysmal behavior. The most troubling were those people whom he accused, like the man who called you."

"Whatever happened to him?"

I hesitated. "Clyde Stone was his name. He's dead. Committed suicide." The image of his body in the pickup, dead and cold, came to mind.

She sat back and stared into my face. "Suicide?"

I nodded.

"Because of the letter?"

"The letter caused his life to disintegrate in a way. So, yes. If we hadn't delivered it to him, might he still be alive? I think so. Then again, what he had done was even worse than what you read in the letter to Katherine Smythe."

She shook her head then handed the letter back to me and stood up. "Let's feed you. I made your favorite, chicken and dumplings. Then you can have a nice hot bath and be back in your own bed."

"First I need to contact the woman and set up a time to call on her tomorrow." I held the letter. "Are we okay? Have I made my plea clear?"

She tipped her head back; her expression was one of having turned a page of some sort. "It's a start, isn't it?"

"A start?"

"Yes. In its own way, it's a gift."

A gift. Somehow I felt the worse in deserving that comment. Mending what I had wrought, that would take time.

The clock on the desk in the parlor read 8:25 when I dialed Katherine Smythe. After four rings a male voice answered, evidently the husband. I asked for Mrs. Smythe and was told to wait a moment. Then she came on the line, Yes? I considered the crisp voice of the person to receive the final letter. When I didn't speak immediately, she said Is someone there? The tone was of a person who brooked no antics.

"Yes," I answered, feeling a moment of breathlessness like I'd experienced with each previous call. "Is this Mrs. Smythe? Katherine Smythe?"

"Yes. Who is this?"

"My name is Michael Sanborn."

There was a brief hesitation. "What is it you want? Are you selling something?" No nonsense allowed.

"No." I offered a chuckle to counter her suspicion. "Not selling anything. I wonder, Mrs. Smythe, if you might remember my father, Randolph Sanborn?"

At first, she said nothing then, "Sanborn," she said guardedly. "Yes, maybe I do. Randolph, you say?"

"That's right."

"It's been some time. What is it you're calling about?"

"It's a personal matter. I wonder if I might call on you tomorrow? Perhaps in the midmorning hour?"

"Personal? But I haven't seen your father for many years. Whatever is this about?"

"I have something to give you from my father."

Another moment of hesitation. "What is it?"

"A communication that I would like to deliver personally."

After several more minutes of pausing and wondering and curiosity, she acquiesced to seeing me at 10:30 the next morning—but just briefly, I was advised.

I reached Johnnie at the mortuary, and she agreed to pick me up at 10:00 the next morning. Though it had been less than two hours, her voice was familiar and reassuring.

Then I had my first home-cooked food in two weeks. As Nadine had promised, I enjoyed my favorite meal: chicken and dumplings. After two helpings, a green salad, and a glass of chianti, I followed that scrumptious meal with a hot bath and nearly fell asleep in the warm soapy water. Even putting on fresh pajamas was a luxurious treat.

When I walked into our bedroom she was there, sitting at the vanity table brushing her hair, as she always did, and wearing a nightgown; I guess it was an aquamarine, maybe cotton, not sure. Hell, I never took note of what she wore, let alone her nightwear. I stood in the bedroom doorway and watched her go through the motions, a nightly exercise I was sure. She caught sight of me in the vanity mirror and lowered her brush. We looked at one another via the mirror for a long moment before she turned on her seat and faced me. I smiled, she smiled. Finally she stood and said, "Feel good, being all clean and scrubbed, wearing fresh jammies?"

I smiled and walked to her. Up close we looked into each other's eyes. I saw again what I'd overlooked, ignored, even excluded from my daily existence: that she was a beautiful woman, a person of substance. When I reached out for her she remained still, her eyes questioning, eying me curiously when I took her hands in mine.

"You must be tired," she said in a voice that seemed a buffer between us.

"I am bushed." I released her hands and drifted over to our bed, pulled the bedding back on my side, and turned to my wife. She stood but remained where she was, so I slid in between the sheets on the left side as always, pulled up the eiderdown quilt, and reached up to turn off my bedside lamp.

The bed dipped a bit when she got in on her side. After a moment, she turned off the lamp next to her, throwing the room into darkness—and there we were. I turned on my back and stared up, considering what getting into bed with my wife had been like only two weeks ago. I knew the usual course of events each night: I was a hard sleeper, so I turned off the light immediately on getting under the covers. She on the other hand was a light sleeper and tended to read before sleeping, often fitfully. On this night she had not reached for the book on her nightstand nor left the light on. I crossed my arms on top of the bedding and my mind ran through thoughts of intimacy. How long had it been since she and I had made love? And what did that mean? But of course I knew; we made love when I was in the mood, as was my prerogative, right?

When I reached out, I found that she was lying on her side, facing away from me. I turned on my side behind her back and rested my left hand on her shoulder. She didn't move, but I was sure she wasn't yet asleep, that much I knew of her. I felt the warmth of her skin and its smoothness and knew that I had not often reached out to let her know that I wanted her and to earn the privilege of sharing her body—and not just because I could. I kept my hand resting on her, gently circling my thumb, to no response.

"You there?" I said.

"I am. Not drowsy yet."

"Me either. Can we talk?"

"About what?"

"Us."

"We did that, didn't we, just a while ago?"

"There's more to say."

She turned toward me. "Like what?"

I hesitated. "Children?"

She sighed. "Michael, we had that conversation. Ages ago."

"I know, but didn't you want children?"

"Why do you ask now?"

"It was my choice to not have a child, wasn't?"

"You know the answer to that."

"I do, of course. Would you want to now?"

"Much too late, besides I decided against it some time ago."

"Why?"

She grew quiet, then said, "Raising a child requires a willing partner."

"And I was not that person."

"No. You were not. You said as much back in the moment we considered it."

"I'm sorry. I really am."

She reached out and placed a hand against my chest. I ceased talking. We both were silent, two people: wedded partners, lovers when my manhood called for it, and sharers of the same abode. But we had become separate people living more parallel than together. My mind drifted at that point; I was reimagining that I was back in the coach, somewhere in Arkansas, I thought.

"What is happening?" she asked on a whisper, pressing gently against my chest.

How to put it into words. "I was recalling a moment, on the trip."

"Something upsetting?"

"In a way," I answered. "Yes, in a way it was...and is. We were in Arkansas. Pine Bluff. We'd stopped for the night, Johnnie and I. We each called home. Do you remember?"

"No, not really. You made several calls."

"It was before you knew that Johnnie was a female."

She took her hand away. "Maybe I do remember that. It was early in the trip."

"Yes."

"What about it? You regretting not telling me about her?"

"Well, yes, but that's not what I'm thinking of."

"All right, what then?"

I closed my eyes and took in several slow breaths. "It was then, during that phone call, that I began to recognize my own mistakes."

"My, my, new behavior."

I inhaled. "A well-deserved observation. I remember the caustic judgement you gave me on that call, saying the trip was a travesty. Remember?"

"Vaguely. And it was."

"Maybe. But it was also a revelation, an unveiling of past actions I regretted but had long ago set aside. It was right there, in Pine Bluff, that I began to understand some things, but mostly I thought of us and how little I had invested in our marriage."

She held her hand against my chest but said nothing.

"Even when you berated me for, as you put it, running around the country with Dad's body like a last rites tour. I remember your words. They have stuck with me. Because it was then that I saw a bit of the truth about us. For once, you took me to task—you expressed your own opinion, for god's sake."

"I remember that outburst and how I trembled after we hung up."

"But why should you have...trembled?"

She breathed a soft laugh. "And the answer? You've never known how I have had to harbor my feelings, have you?"

"What an arrogant ass. Again, can you forgive me?"

She rubbed my chest. "It's been a long time, Michael."

"Meaning, no?"

"Meaning while you've been out there going through a breakthrough of self-revelation, I've been here living in the same old way, expecting your return to be as things were. And suddenly you come through the door all renewed and seeking a pardon."

"Not good enough?"

"How do I know that you're not just under the influence and after a raging hangover will reclaim your former role in my life?"

I couldn't speak.

"You know, don't you, that we've never had a discussion like this in all of our eighteen years."

Chapter Thirty Six,

I rolled onto my back. Her hand dropped away from my chest. It was quiet in the house. After some time I turned onto my left side, pulled the quilt up over my shoulder, and closed my eyes, not to sleep but to hide out.

At first, I didn't detect her presence, until I felt her breath on my neck. I opened my eyes, to see nothing but to wonder. There it was again. I turned over and sensed her face in the dark; she must have been looking at me in the same way.

"That doesn't mean we can't have more than one conversation every eighteen years," she said.

"I suppose that's true," I responded.

"It is true. And there will be much more to say."

"True again."

She found my left hand and kissed my fingers. "In the meantime, perhaps we can rediscover something else that had been lost...or at least diminished."

I wondered how long it had been since I felt real passion when having sex with my wife. Prior to that night, it had been when I was in the mood, felt the urge; and usually I was abrupt, finished quickly, then to sleep. On this occasion, we rediscovered the elation of exploring our bodies with mutual passion and loving the moment. We awoke in the morning to smiles, holding each other tightly beneath the quilt; she even shrieked when I bit an earlobe.

We shared a tub shower, which was raucous fun; afterward, she scrambled us eggs and cooked bacon while I brewed coffee and made toast. It was an incredibly happy moment. Could it be like that all the time? I didn't know for sure, but maybe.

I dressed in a blue serge suit, white shirt, red tie, and brown wingtip shoes. Back in uniform. When Johnny tapped the horn, I kissed Nadine, a real kiss, retrieved letter number seven, and stepped out onto the porch. There it was, all clean and shiny, the Meteor ready for its final correspondence delivery. The sun was out. Nadine walked out with me to meet the woman I'd shared company with for thousands of miles. Johnnie stepped out of the coach, and they smiled at each other, made pleasant comments about finally meeting one another, and shook hands. A man who lived three houses away, whom I knew only as Bill, happened by, walking his Airedale terrier on a leash. He nodded but said nothing, just strode on by, pulling the poor animal down the sidewalk. The hearse still held its morbid mystique.

And then we left, Johnnie and I. We said little, except that it had been nice to be back in our own beds. I'm sure she was curious about how it had gone between Nadine and me, having listened to my regrets too often and over too many miles. Then again, I wondered about her own return. We discussed the route, across the Sellwood Bridge over the Willamette River, through the city up and over the Vista Bridge into Portland Heights, where the well-to-do lived in stately houses. Johnnie drove slowly, coursing uphill through gentle curves until finding the address we were seeking. It was an immense Colonial, painted in ivory, sitting astride a huge lot carefully landscaped and adorned with hedges and trees and gardens and groomed lawns. Finding a wide driveway, Johnnie pulled up to a four-car garage behind the house and turned off the ignition. We sat quietly, as we had done all of those other times. I pulled the letter from my inside pocket, held it up, the final delivery. She laughed and wished me luck. We shook on it.

I walked across a brick courtyard to what I assumed was the rear entrance and rapped my knuckles on the glass of double French doors. Moments later, a woman came in response and opened one side and peered out at me. She was wearing what looked to be a housekeeper's dress and an apron. I told her who I was and that I had an appointment with Mrs. Smythe. She nodded as if she knew and led me through the house, room after spacious room, past a central staircase, moldings, hardwood floors, and oversized windows into what appeared to be the main living room.

Mrs. Smythe would be with me shortly, I was advised.

I was sitting in an upholstered armchair when I heard the clipped sounds of heels on hardwood and stood. Katherine Smythe was a slender woman. She had large brown eyes, a slight frame, carefully styled short brown hair. She wore a high-necked dress in a dark gray fabric—expensive.

"Mr. Sanborn," she said in rather brittle voice. "Thank you for being prompt. I have a luncheon to attend a bit later."

Of course she did. "Thank you for seeing me. This won't take long."

"Please, be seated," she said, gesturing and sitting across from me on a large white couch.

I sat, holding the envelope down next to my right leg, and gave her my most sincere smile. She tightened her thin lips into a reciprocal smile and folded her hands in her lap. I waited, assured that she would speak if I said nothing; I'd grown accustomed to such an approach.

Finally, after a modest clearing of her throat, she spoke. "Randolph Sanborn. You caught me off guard when you called, as it has been many years since I've seen him."

I merely nodded.

She hesitated. When I didn't carry on from there, she went on. "You said you have a communication for me...from you father?"

"I do."

She brushed something not evident from her dress and said, "You could have mailed it."

"I know, but he wanted me to deliver it in person."

"How odd. Just what is this communication, as you call it?"

I lifted the envelope so she could see it. "It is a letter."

"A letter? From your father?" When I nodded, she added, "Whatever in the world for? Why didn't he deliver it?"

"It's all in his letter."

"I see." She looked at the envelope in my hand as if it were a summons but gave no indication of wanting to accept it.

Finally, I stood and stepped forward and held it out. After an awkward hesitation, she leaned out and took it from me. I returned to the chair and watched this final event unfold. Like others had, she examined the envelope before withdrawing the letter. I crossed one leg and leaned back as she began to read.

RANDOLPH E. SANBORN
FLORHAVEN ESTATES
JUPITER, FLORIDA

February 1952

Katherine Smythe
2131 SW Vista Avenue
Portland, Oregon

Dear Katherine,

Yes, it's me, Randolph Sanborn, a friend and colleague of Walter Rumley's, as you may recall. You also may remember that he and I worked together at the old Ladd & Tilton Bank lo those many years ago. You have just met my son Michael, who brought you this letter. I have recently passed on, dying of a cancer. I'd been living in Florida for some time when my wife Melba died, and soon thereafter I fell ill. Michael agreed to transport my body back to Portland. The proviso being that he make seven stops along the way to deliver letters I had written in the months before my death. The seventh letter being yours. You will note that my remains are resting outside your door at this very moment.

Each of the letters was written to people who played a unique role in my life. You may be wondering how you fit into that picture. Well, some letters were written in an attempt to make amends to people I had wronged. Others were directed to persons deserving redress. I cast you among the latter, Katherine. At the end of this journey, I am here to condemn you on behalf of Walter Rumley, the first man you accepted as your life mate. I wasn't the most admirable friend to Walter. In fact I rue that I did not support him more during those days when you cast him out of your life. No, he wasn't going to rise to be president of the bank, but he was a capable man, and he loved you dearly. But you tossed him aside. You traded him in for more of what you deemed a superior life by marrying more money. He lost everything: you, his daughters, and his self-respect.

I remember painfully the day Walter jumped from the Vista Ridge Bridge, ironically just down the hill from where you live now. I hope this brings that black day back to you as well. It was Christmas Eve 1935. Remember? You took his life away.

May you never forget,
Randolph Sanborn

She read slowly, perhaps going back over certain parts, as others had. At one point she looked up at me, probably when reading that my father had died or that he was parked outside. In the end, she let go of the letter; it dropped onto her lap. She stared across at me. Neither of us spoke. From somewhere in the house came the whir of a vacuum cleaner. We ignored the sound. She looked at the letter again, shook her head, and stood; the letter floated slowly to the floor. From there she turned, took several strides to the large fireplace at the end of the room, and stood in front of a brass fire screen. The vacuum cleaner continued then suddenly ceased. Katherine Smythe stood immobile for some time before suddenly cursing.

"Damn you!" she called out and spun around. "Damn you to hell for this...this invasion of my life."

"I can understand," I responded.

"Oh really. And just how can you understand, Mr. Sanborn?"

I scooted up in the chair. "I don't know, being blind-sided by something this cruel from your past."

"Cruel. And who was cruel in this...in that letter? Your father or me?"

I shrugged. "That's for you to decide."

"Is that right?" Her voice rang out with venom, having lost its cultured bent. "And now you bring him here, to my door. His...body?"

"Yes."

It was just then that a large-bodied, white-haired man wearing a vested gray suit and red and green tartan tie along with a melancholic expression entered the room. He was tall, taller than my six feet. He pushed up on a pair of gold wire-rimmed glasses poised atop a reddish nose and approached Katherine. I assumed he was her husband. She fell against him; he held onto her, and they stood that way for some time, while I tried to appear smaller in the chair.

Eventually he released her and turned to look my way. He smiled sympathetically and walked over to pick up the letter from the floor. After he'd read it, his eyebrows rose; then he placed it on the table in front of the couch.

"Mr. Sanborn, is it?"

"Yes, Michael."

"I'm Thomas Smythe. Welcome." He felt his wife come up behind and reached back to hold a hand, then gestured for her to sit on the couch. She did, and there we were, a triumvirate of disparate points of view on the matter of the contents of a given letter written by a dead man.

"It seems you've traveled far to deliver this letter," the man said.

"It has been quite a trip."

"So it seems. I'm sorry for your father's passing." He paused and seemed to consider me for a moment. "And now, Katherine is the last in line. But you know, she has been expecting this call for redemption for some time. We both have. Since 1935, as noted in your father's letter."

"I don't understand," I said.

"What you father alleges is quite near the truth. As you can see, I am quite a bit older than Katherine. So—"

"Tom, don't," she said.

He kept his eyes on me and reached behind his back to pat the air. "No, my love, this is the moment we've talked about. We may have thought, hoped even, that it would never happen, but here it is." He stood before me and looked down, sadness in his eyes. "You see, Michael, back in those days, Katherine sought to guarantee a good life for her daughters."

"Walter's daughters as well," I broke in.

He smiled benignly. "Of course. That goes without saying. Forgive me."

I nodded, and he went on; his voice had a pleasant baritone modulation to it. He spoke slowly. "They say that truth is something known and admitted to. But does it remain the truth even if it's never acknowledged out loud? That has been our quandary. We, Katherine and I, we knew the truth surrounding Walter Rumley's death."

"Oh, Tom," Katherine broke in, "you knew nothing of it. Nothing of what was happening between Walter and me before you and I met. You were an honorable, kind man who accepted only what you knew of my plight. Or thought you knew."

He turned to look at his wife. "I knew more than you realize, my sweet. You see, Michael," he said, turning once more in my direction. "Sometimes with truth comes confession."

"My word, Tom," Katherine said, rising from the couch and coming to his side and gripping an arm. "Stop this. This man has done what he came to do, and he can now leave us in peace. Be on his way. It is over."

Thomas Smythe stood quietly, a gentle smile still on his lips. He reached out and took his wife's hands in his own. "It will never be over and never forgiven, because the wronged party is no longer in our midst."

Katherine Smythe drew up to her full height, eyes flashing, and slapped her husband across a cheek. He flinched, but his smile remained. He reached for the offending hand and held it to his chest. He looked upon her as one would a son or daughter who had misbehaved in an old-school way. He even raised the hand and kissed its fingers. Still she was having none of his self-reproach.

"I wonder if we could finish this over a cup of coffee in the kitchen," he said. "I'm sure Imogene could brew us up a pot, don't you think, Katherine?"

She stood flat footed, studied her husband's face, finally agreed, and walked off to attend to the matter. Thomas Smythe folded the letter and put it into his breast pocket then gestured for me to precede him toward the rear of the house.

Chapter Thirty Seven.

The housekeeper soon had coffee ready and brought the service over with yet another a plate of cookies; we were all seated at a long walnut table in the spacious kitchen. The woman they called Imogene left us, and in turn, we each filled our cups and doctored them to our tastes. Thomas Smythe took a cookie, as did I, but Katherine did not; her face still that of one aggrieved. We sipped and quietly waited, each alone with our own thoughts.

It was Thomas who broke the calm. "You know, we assumed this day would never come. At least I did. You, Katherine? That we would never have to face our culpability?"

She picked up her cup again, lifted it to her mouth, but did not respond.

"You may not need or even want to hear this, Michael, nor Katherine want it told, but I fear we must." I met his eyes but said nothing. "Very well, then. As I was about to tell you, Katherine is very much younger than I am, some fourteen years as a matter of fact. She is quite lovely, is she not?"

"Oh, Tom!" she spat out in obvious distaste of such a comment.

I held back on responding, merely smiled innocuously.

"To reiterate, Katherine had real concerns about what lay ahead back then and felt her children needed an ensured future that seemed unlikely at the time." He set his cup down and clasped his hands on the tabletop. His smile faded away. "My god, it all seems so cold to me now, spoken out loud. Katherine," he pleaded.

She set her cup down also and drew her lips in. "You big softie," she said. "Leave it to me to go there then, is that right?"

He blinked, and his large face softened.

"All right, Mr. Michael Sanborn," she said looking directly at me. "Here it is. I cared for Walter, but I wasn't in love with him—not after eight years of his struggling to get ahead. He just couldn't build us the kind of life I wanted." She leaned forward. "Here's the cold, hard truth. I wanted more…of everything. Walter would never have been able to give me and my daughters everything. My parents had never taken to Walter, wondered why I'd married him, if you want to know. They had wished more for me than a mid-level banker going nowhere. Cold?"

I nodded. "Yes."

"They connived, my folks, and I with them. It was the Depression. Walter was barely hanging on to the modest job he had. It was hard, as you know. My family had money from my father's inherited wealth, and they wanted nothing less for their only child—me." She sat up and stared hard at me. "You getting the drift here?"

"I guess."

"You guess. Well, here's the rest, the unvarnished devious scheme."

"Oh, I wouldn't go that far," Thomas Smythe roused to say.

"Tom," she snapped, "if we're going this far, we don't get to deny the damn truth. It was a scheme, and you were part of it. Face it, I wanted you because you were wealthy, and you wanted me because I was desirable—I guess."

Thomas reached out to pour himself a fresh cup of coffee; his hand shook, and his face was downcast. His nonresponse to her admission confirmed the truth of it. I sipped my cooling coffee, and she went on.

"The cold truth of it was my parents knew Thomas Smythe, a widower, whose trucking and transportation company had made him a man of means. Even during the Depression, things had to be moved." She closed her eyes and pulled her lips in. "And to connect me with that wealth—and my security—we actually discussed the likelihood that a mutual understanding could be reached. I met Tom at several social functions, and we soon found ourselves attracted to one another. Or rather we accepted what all parties wanted: to get rid of Walter and clear the way for our eventual marriage."

"My god," Thomas Smythe almost sobbed the words. "Please, Katherine."

"Well, that is damn well what we did. We disposed of him."

Thomas Smythe sighed and leaned forward on his elbows.

"How?" I asked.

"You want the grisly truth then. All right, my father, Harvey Brown, if you're taking names, he gave Walter the hard news. To this day, I don't know what he did to convince my husband to grant my freedom from him. I knew an offer of compensation was discussed, but I've never known the outcome of that."

"He refused," Thomas said softly. "He was an honorable man. He would not accept being bought off." He tossed off a little laugh. "Told Harvey to stuff that big fat check."

"I never knew that," she said. "Not surprised. He was principled in that way."

"Have you been happy?" I asked, looking between them. "With the outcome of your scheme."

Neither of them responded to my probe. The coffee was cold, the cookies mostly untouched, and the kitchen was soundless. Off somewhere else in the huge house came a clunking sound: a door closing or some other activity being conducted by Imogene.

"Happy?" Katherine said. "What a question."

"Yes," Thomas responded, "but what is your answer, my love?"

She sat up straighter, looked first at her husband then at me. "Happy. That is a word I haven't considered for some time." She laughed. "I've been too busy being secure and living up to my station in life."

Thomas Smythe's expression collapsed in despair. Everything: his eyes, his mouth, the flesh of his face, revealed a deep sadness. I considered that it was a sorrow that may have been part of him for some time.

The man turned his distinguished head and stared at his wife. "I guess I should acknowledge that reality as well. I knew from the beginning what we had agreed to was a contract of expediency. You see, Katherine, I knew you didn't truly love me, but as you said I offered you and the girls security. But I can now confess that I've never loved you in a passionate way either. But I coveted how you looked on my arm, even though you were often mistaken for my daughter."

She considered her husband, studied his dispirited face, then smiled brightly. "Well, there it is, the unadorned truth. What does that make us? Connivers, manipulators of another person's life?" She clapped her hands. "That is exactly who we are. So, Michael Sanborn, I think your father would be pleased. You have delivered the words he drafted, and its contents have ripped away any sense of decency to which we have felt entitled."

Just then the housekeeper entered the kitchen. Thomas Smythe looked up, waved a hand. "Not now, Imogene. Not now." The woman nodded slightly and went away.

There was something more that I wanted to know. "If I may?" I inquired.

"What more is there?" Katherine said, her smile cold and insincere.

"That Christmas Eve, 1935, when Walter died…"

"You mean when he jumped to his death off the bridge," she bore in.

"All right, then. When did you learn of his death?"

Thomas Smythe put a hand to his chin and leaned on an elbow; he closed his eyes. Katherine's smile was fixed, and it seemed she wasn't breathing.

Finally she expelled a breath and said, "The next day. Like everyone else, we saw it in the morning edition of the newspaper. It wasn't a large article, but it was on the front page. Two paragraphs among several other stories. I can still recall the headline: Man jumps from bridge Christmas Eve." She lifted her chin. "It is indelible, in fact. Etched in my brain where I keep tragic memories. Is that what you wanted to hear?"

"Just curious. What of his daughters. How were they told?"

She shook her head. "You don't let up, do you?"

"Sorry, I'm asking of matters I think my father might have wanted to know."

She scoffed. "Truly? And is your father's…is he really outside?"

"He is."

She considered that. "Yes, the girls were told. They were five and six at the time, so I talked to them in terms that imagined that daddy had taken a long trip and wouldn't be back. They were sad, but as children do, soon got over it. They know better now, of course, both away at college and in the their twenties."

We all fell silent and backed into our own thoughts. Imogene made another attempt to enter the kitchen but quickly withdrew.

"No one knew of his…despair, I guess you'd call it," she said. "There was no letter, no reason given." She looked directly at me. "He was just gone."

I took that as my cue to end things. "Yes. Well, I've taken more of your time than intended. I'm sorry for the apparent stress I've put you both through."

"I'm not," said Thomas Smythe. "I'm not sorry. In fact, thank you for forcing us to face this entire tragedy. And I mean the whole of it. Perhaps now, Katherine and I can accept our guilt on behalf of Walter and consider our mutual lives. The charade between us is no longer. I hadn't thought of the deadening effect a noncommittal marriage can foster. There's been a dead spot in my heart all of these years, Katherine. Have you felt it too?"

As Thomas spoke, Katherine watched the man she called husband as if he was the chairman of a meeting and she an unaffiliated visitor. "No, Tom, I haven't felt that way. Never have, probably never will."

He was crestfallen one more time in the space of my visit. But he managed to form a smile and pick up another cookie. He nibbled. "You know, I've known that about you, about your coolness to affection and commitment to our marriage. And yet, I cared for you. What do we do now?"

She looked between Thomas and me, obviously irritated. "Don't be foolish, Tom. And not in front of this person. More people than you know live completely satisfactory lives in the manner we are used to. We will go on."

That ended it. They followed me outside, where they observed the Meteor coach, knowing that their accuser lay within. I hadn't asked if they wished to view the casket; neither of them seemed curious about that. They watched me get into the vehicle and stood in the driveway while Johnnie turned around and we drove off. I wondered where they would go from that moment on—thanks to my father.

I leaned back in the seat as Johnie drove me back to Sellwood, and thought of what I'd just experienced. It had felt invasive watching two people reach an unforeseen consensus about their sterile marriage. Not that Katherine Smythe hadn't deserved my father's declaration of guilt; still it was sobering to watch them look at each other with new eyes. Johnnie finally asked me how it had gone, as she usually did. She had heard enough of such episodes and seemed to shrug off the seventh tale of seven tales. She returned me to Sellwood, where we sat in the coach as if to discuss the next steps for my father's final appointment. First, she leaned over the steering wheel.

"Michael, I am so glad this is over. This damnable trip."

"Dear Johnnie, my co-conspirator, my guardian, and my fellow-traveler—I feel the same. However, at one time you told me, out on the road, it was the most fascinating experience you'd ever had."

Head down, she answered, "And it was—it was fascinating. But it was also exhausting and mentally wearing. How can I ever look at life in the same old way? Over dinner last night, I tried to tell my dad about it, the trip and all. He kept eating and nodded from time to time but never looked at me all during my telling. My brother, Danny, bless his heart, listened to me smiling as usual but had no idea what I was saying. I was speaking of things outside of what is familiar to him. When my dad put his fork down, he looked at me as if I'd told him a falsehood, like he did when I was a kid—at least it felt that way."

"What did he say, anything?"

She sat up. "Yes, he said that that was some kind of tale. Did it really happen that way? He actually asked me that. I asked him right back if he thought I made it up? Well no, he said, it just seemed bizarre. Then he cleared his dirty dishes, and that was it. I sensed he thought that I'd embellished what had occurred." She turned to me. "Michael, this whole thing: the trip, the people, it's just you and me. No one will ever believe it the way we know it."

"How could they?" I stuck out hand. "Shake, pardner, it's you and me."

"The hell with that." She leaned over, grabbed on, and hugged me, holding tight for a long moment in her strong arms.

When Nadine asked how the delivery of the very last letter had gone, I admitted that I'd witnessed a detached marriage up close—it frightened me, I confessed. She looked me in the eye and asked me why that had frightened me, though I'm sure she knew why. Instead of trying to explain in so many words, I hugged her and merely said, Because. Right then, I needed her like never before, and I wanted her, even more than the previous night. When I took a hand, she followed me with no hesitancy. In the bedroom, we slipped out of our clothing in front of each other—an act we may have done but a few times in our marriage, most notably in the first years. Right then, it seemed both natural and yet uncommon. Mostly our sex had been when we were already in bed, lights out, beneath covers, and I always assumed the role of instigator, with no consideration of her wishes. That day, our act of disrobing before each other was beguiling. Looking upon the woman with whom I'd lived for so long confirmed the years I'd wasted instead of participating in what could have been.

In her nakedness, she was so lovely. I saw her body as I should have all along: the curve of her hips, the roundness of her breasts, the rose-colored areolas, even the hollow of her neck—all of her. She came to me openly. We spent most of the afternoon reclaiming our intimacy. It was effervescent.

The following week, on a Wednesday, there would be a modest graveside service at the Riverview Cemetery. Randolph Evers Sanborn would be laid to rest, finally, next to Melba, his long-suffering wife. I supposed she would be okay with that.

I had called my Uncle Charlie in Reno to let him know of the burial. He thanked me but declined to make the trip. We agreed to remain in touch. I told no others of the internment; however, the funeral home and cemetery listed all funeral services in the newspaper. It was around ten-thirty that morning and in the mid-fifties with a light Oregon mist when Nadine and I arrived. The Gates & Collier Funeral Home had preceded us to complete the graveside setup: fake grass framing the grave site, a few folding chairs, umbrellas, the mechanical device that would lower the casket after a simple observance. No flowers. Johnnie was there with her father; she introduced us. Nadine and I shook hands with Clarence Gates while he looked me over, the man who had ridden across country with his daughter, and likely wondered again if her accounting of the trip was really true. The Meteor was on hand. My father was still within, still wearing his flowered shirt. He had reached his final destination; time to get it over with. With no actual pallbearers, Johnnie, her father, one of the cemetery workers, and I carried the casket from the coach to the grave site.

The Episcopal priest I had asked to say a few words over my father was waiting. I chose the man because my mother had attended his church. We too shook hands and briefly discussed what would be said; I'd given him a page of biographical details about my father: birthplace, date, wife, child, career, death—that was it. No proselytizing, no aggrandizement, a succinct invocation—over.

Counting the priest, a couple of cemetery workers, Johnnie and her father, Nadine and I, and two guests, there were nine in attendance. Nadine's parents, who lived in Seattle, would not attend. The guests included Samuel Painmayer, my employer; he offered his condolences, and I confirmed that I would return to work immediately. Surprisingly, Katherine Smythe also materialized; she came dressed in a stylish black outfit, wiped off one of the folding chairs with a handkerchief, and sat down. We did not acknowledge one another. At eleven o'clock, the priest stepped forward, smiled, and did what I was paying him to do.

By the time he had finished the sparse eulogy and ended the observance with the final amen, eighteen minutes had passed, and the mist had turned to light rain. Umbrellas popped open, and one by one the guests were gone. I handed the priest an envelope with his compensation, nodded to Johnnie and her father then Nadine stood beside me, and we watched when the lowering device was activated. As the casket descended slowly and gracefully into the grave, she gripped my hand. Randolph Sanborn was at his final rest. I thought, Happy now, Dad? I stood over my mother's grave for a moment; then we walked to our car. It was done. A matching headstone would be installed the following week, adjacent to my mother's marker. I had no plans to be on hand when it was set in place.

Chapter Thirty Eight,

Two days later, among the mail was a confirmation from the Realtor in Jupiter: the cottage had been sold. There was also a letter from Jupiter addressed to me. The name and address on the upper left hand corner of the envelope were those of Randolph E. Sanborn. The ivory-toned envelope was identical to the ones we'd carried from Jupiter to Portland, right down to the typed lettering. It was unsettling. I held it in my hand; there was nothing unusual about its weight or thickness. The postal cancellation was dated March 21. After a moment's thought, I determined that had to be when Johnnie and I were in Reno, ironically visiting his brother.

When I looked up, Nadine was watching me closely. "How can that be?"

"He had someone mail it after I'd left on the trip."

"Still, it's eerie."

I bounced the envelope in my hand. "How about some coffee. I need to think on this before I open it."

She nodded, touched me on the arm, and went to the kitchen. Once the percolator had finished bubbling, we sat at the table where I'd had so many meals and doctored our coffee. I stared at the envelope lying before me.

"What if I simply tore this up and tossed it away?"

She smiled and stirred her coffee some more. "Is that what you want to do?"

"Part of of me is angry that he would send me a letter to arrive just now after the fact. Yes, I do want to destroy it sight unseen. Several who were handed one of his letters felt the same. But they all read what he'd written."

"And you?"

"Fascinated. Curious. And pissed, because he planned for this letter to arrive after he's in the ground."

She smiled. "I'll bet curiosity wins. Always does in life." With my eyes still focused on the envelope, she added, "But then again, are you prepared to deal with whatever he says to you?"

I laid an open palm over my name typed on the face of that rectangular hunk of paper and held it down. "I don't know. Can't be good. It sure as hell won't be a thank you note."

She laughed and pushed her chair back. In a few moments she returned and handed me our bone-handled letter opener. "Maybe this will help your resolve."

I slit the envelope open. The page unfolded as had all of the others, and I read:

RANDOLPH E. SANBORN
FLORHAVEN ESTATES
JUPITER, FLORIDA

```
                                         February 1952

Michael Sanborn
901 SE Sellwood Blvd.
Portland, Oregon


Michael,

So here you are, back in Sellwood. It was a long
trip, was it not? And yes, this is a letter for you,
call it number eight. I'm assuming that you com-
pleted the trip as agreed and that I am now under-
ground. After writing the seven letters, I wrote
these words just for you. The real estate agent
agreed to mail it after you left.

When you made your first trip to Florida, and I'd
laid out my proposition, it was obvious that you
```

agreed against your best instincts to carry my dead carcass across the country and go face-to-face with a collection of total strangers. Even my brother Charlie was a stranger to you. I was truly surprised when you agreed to my crazy scheme.
How I would love to sit down with you now and discuss the trip. For you see, I fully intended the journey to be an emotionally distressing experience for you. And if you followed through as planned, I'm sure it was. I can just imagine how hellacious it must have been to face each person. First were the reactions to pleas of forgiveness for my blatant wrongdoings. But mostly I'm grinning about you going nose-to-nose with those bastards I accused of evildoing. Oh, to have been a fly on the wall on those occasions. What repercussions did you experience?

Now that you've concluded the trip, how did it feel? What did you learn about your father? That I was a disappointment, a vile person, who had associated with other vile people? That I shamelessly ruined lives and stuck a splinter in the eye of those whose deeds were without redemption?

And what did you discover about yourself, Michael? To tell the truth, that was the whole purpose. I could have written those letters, sent them off, and had my body shipped home. But I didn't do that because I wanted you to perhaps see something of yourself in the callous acts for which I would seek vindication in absentia. Or be my accuser by proxy.

As you grew up I noted that some of my dishonorable traits had been passed on to you. But mostly, and here is the crux of the matter, this misadventure is to let you know that I was fully aware that in our shallow father-son relationship your knowledge of me, who I was as a person, was drawn solely from your mother. Melba and I had a tedious marriage, barren of energy let alone passion. We merely co-existed. I focused on building my career, and, as you found, dallying in the extracurricular. That left your mother to her one allegiance, you, not counting the memory of the stillborn child, who also lived among us. At times, the display of her love and devotion to you was insufferable.

And through it all, I knew my story was being told to you as if by the Brothers Grimm. While I was by nature a stoic human being, to know that I was not loved by my wife and son was still humiliating. Not that I cared, but to be considered unacceptable in my own home was offensive. I know I had it coming and yet, as soon as I was diagnosed with cancer, I had days on end to devise a way to reverse course, to get back my sense of redress. And so I did.

While I know it was my due, your disgust, in a twisted way the trip set things right. Knowing what you experienced makes me smile.

Adieu,
Dad

P.S. Hello to Nadine, if she's still with you.

I read it through again, just as I'd seen the other recipients do, and refolded it. It was quiet in the house; then we heard the clatter of the garbage truck—it was our pickup day. My coffee was cold. I was tired of sitting so rose and walked to the sink to draw a glass of cold water. I drank it down, set the glass on the counter, and turned around. Nadine had her elbows planted on the tabletop and clasped hands beneath her chin. We looked at one another until I guess her desire to know broke through.

"What did he say?" she asked finally.

I pointed to the letter lying on the table. "Read it. He asked about you."

Her eyebrows went up. When she started to read, I left the kitchen and went out onto the front porch, sat on the swing hanging there, and pushed off gently; the chain links groaned. The air was cool, but I didn't feel it. My mind was elsewhere. I was still replaying several lines of the letter when Nadine came out of the house and sat beside me on the swing. She had the page.

"I am," she said. When I turned my head, she added, "still with you."

"But why would he ask that question? He must have thought there was reason to."

She hesitated, then said, "It's curious, isn't it? That your father, who hardly ever participated in our lives, would have noted something as crucial as the state of our marriage. I always assumed, by virtue of his detachment, that he truly gave us no thought at all."

"He was an observer. He didn't miss much. I can imagine that on those rare occasions when we were with them, our marital demeanor was easy enough to pick up on."

"Meaning he assumed what?"

A neighbor kid pedaled by on his knee-action Schwinn bicycle. Looked like unbridled fun. "I suspect he was assuming that I was the same brand of husband he was. That's what I think."

"You mean the tedious, barren marriage he described?"

I thought on that question. "Nadine, have you ever considered leaving me?"

She fiddled with the letter for a long moment, seemed to read, then rose from the swing and stepped to the front porch railing. She turned around. "What about you, Michael? Have you ever thought about ending our marriage?"

Chapter Thirty Nine,

On November 4, Eisenhower easily won the presidential election. I had voted for Adlai Stevenson, even though I knew he would lose; I just liked the guy. But by then the election meant little to me because on the day before, while working at my desk, a messenger had hand-delivered the legal documents that would end my marriage to Nadine. I signed where designated and handed the pages back; the messenger left, and I leaned forward on my elbows. The air had gone out of my office. I felt short of breath. My life had taken a lurch from the predictable to something totally unknown.

That day, my mind awash with regret, I had absent-mindedly scribbled down March 12, the date that I had flown to Jupiter. My father had died; time to initiate the game plan. Not quite eight months before my divorce, I had retrieved his body, and with Johnnie at the wheel, set off on that macabre road trip. In the end, my old man told me in his letter that he had set me up to endure an emotionally distressing experience. And that's how it worked out.

In that letter, he had also acknowledged our shallow father-son relationship. But mostly he had used the trip as a ploy to exact retribution for a long-held slight: his belief that my mother and I had conspired against him. Even though he was a detached father and husband, it was degrading to him not being respected in his own home. He found that offensive and had orchestrated his revenge, taking my marriage along with it.

That day on the porch, after the funeral and after my father's letter had landed, I had answered Nadine's question: Michael, have you ever thought about ending our marriage? I had responded: Of course not. Have you? I recall that she leaned against the porch railing and studied me. It was then that I knew. I have, she had answered.

It was eerie, sitting there on the porch swing, looking at the woman who had endured our eighteen years together, with her words, I have, ringing in my ears. Like my mother had, I thought then and now that Nadine would have stayed the course but for that question. The question brought on by the postscript in my father's letter: if she's still with you. As I signed the divorce decree, I knew I had it coming. And just when I had anticipated a rejuvenated marriage, my wife had reached the end of enduring the marital status she'd been subjected to; she had waited too long for too little. There would have been too much baggage to unpack and resolve. My personal breakthrough, that I was ready for a better marriage, was too late.

The one person with whom I could confide was, of course, Johnnie. After my father's burial, we met for lunch at least once a month at Henry Thiele's Restaurant out on Burnside Street for its barbecued pork sandwich she favored. The day I told her of the divorce, she set her sandwich back on the plate and studied my face.

"His letter to you, that's it, isn't it?"

"I think so. He asked the question Nadine had been harboring for a very long time. She answered it."

"Like I said before, he set you up," she accused. "The whole damn thing was a con job."

"Yes, I'm certain it was. But his most cunning ploy was to probe at my most vulnerable point: our marriage."

"That's tough."

"Yes. Like they say, you don't miss something precious until it's taken from you. I'm adrift, and I had it coming."

She shook her head and picked up the sandwich. "Maybe. But don't we all." She took a bite then wiped barbecue sauce off her fingers. "Suppose it will work out—life has a way of doing that. I see it everyday, loss and moving on."

I chuckled. "You know, some days I wish we were back out on the road, covering miles in the Meteor again. A peaceful thought right now."

"Yeah, it had its moments. By the way, you remember Maples Mortuary in Boulder, Colorado? There was a fellow who worked there, Toby Ellis?" I nodded. "Well, he's working for us. Showed up a few weeks ago. Remember him?"

It came to me. "Yes. I do now. As I recall, he was taken by a Miss Gates."

She grinned. "Yes, there was that. Anyway, my father took to him and hired him almost on the spot. We're seeing each other on the side."

"Your father clued in?"

"I think he's getting the idea. Hasn't complained."

We gave each other tight hugs when we parted. As I watched her drive away, I was suddenly aware that we had switched places in a way. She was launching a new phase of her life, and I was facing a blank wall.

I suppose it was a month later when I rolled a sheet of paper into the typewriter at my desk. For some time, I'd been contemplating writing the letter I crafted that day.

MICHAEL J. SANBORN
901 SE SELLWOOD BOULEVARD
PORTLAND, OREGON

December 15, 1952

Richard Charles, Vice President of Finance
Sears, Roebuck and Company
925 S. Homan Avenue North
Chicago, Illinois

Dear Dick,

> It has been a long time since our years at OAC in
> Corvallis. I enjoyed that time and having you as
> a college classmate. Congratulations on your very
> successful career at Sears Roebuck.
>
> Much has changed. The years have gone by quickly.
> Some lives have prospered, some have failed, others
> are gone. We are long past being wide-eyed college
> graduates set to save the world.
>
> All of that said, I am writing to you for one
> simple reason. I betrayed you back in those days
> and wish…

I emptied my soul. He never responded.

So that's how it played out. I was disheartened the day I signed the divorce papers and had no idea where I would go from there. I felt relief on Nadine's behalf, but it was a bitter pill to swallow. Knowing that the blame for my sudden isolation lay at my own feet was crushing. I was alone: parents gone, spouse gone, the children we never had missing.

At first, I focused solely on my job and thought nothing about options or life choices beyond that sad ending. It took time. I resisted reaching out beyond the daily life I knew and felt some comfort in. It wasn't until nearly a year later that someone new and different entered my life. By happenstance, she simply appeared. I wasn't ready; who's ever ready? She was just there one day. I was reminded of Clyde Stone being accepted by someone after all. Was that me? I didn't know. We're still exploring, she and I, and considering. It frightens me. But there is promise.

Acknowledgements

I am indebted to the Playa Art & Science Residency Program, an artistic retreat venue in the Oregon Outback near Summer Lake, Oregon. At Playa (pronounced "ply-uh"), I enjoyed seclusion in a natural environment and quiet accommodations to work. It was at Playa where I spent a month in March of 2016 and began the writing that became *Summation*. My time there was spent crafting what would become the core of this novel, the seven letters which drive the story. I so appreciated being accepted at Playa and extend my gratitude for that unique opportunity.

Once again, I am so appreciative of my editor Karen Brattain for clearing the clutter and holding my work to account. Thanks as well go to Abbey Gregory for her creativity in designing the interior and exterior of Summation to make it look its best.

And to Betsy, my wife and first reader, who through the down-time of Covid, and subsequent years of lag time, encouraged me to keep on trucking until this work was done.

About the Author

The son of an embalmer became a novelist. George Byron Wright was born on the banks of the Columbia River in The Dalles, Oregon, lived there until age seven, followed by short periods in Baker City, Tillamook and Roseburg, Oregon while his father practiced the art of funeral director and embalmer. George's a career was in the nonprofit sector, eventually serving as CEO of the American Lung Association of Oregon. He also found time to own a bookstore, write a newspaper column, consult in the not-for-profit sector, publish a national newsletter for nonprofit CEOS and produce two books on nonprofit management. But the long held passion for stories brought George back to writing several novels set in the towns of his youth. His first novel, *Baker City 1948*, was followed by *Tillamook 1952*, and *Roseburg 1959*. George then continued to pursue his passion of writing stories: Summation is his eighth novel. Wright lives with his wife and first reader, Betsy, in Portland, Oregon.

Printed in the USA
CPSIA information can be obtained
at www.ICGtesting.com
LVHW040133250724
786462LV00031B/238